BRIAN PINKERTON

THE GEMINI EXPERIMENT

This is a **FLAME TREE PRESS** book

Text copyright © 2019 Brian Pinkerton

FLAME TREE PRESS
6 Melbray Mews, London, SW6 3NS, UK
flametreepress.com

Distribution and warehouse:
Baker & Taylor Publisher Services (BTPS)
30 Amberwood Parkway, Ashland, OH 44805
btpubservices.com

Publisher's Note: This is a work of fiction. Names, characters, places, and incidents are a product of the author's imagination. Locales and public names are sometimes used for atmospheric purposes. Any resemblance to actual people, living or dead, or to businesses, companies, events, institutions, or locales is completely coincidental.

Thanks to the Flame Tree Press team, including:
Taylor Bentley, Frances Bodiam, Federica Ciaravella, Don D'Auria,
Chris Herbert, Matteo Middlemiss, Josie Mitchell, Mike Spender,
Cat Taylor, Maria Tissot, Nick Wells, Gillian Whitaker.

The cover is created by Flame Tree Studio with
thanks to Nik Keevil and Shutterstock.com.
The font families used are Avenir and Bembo.

Flame Tree Press is an imprint of Flame Tree Publishing Ltd
flametreepublishing.com

A copy of the CIP data for this book is available from the British Library
and the Library of Congress.

HB ISBN: 978-1-78758-229-3
PB ISBN: 978-1-78758-227-9
ebook ISBN: 978-1-78758-230-9
Also available in FLAME TREE AUDIO

Printed in the US at Bookmasters, Ashland, Ohio

BRIAN PINKERTON

THE GEMINI EXPERIMENT

FLAME TREE PRESS
London & New York

CHAPTER ONE

Tom Nolan stared into his own eyes. They did not blink. He examined his face, a perfect mirror image. It took his breath away.

The color and texture of his hair was a striking match, blond and wavy. His lanky frame — the six-foot height, broad width of his shoulders, narrow waist — measured up like a crisp reflection. Yet this was no illusion of light and glass. Fully clothed, his double stood in three dimensions with lifelike features and flesh tones. Everything down to shoe size was immaculately scaled.

Tom reached out and lightly grazed the cheek of his other self. Then he touched his own cheek. There was no difference in texture and temperature.

"I feel like I'm having an out-of-body experience," he said. "Like I'm a spirit, looking back at myself. This is completely disorienting. I can't put it into words."

Steven Morris stood beside him in round glasses and a long, white lab coat. "Perfectly understandable. It's like nothing you — or anyone else — has ever experienced before."

Steven had promised the 'great reveal' would exceed all expectations. He said even Tom's own mother would not be able to distinguish him from his duplicate. Tom originally accepted those words as hyperbole. Now he truly wondered if his mother could tell the difference.

Tom kept returning his gaze to the uncanny likeness of his face. Every physical detail was painstakingly recreated, down to each mole, bump and tiny scar. As he circled his replica, it remained motionless, standing in perfect balance with exact posture.

"This is the most sophisticated body scan and skeletal reproduction ever undertaken," Steven said. "The surface material is the most lifelike ever developed from synthetic elements."

"It's too bad you scanned me at thirty-four instead of twenty-four," mused Tom. "I was in better shape ten years ago."

"This wasn't possible even one year ago. We've made giant leaps in science and technology. Then there's the financial commitment. We have the funding we need, which is a lot."

Tom broke his gaze from the replica to look at Steven. "How much did this cost?"

Steven just smiled. "Don't worry about it. We're privately funded by a sponsor that's sparing no expense to make sure we succeed. We're halfway there, and the best is yet to come. The team is busy preparing for the next stage. Your twin here is not complete. You know what he's missing?"

Tom nodded and lightly touched the wisps of hair that fell over his replica's forehead.

Steven began humming a familiar tune from *The Wizard of Oz*.

Tom smiled. "If I only had a brain."

"*That* will be the most remarkable advancement in modern science," said Steven. "The finishing touch in creating the first duplicate of a living human being entirely from technology."

"So when do you open up my head?" Tom asked.

"We're still a few months away from pure digital cognition. We have to conduct several more tests. So far, we're encouraged, but it's not ready for prime time. We have an amazing crew working around the clock. Everything we're doing is revolutionary."

"When can I tell Emily?" asked Tom.

"Not yet," Steven said. "We'll bring her into the inner circle before we start the brain mapping. But not before. Confidentiality is very tight, it's beyond my control. This experiment has gone further than anything like it anywhere in the world. We can't risk interference – disruptions – from outside interests. If this project was wrapped up in regulations, bureaucracy and red tape, we'd still be talking about it with nothing to show. You can imagine how quickly it would become mired in political games, media scrutiny and public pressures...." Steven turned to Tom's replica and placed a casual hand on its shoulder. It did not flinch, eyes frozen open. "We have to look out for our friend."

Tom nodded, still studying his replica and marveling over its stunning likeness. "You know," he said, "this is the best I'll look for the rest of my life. It's all downhill from here...."

★   ★   ★

Tom's world began to change when he dropped a jar of salsa that shattered on the kitchen floor. It wasn't the first example of his odd onset of fumbling and stumbling, but the one that finally caused him to seek medical advice for the curious disobedience of his muscle coordination.

For several weeks, he had suffered muscle cramps and stiffness with awkward difficulties conducting simple tasks. He struggled occasionally with buttoning a shirt, twisting a key to open a door lock, and holding a fork or spoon. Then one of his legs started to bother him, sometimes falling out of sync with his stride, acting irrational, as if it was possessed.

While generally familiar with motor neuron diseases, the thought never crossed Tom's mind. He visited his regular doctor, who suggested he see a neurologist. A series of tests were conducted to rule out a list of possible ailments. As the muscle weakness worsened and EMG and MRI tests could not uncover any other possible explanation, the words *amyotrophic lateral sclerosis* surfaced with grim likelihood.

Ultimately, Tom was diagnosed with a progressive neurodegenerative disorder known as Lowrey's disease. In a similar fashion to ALS, Lowrey's disease culminated in an irreversible communication breakdown between upper and lower motor neurons, disconnecting signals that united the brain, spine and muscles.

Tom and his wife Emily read everything they could about the disease and sunk into an immediate, dizzying feeling of terror and helplessness. There was no cure and the typical life expectancy was three to five years of worsening health. Lowrey's was attacking Tom's ability to control movement, poised to gradually accumulate more victims in the list of Tom's muscle activities including walking, speaking and, ultimately, breathing.

Tom and Emily pursued a second opinion, then a third, but the prognosis remained the same. They followed the journeys of others afflicted with motor neuron diseases who shared their stories online. "It's one of the cruelest afflictions," reported a former athlete on his blog as he entered his second year of struggles with ALS. "Your body atrophies while your mind remains sharp. You're fully cognizant of everything that's happening to you as you gradually lose control of your movements. You just wither away."

Tom fought to remain cheerful and optimistic, if nothing else for the sake of his wife and their seven-year-old daughter, Sofi. Tom and Emily chose to postpone telling Sofi until she was older and the symptoms were more obvious. They worked hard to act like nothing was happening around her. 'Clumsy Daddy' became a common phrase around the house and the extent of their acknowledgment that something was wrong.

For everyone else, it wasn't so easy. Tom, Emily and Sofi flew to Phoenix, Arizona, to spend time with Tom's parents and allow Tom an opportunity to disclose the news to them in person. He tried to remain his regular jovial self, feeling guilty for battering his aging mother and father with such sorrow. "It's not going to happen overnight," he told them, holding back tears. "I'm still here. I actually feel pretty good. We're going to take this a day at a time. They have drugs that can slow this thing down. I'll be in physical therapy. With so many advances in science and medicine every day, who knows?"

After completing conversations with close family members, Tom revealed his condition to his colleagues at the law firm where he worked in downtown Chicago. He minimized talking about his disease and instead focused on the transition plan for his clients.

"Short-term, I'm still here for them," he insisted. Aside from the minor and sporadic coordination issues, he could still conduct his work for the small businesses and nonprofits he counseled. He could even continue some of the pro bono work and mentorships he was passionate about. It would be business as usual until that was no longer possible.

"Long-term, we'll work together to move my clients to new partners," he said. "We'll start a shadowing process to bring you up to speed and ensure everything is seamless. We'll have plenty of time to do this right and minimize disruption."

Of course, no one at the office wanted to talk about the impact on clients – they wanted to express their feelings about his condition. Tom actually preferred the former, but understood their need to come to terms with the latter.

His bosses encouraged him to minimize his hours immediately, but Tom desperately wanted to cling to some routine. Also, his family needed the income. Emily worked as a grade school teacher's assistant, not earning enough to cover the mortgage of their Wilmette home. The life insurance payout would help, but she was still young and there was so much to worry about – including saving for college for Sofi.

Tom knew he would not be alive to see his daughter graduate from high school or college, or see her get married, and that was by far the hardest reality of all. He planned to create videotaped messages for her that she would receive at each of her life's milestones – including the birth of his first grandchild.

Emily turned to prayer. They were both devout Catholics, but Tom's unexpected fate had Emily searching for answers.

"Why you?" she said to him late one night in a soft voice. "You're good, you're kind, you're caring. You give back to the community. You worship and serve at your church. I know bad things happen to good people. But where is God's mercy at a time like this? How can He allow this to happen?"

"Life is tragedy and miracles," said Tom. "Sofi is our miracle. Let's not forget that. The doctors said we couldn't conceive and look what happened. The Lord is always present. We will stay strong."

Having informed his family and work colleagues, Tom next began to tell his friends. Some of them were already hearing about his condition through the grapevine. He divided the names into categories: phone calls or personal visits, with or without Emily. He went through his address book and built a routine, now able to share his condition in a well-rehearsed dialogue that no longer felt strange and agonizing – it was the new norm.

Most of Tom's friends easily followed Tom's gentle steering of the conversation away from the uncomfortable particulars of motor neuron disease, content with quick references to Lou Gehrig or Stephen Hawking. One old friend, however, took an interest in delving deeper into Tom's condition and discussing the precise stages of his affliction. Steven Morris was an old high school classmate who now taught at the University of Chicago. They met for dinner at an Italian restaurant downtown. Steven's specialty area was neuroscience. He was familiar with the latest advances to treat brain trauma victims and wanted to help. He told Tom, "There's an entire field of study that looks at ways to record signals generated by the brain and turn them into technical commands – for instance, controlling a wheelchair or speaking through a computer."

"Can something like that help me?" Tom asked.

"It can't stop the muscle degeneration but it can make certain tasks easier. We're using it with wounded veterans. There are advances in intelligent prostheses – artificial limbs that can respond to brain commands. It's a growing field called neurotechnology."

Steven hesitated for a long moment, glancing around the dimly lit restaurant before returning his eyes to Tom with his voice lowered.

"There's something you don't know. I'm on a sabbatical right now from the university. I'm part of a team working on an experimental treatment. I can't say much more than that right now. But you – if you're interested, you could be part of our test. In fact, you're rather perfect for it. There are no guarantees. We're trying things that have never been done before. But...we *are* making advances. It's a big gray area with a lot of possibility. I'm mentioning this as a friend. Is it something that would interest you?"

"Sure. I'd be willing to look into it," said Tom. "At this point, I don't have a whole lot to lose."

"I'm under a strict confidentiality agreement, so I have to

ask that you please not mention this to anybody right now. Not your doctors, not even Emily."

"I can do that," Tom said. "I mean, I barely know what you're talking about."

"We'll stay in touch," said Steven. "This could be very interesting for both of us. I want to help you. And I think you can help me."

Several days passed and Tom researched neurotechnology online. He read about brainwaves and robotics. It provided optimism for retaining some control over movement and activities as Lowrey's disease shut down the communication between his brain and nervous system. But the death sentence still loomed with inevitability.

Steven arranged for their next meeting at a restaurant twenty minutes from Tom's house. When Tom pulled up, Steven was waiting out front. He immediately led Tom to his car. "We're not staying. I'm going to take you to meet the team."

"Team?" Tom said.

"I'll explain in the car."

"Well, this is mysterious."

"Trust me."

Tom climbed in the passenger seat of Steven's Camry.

Before Steven started the engine, he handed Tom a clipboard with some papers and a pen. "It's a nondisclosure agreement. Being a lawyer, I'm sure you're familiar...."

"Of course."

"I can't leave until you've signed them. I hope you understand. Take all the time you need."

Tom read them carefully. He was under no obligation to participate at this stage; it was merely a promise to keep everything he was about to see and hear confidential. It was slightly ominous, but nowhere near as intimidating as his condition. Tom fumbled a moment with the pen – cursed his hands – and signed the sheets.

Steven started the engine and headed for their destination. During the ride, he outlined what to expect. "I'm bringing you to a facility where we are conducting highly confidential lab work to test the physical integration of technology and human biology."

"Sounds very sci-fi," Tom said.

"Perhaps. But more science than fiction at this stage," said Steven. "I think you'll be impressed. When we get there, you'll meet the staff and we'll give you a more complete picture of the work we're doing. One year ago, I was recruited to join a team of top scientists in their field – neuroimaging, neuroscience, robotics, prostheses. They come from Stanford, Berkeley, Carnegie Mellon and major research centers across the country. We're independent, fully funded and all focused on one outcome: the technological reproduction of a living human being. Not only physically, but enabling the transfer of mind and memory through highly evolved digitization."

"Like a clone?" asked Tom.

"Not exactly. A clone would indicate a duplication, a set of twins. This is more like a transfer. It involves the physical reconstruction, artificially, of the source to create something virtually identical that, I suppose, could be considered a clone. But the most important part is the relocation of consciousness. Once that takes place, the original source expires. It is no longer functioning."

"You move the brain?" Tom began to feel queasy. The whole thing sounded improbable, like an old Frankenstein movie. In all the years Tom knew him, Steven had never seemed crazy – meticulously rational, in fact – but this was mad-scientist material.

"We don't relocate the brain," said Steven. "We replicate it. We penetrate the brain tissue. We pick up electrical fields generated by the brain. We record the electrodes. We fully map the interior. We reimage it. It's very invasive and creates irreversible damage. The original brain does not survive."

Tom's head was swimming. "So is this artificial intelligence?" he asked.

"No. The intelligence is human and real. It's just 'backed up' to a new hard drive, as it were. The body is artificial."

"And this is the experiment you want to recruit me for?"

"Yes," Steven said simply.

Tom couldn't get over a small but real feeling of rescue. Perhaps God was watching after all and had sent him a miracle.

"Everything I've described," said Steven, "is a best-case scenario. I want to be upfront about that. At the end of the day, it's one big experiment. We're guessing. We don't know what will happen. And there are risks. This is a delicate process."

"I understand."

They arrived at a medium-sized building at the back of a dull, quiet industrial park in the Chicago suburb of Lake Forest. The building drew no attention to itself, aside from a plain, innocuous-looking sign that said 'Perking Institute'. Five other cars were parked in front.

"Who's Perking?" asked Tom.

"Nobody," Steven said. "It's made up."

Steven led Tom inside. After passing through two levels of security, requiring codes and thumbprints, they entered a long, narrow lab space. The area was filled with computer equipment. Several people in white lab coats came up to greet them.

"Tom signed the papers and I've given him a general briefing, so you're safe to talk with him about the Gemini Experiment," announced Steven. "Tom, this is our dream team."

"Hello, I'm Alan," said a middle-aged man with dark hair, a thick beard and heavy eyebrows. He offered his hand.

"Alan is one of our team leaders," Steven said. "He's a brilliant scientist."

"On some days, perhaps," Alan said with a modest smile.

Tom shook Alan's hand and met several others in a short receiving line. The team members commented on hearing about Tom from Steven and expressed their hopes that Tom could support their research. Soon, the discussion deepened, with probing questions about the stage of Tom's disease and current mobility and health. They outlined a potential sequence of steps for the coming weeks, beginning with a full-fledged physical and advancing to a process they called 'body scanning'.

Before Tom left for the day, they took him to a smaller, adjacent room dominated by a long white container that looked like a tanning booth – or a slick, rounded coffin. A web of cords and wires connected the booth to computers and monitors that smothered the length of one wall.

"That's the scanner. It will give us an extremely detailed mapping of your dimensions – your body mass, skin tone, skeletal and muscular structure, everything down to the size and shape of your fingernails. We'd like to set up a time for scanning as soon as we can, to preserve your current appearance."

"Before I start to deteriorate," said Tom.

"Yes," Steven said. "We're on a time clock, and the clock is ticking. I don't need to tell you that. Your mind – we have more time. Your body – not so much."

"So," Alan said, clasping a hand on Tom's shoulder. "Have we scared you away yet?"

Tom shook his head. "No. I'm not scared. I'm…grateful." He thought about the possibility – however small – that this process and technology could suspend death long enough for him to see his daughter grow up. He felt something he hadn't felt since his doctor's shattering diagnosis – hope.

Six weeks later, Tom stood in the same lab feeling more than hope – the possibility was moving toward reality. The rest of the lab had stepped away to allow Tom and Steven a private moment with Tom's full-sized duplicate. The artificial 'shell', as Steven called it, appeared to be a total success in recreating his shape and form.

Tom wanted to ditch his diseased body and live in this new one as soon as possible.

"We call it the Gemini Experiment, after the Dioscuri," Steven said. "Do you remember your Greek mythology? The Gemini twins are Castor and Pollux. One is mortal, one is immortal."

"So this is my immortal twin," said Tom. "Amazing. I'm speechless. Thank you."

"Don't thank me yet," Steven said. "We still have a long way to go. But I hope you can go home tonight…feeling good. We're all dedicated to making this work."

"This *is* a miracle," Tom said, his spirit lifted.

★   ★   ★

That night, as Tom lay in bed with his wife, Emily, his mind continued to wander restlessly long after she fell asleep. Her arm rested across his bare chest, comforting and affectionate. He wondered how she would react if one day that same arm was draped across a synthetic simulation of his chest, fake versus real flesh, and would she feel any different toward him?

Tom struggled with the religious implications. What would his church think? *God created man.* But what happens when man gets sick? Tom thought: *We've accepted centuries of medicines and vaccines and moved on to artificial limbs, pacemakers and lung machines.* Was this truly sacrilege or simply taking the art of healing to a new level?

For Tom, the arguments in his head persisted but he kept reaching the same conclusion. *I don't want to die.*

CHAPTER TWO

Groucho waited behind the wheel, watching the scene around him, feeling a chilly tingle of perspiration stick to his clothes. The silver Mustang idled at the curb in front of Elgin First Bank, car windows tinted at twenty percent, doors unlocked and ready to welcome three passengers – Stan, Ollie and Charlie – to complete the classic comedy foursome.

The police scanner crackled with tight, tense voices describing a bank robbery on the other side of town – a madcap scramble of Keystone Kops reporting to the foursome's first crime, the perfect diversion to clear the way for this second heist.

A meticulous, minute-by-minute plan was being executed with precision to hold up two banks in rapid succession in Illinois' eighth-largest city. The town was big enough for a big haul, yet scaled to the right size for a fast getaway without the heavier congestion and bulkier police presence of nearby Chicago. Elgin was surrounded by rural areas and main arteries, allowing many miles of distance to be covered in minutes. Every consideration – time of day, traffic patterns, bank activity, police proximity – factored into the final agenda, largely developed by the foursome's organizer and ringleader, Charlie.

It was Charlie – Chaplin – who came up with the idea to disguise themselves in throwback Halloween masks bought anonymously on eBay, gleefully choosing the old-time comics theme over other options such as classic monsters or US presidents. Charlie looked forward to the press coverage of his novelty choice and the funny look of the security camera footage, playing out like a grainy, pantomime movie of the slapstick era. Charlie brought together his holdup team with the insistence they only know one another by these stage names, so that after they split with their shares of the haul, they couldn't reveal each other's identities, even if under tremendous pressure. The entire operation, rapidly assembled less than twenty-four hours before, was to be conducted under a strict shroud of anonymity. Only Charlie, their recruiter, knew everyone's true names.

Charlie was also very deliberate about the numbers – three on the inside, one waiting outside. "We'll be ready for any asshole who wants to be a hero. They'll think twice before doing something stupid. If anyone tries to be a hero, they'll be a dead hero."

Groucho checked his watch: two minutes to go. One hundred and twenty seconds. He itched for a quick cigarette. He wanted to peel off the idiotic mask and light up, but the pleasure would have to wait. He had been hired for his fierce concentration and driving skills to transport people and cash at lightning speed. He possessed an uncanny talent to tune out all distractions. If he didn't perform at the top of his game, he endangered them all and his stellar reputation.

A little girl in a sundress entered Groucho's view. She crossed the street directly in front of the getaway car, carrying an ice cream cone. She moved excruciatingly slowly, careful not to upset the balance of her two scoops. Groucho tensed up. This pint-sized obstacle was not expected or acceptable. She needed to move *faster*.

From the other side of the tinted glass, the little girl could not see his funny face – big eyebrows, big glasses, big mustache. He was just a shadow.

Groucho applied pressure to the gas pedal while parked, creating a small roar of impatience to accelerate her pace.

Instead of stepping more quickly, she stopped cold. She turned to look into the windshield, curious. A melting streak of ice cream dribbled onto her fist.

"*Move!*" screamed Groucho.

At that moment, Stan, Ollie and Charlie rushed out of the bank, each carrying a bulky canvas bag.

The little girl's head turned from the Mustang to the comedy trio running toward the car. She stared at them in awe.

The car filled up with clowns, doors opening and slamming.

Groucho adjusted the gear shift. He weighed his options at lightning speed:

1. Wait for the girl to move – not really an option.

2. Blast the horn to chase her away and draw attention.

3. Back up and circle around her, trimming precious seconds off the getaway time.

4. Run the damned kid over.

"Run her down!" Charlie shouted in the front passenger seat. Stan and Ollie nodded vigorously in the back seat.

Groucho slammed the accelerator.

The little girl jumped out of the path of the advancing car and fell to the curb, bursting into tears as her ice cream cone exploded on the pavement.

Groucho would not allow himself a glance in the rearview mirror – he had an upcoming intersection to contend with – but Charlie twisted around for a look and reported, with no real emotion one way or the other, "She's fine."

Inside twenty minutes at breakneck speed, the Mustang arrived in small, sleepy Sycamore, Illinois. The vehicle returned to the previous night's makeshift headquarters, a vacant house on a country road with a toppled 'For Sale' sign. Ongoing monitoring of the police scanner provided reassurance that no one had picked up their trail.

Groucho pulled the Mustang into a large, dilapidated garage, essentially a shack of brittle wood. He parked alongside Charlie's Chevy, which would take them back into the city after the loot was divided. The stolen Mustang was officially retired. They climbed out and entered the old, empty country house and its layers of dust.

Charlie took control of the money, unloading the bundles of cash on a table in the center of the living room. True to his plan, exploding packs of dye had been purposefully excluded, following his cold-blooded promise to the tellers: "If you include the dye, you will die. My brother has instructions to kill your family if there's even *one drop* of blue ink. He has your home addresses and the names of your children. Make the wise choice."

Ollie collected the rubber masks and burned them in the

fireplace with a generous squeeze of lighter fluid. Stan popped a celebratory bottle of champagne he had reserved for their return.

Groucho, still all nerves from the getaway run, craved his cigarette now more than ever. "I'm going out back for a smoke," he said.

Charlie looked up from where he had been counting the money. "I'd rather you didn't," he said.

"Why?"

"I think it's best we stay together in this room."

Groucho frowned. "The money's here with you. What's your problem?"

"I don't have a problem. I'm just making a request."

Groucho's voice lowered a notch and growled. "You're no longer the boss. The job is done. I'm going out for a smoke. It's a hundred degrees in here."

Groucho turned away, not interested in continuing the debate. Little Charlie had dictated every step of the bank robberies, told everyone what to do without soliciting their input, and that was fine. But denying him a smoke after it was all over — that was just unnecessary. The overreach of a control freak.

Groucho stepped out of the house, letting the screen door slap shut behind him. He descended a small set of wooden steps into a secluded backyard. It was a grassy, overgrown plot of land that quickly gave way to a sprawling forest preserve. The yard was welcomingly cool and breezy, offering tranquility and isolation. The pleasant chirp of birds accompanied a gentle tussle of sweeping wind.

As Groucho walked toward the forest, sucking on his cigarette, he began to run numbers through his head. Charlie had anticipated a haul of six hundred thousand dollars across the two banks. Divided equally among the clowns, the take-home pay would be approximately one hundred and fifty thousand big ones. Based on his average annual earnings over the past few years, working in such glorious jobs as dishwasher, bartender and janitor, that would mean he had earned more in one day than he would ordinarily take home…in about six years.

Wait a minute. The money was tax free. Make that eight years.

Groucho smiled. The cigarette tasted fantastic. Very soon, Charlie would drive them back into Chicago and they would scatter with their individual bounties, never to see one another again. He would hop a train to leave the state, head into northern Minnesota, maybe buy a small cabin and....

"Whoa," he said. Entering the forest, he nearly stumbled into a big hole.

He froze in his tracks. He examined the opening. It was a large, manmade excavation, rectangular and deep, about the size of a—

Crack.

Crack. Crack.

Loud staccato pops disrupted the calm, sending birds fluttering from the trees.

Studying the scene in front of him, Groucho realized he had found not just one hole, but three of equal size. If there was even a moment of mystery around their intent, it had been quickly erased by the sound of gunshots.

Groucho turned and ran away from the woods.

Charlie emerged from the back door, descending the steps with banging footsteps, pistol in hand.

Groucho immediately circled toward the side of the house. A bullet kicked up dirt at his feet. His own gun was tucked deep into a holster under his shirt. He couldn't slow down yet to dig it out. He needed to create more distance.

At the side of the house, he reached the garage. He discovered an external door that led to the cars. He had a split second to make a decision.

The key to the Mustang remained in his pocket. He had instinctively pocketed it after they parked. Should he stay for a shootout or attempt an escape?

He knew his driving skills were better than his shooting skills. Decision made.

Groucho rushed inside the garage. He jumped in the Mustang and started the engine. As the motor roared, Charlie burst into the garage. He fired his gun, shattering one of the Mustang's windows.

Groucho floored the car in reverse, smashing through rotten wood, spilling into the driveway. He backed up in a fast, straight line, eighty feet to the main road, and then threw the car into drive, kicking up dirt and gravel.

A new getaway had started. He was in his element.

Groucho pushed the Mustang as fast as it would go, roaring down the main road, grateful to have no other vehicles in his way.

"Son of a bitch," he said over and over. This had been Charlie's plan all along – enlist their help, then kill them off and escape with all the money.

In his rearview mirror, he glimpsed the inevitable – a car coming after him, the Chevy belonging to Charlie. Charlie was not going to allow this loose end to spoil his master plan.

Okay, thought Groucho. *So it's me against you, winner takes all.*

He maneuvered in his seat, reached under his shirt and brought out his gun.

One hand on the wheel, one hand on the gun, Groucho began to slow down.

Come and get me.

Years later, the citizens of Sycamore, Illinois, would recount the events of that day with mostly accurate grandeur. It was easily the most memorable drama to ever unfold on their quaint and cozy Main Street.

Two speeding cars containing bank robbers engaged in a shootout, each looking to wipe out the other for more than half a million dollars in prize money and, ultimately, both losing. The one nicknamed Groucho did not survive, riddled with bullets and pulverized to a pancake as he crashed into parked cars at eighty miles per hour. The other, ridiculed in the press as 'The Little Tramp', absorbed multiple bullets and crashed, too, wiping out the front of Argento Pizza, and suffered a collection of broken bones but didn't die. He wound up in Stateville Prison, serving a life sentence for the murder of Laurel and Hardy.

★　★　★

"Call me Charlie, everybody else does."

The prisoner spoke plainly, seated on the other side of the glass partition in the inmate visiting area. He cradled the phone receiver in his shoulder, staring at the stoic, neatly groomed man who had just addressed him by his proper name, Louis, and introduced himself as Cooper.

"Charlie...?"

"You know why I'm in here?"

"Yes," responded Cooper. He sat on a stool, speaking into his end of the timeworn phone and staring through the smudged glass. He wore a formal suit and tie, noticeably out of place in this house of orange jumpsuits. He appeared nervous but purposeful. Louis had agreed to meet him without asking his agenda. He didn't get visitors every day.

In fact, Louis never received visitors. Not since those meetings years ago with the oily lawyer who represented him and failed to reduce his sentence from forever. Louis had no family, no friends. The no friends distinction carried over into the Big House; he didn't seek companionship and companionship didn't seek him. He was small and private. The other inmates made fun of his bungled bank robbery and silly character choice, which were widely covered in snarky media coverage.

If he became Charlie Chaplin for the rest of his life, so be it. He never cared for 'Louis' much anyway, a name bestowed on him by parents he detested.

The man sitting across from him remained serious, probably not a comedy fan. "To be honest, your circumstances for being here are of no interest to me," Cooper said. "It's your medical condition. It's the cancer."

Louis stared hard at the man. It was a topic he didn't really care to discuss. Yes, he was dying. So what.

"Illinois doesn't have the death penalty, so the man upstairs gave it to me instead," said Louis in a wry tone.

"I'm sorry," Cooper said flatly. If there was sympathy, it didn't reveal itself.

"Why does my sickness interest you?"

"You're a candidate for a special medical procedure. It's an experiment. There are no guarantees, of course, but we might be able to treat you and extend your life."

"Lucky me."

"Perhaps," Cooper said.

"Well, I'm afraid you don't have much time to do your experiment. The doctor gave me six months to live. The cancer's spreading. It's weaving its wicked web as we speak. It won't stay put."

"We can work with that."

"Who's paying for this?"

"We have a sponsor."

"What's the catch?"

"The treatment is new and aggressive. If it doesn't work, you will die...sooner than your six months."

"And if it does work?"

"You will be freed of your cancer."

Louis, as much as he tried, did not feel hope. He just felt puzzled.

"Why me?" he asked. "There must be a ton of other cancer patients out there – ones without a murder rap."

"I will be upfront," said Cooper. "Our methods are very new. They're not recognized by the general science community. We need someone who guarantees us a high amount of privacy. Meaning no attachments."

"No family."

"Yes."

"So if I participate in your experiment.... I could die faster or live longer?"

"That is correct."

"What are the odds?"

"Hard to say," said Cooper. "Maybe fifty-fifty."

Louis nodded, and then he smiled. "So I could die from it. And miss out on spending the rest of my days in this high-end resort?"

"The procedure will take place outside the prison, yes."

Louis stared at his visitor for a long moment. Then he said, "Mr. Cooper, I'll be your lab rat."

Cooper responded quickly. "Good. We'll begin the paperwork. Our only request is that you keep this confidential, given the proprietary nature of the research and tests."

Louis smirked. "Who am I going to tell? My cellmates? Get real. If word got out that I might get cured, my so-called friends here.... They'd probably kill me."

CHAPTER THREE

Cooper pulled up his sedan and waited at the front gate of a lakefront mansion in Glencoe on Chicago's North Shore. The cameras swiveled to get a good look and then the gates split apart to admit him.

The long driveway led to parking spaces alongside a broad garage, which was roughly the size of a small house. Cooper parked, took firm hold of the handle to his briefcase and reported to the mansion's front entrance.

Cameras observed him one more time before the door opened and a beautiful young woman in her twenties, dripping with jewelry and dressed with casual elegance, admitted him inside.

"Cooper, so good to see you." She gave him a quick hug and faint kiss on the cheek. "They're in the den."

Cooper advanced through a large, open living area of overstuffed, underused furnishings, occupied only by an orange cat and the frozen stare of portrait paintings. He crossed a set of open doors and entered the warmly lit den. Two men promptly stood from their chairs to greet him.

"Cooper!" thundered Giamatti, a heavyset man in his early sixties with a bulky white beard and balding head. He was stuffed in a black vest and wore slippers. "Please join us. Would you like a drink?"

Cooper politely declined. He eyed the second individual in the room, a handsome, middle-aged man in a relaxed sweater, wearing round glasses with silver rims.

"Cooper, this is Steven Morris, our lab team coordinator." Giamatti took a step back to allow the two to shake hands.

As the three men settled into seats, Giamatti told Steven, "Cooper has been my business associate for twenty-five years. He helped build the corporate empire that made me what I am today and allows us to fund this very special project. We're bringing him into the fold."

Cooper sat with the briefcase in his lap. Giamatti pointed to it. "You have the consent forms?"

"Yes," Cooper said. "He signed all the papers in front of me. We're in good standing with the prison. The test subject is ready as soon as you need him."

"Very good," said Giamatti. "Is he excited?"

"He's receptive. Naturally, he feels he has nothing to lose."

Giamatti leaned back in his chair. "I appreciate that kind of optimism. But our man Louis will not survive, even if our experiment is a total success." He glanced over at Steven. "Am I right?"

"The inmate is only a stepping stone," said Steven. "A means to an end."

Cooper awaited further explanation. He said, "I'm afraid I don't understand."

Giamatti responded, "The man's a killer. He has terminal cancer, and he's donating his body to science. It's the most noble thing he'll ever do. But this isn't about cancer research or saving him. It's something much more." His expression brightened. "Cooper, I know we can trust you. That's why I'm bringing you into a very exclusive inner circle. Together, we're going to make medical history. This is the biggest thing any of us will ever be involved in. We are bringing together science, human biology and technology to unlock the secrets to immortality."

Giamatti studied Cooper's reaction. Cooper's face remained stoic with a tilt of uncertainty. Giamatti turned to Steven. "Explain our plans for the inmate. Start at the beginning. And Cooper, what's said in this room stays in this room. I know you're used to our confidentiality agreements for mergers and acquisitions and financial disclosures, but this is in another league entirely."

"Understood," said Cooper.

Giamatti sat back in his large, plush chair and gestured for Steven to begin.

Steven spoke slowly and thoughtfully. "This is a very

special project. It's unlike anything that's ever been done before. We've crossed a critical threshold in understanding the human mind and how it works. We have years of research into neurons and how they control body movement – the brain's version of electronic codes and signals. The latest advances in technology have brought us to a point where we can actually mimic those codes and signals outside of human biology. We have sophisticated theories for how this could play out, and they've been in development for some time, but we've never had the ability to put it into practice for a host of reasons: the astronomical cost, the need for a very specific team of cutting-edge talent, and the availability of test subjects who may live or die. Above all, it requires an extraordinary level of secrecy. We can't afford interference of any kind that could lead to a loss of control to outside authorities that feel they should govern, advise, co-opt or otherwise insert their special interests into our processes and decision making. We need the freedom to explore. We are blessed by Mr. Giamatti. His funding, of course. That goes without saying. But also his savvy and relationships to pull the right strings, tap the right people and secure us a clear runway without making a ripple in the broader science and technology community. His stewardship gives us the ability to conduct our test in a way that maximizes its potential for success."

Giamatti held up a hand. "You're very kind, but enough about me. Describe what's in store for our friend Louis."

"Of course," said Steven. "Louis is the start of a six-week journey. We're headquartered in a private lab space not far from here. We're going to conduct a very invasive operation on Louis Karp's brain. We will penetrate his brain tissue. We will create a multidimensional image map of every contour and neuron that controls his thinking, his memory and his movements. We will replicate it digitally. The amount of detail required to do this means we'll ultimately dissect the brain in a manner that will kill it…with the goal of acquiring everything we need before it stops functioning. If phase one succeeds, Louis, as a human being, dies. But his consciousness is recreated and resides inside a computer."

Giamatti looked over at Cooper with a smile. "Are you sure you wouldn't like that drink now?"

"I'm fine," Cooper said. "I want to hear more."

"There's so much more," said Giamatti. "Because we're not just computerizing the human brain. Steven, please continue."

Steven nodded. "If phase one is successful, we'll have transferred Louis's consciousness to a computer. If it's not successful, we'll have done nothing more than accelerate Louis's terminal condition and the prison will be informed he did not survive the treatment and died on the operating table. If that's the case, we close down and there's barely a blip on the radar. But—"

"Now we get to the good stuff," Giamatti said.

"But," continued Steven, "*if* we are successful with the transfer, we can begin phase two. Phase two is the installation of that consciousness, the digital duplication of an active brain, into a highly evolved robot that precisely mimics the appearance, functionality and texture of a human being."

Steven bent forward to pick up a manila folder from a low table. He handed it to Cooper.

Cooper opened it and stared at a color, 8 x 10 photograph of a blond man, mid-thirties, stripped down to his underwear and standing against a blank background.

"Who's this?" he said.

"Currently, it's nobody," said Steven. "It's an empty shell. A life-size duplication of a young attorney who lives in Wilmette and works in Chicago. He was carefully selected and screened, put through a rigor of clearances, to ensure he was a man of good standing who could be trusted. I've known him for a long time and can vouch for his character. We brought him in and scanned him using the most sophisticated methods available. Then we reconstructed him, his every dimension, so that you could place the two of them together and not tell them apart. It's a synthetic clone, but missing one very important feature: mental faculties."

"That shell you see — it's the first of its kind," Giamatti said. "It cost ninety million dollars. Human anatomy, the bones, the muscles, the flesh – recreated by man. You can imagine the public response, especially in the heartland, if word of this got out while it was still a work in progress. But once we're able to offer immortality…. I think some of those naysayers will become customers."

"Yes," said Steven. "And that's phase three. The marriage of the digital consciousness with the android anatomy. If – and please understand me, it's a massive *if* – if we can preserve the brain and duplicate the body – we can save human beings from the ticking clock of biology and extend life indefinitely."

Cooper put down the folder with the photograph. "Why him?"

"He's the ideal test subject," Steven said. "His name is Tom Nolan. He was recently diagnosed with Lowrey's disease. It's a terminal motor neuron disorder. His mind is sharp, but his body is in the early stages of degeneration. If we can successfully digitize the mind and memory of Louis Karp, and if we can successfully transfer that consciousness to the shell we've created for Tom Nolan…then we will have the confidence and precedent to free Tom mentally from his human form and place him in his new body."

"Then what happens to Louis?" Cooper asked.

"Louis is proving the hypothesis," said Steven. "If everything works, we conclude his participation in the experiment."

Giamatti leaned forward in his seat and looked into Cooper's face with raised eyebrows. "We erase him."

"Louis dies either way," Steven said. "Either the brain transfer fails and he dies during surgery, or the brain transfer is successful and we wipe the hard drive clean and proceed to save the man who deserves to be saved, Mr. Tom Nolan."

Giamatti added, "We're not spending hundreds of millions to preserve a murderer. He's just the cheap meat for a trial run. The prisoner has stomach cancer," he said matter-of-factly. "He's dying already. We're not doing anything that isn't already coming to him."

"I have no sympathy for Louis in this process," said Cooper. "I'm just taking it all in so I understand. If everything works… and Tom Nolan is saved…then what?"

"Then the door opens to unlimited possibilities," Giamatti said. "Rescuing brains at the onset of Alzheimer's. Curing paralysis. The list goes on." He smiled broadly. "Cooper, how long have we worked together at the corporation?"

"Twenty-five years, sir."

"And in that time, I have trusted you like no other. You're a good man. You're like the sibling I never had. So, I'm going to share one more part of this project with you."

"There's more?" said Cooper.

"This is my favorite part," Giamatti said. "Stand up, we're going on a little walk. I want my wife to join us." He shouted, "Bella."

Giamatti's young and beautiful wife appeared at the door in a sleeveless dress. Her rolling blond hair rested on bare shoulders.

"We're going to pay a visit to the vault," he said.

She smiled and joined his side as he stood from his chair. The couple led the way out of the den and into a corridor.

"Are you sure you don't want that drink?" Giamatti asked Cooper.

"Maybe later."

"We'll all have a drink later."

Giamatti walked slowly, limping noticeably under the weight of his frame on aging legs. He took out a key and unlocked a door that led to a set of stairs descending to a windowless, underground level. He stepped carefully, gripping the banister, followed by Bella, Cooper and Steven. The basement space held no furnishings and the walls were plain. He advanced to a door with an electronic keypad and punched in a code, followed by the press of his thumb to validate his identity.

The door slid open. In the darkness, two shadowy human shapes stood motionless before them.

"What—" said Cooper, startled by the outline of apparent prisoners. Giamatti flipped on the light.

Exact replicas of Giamatti and his wife, Bella, stood propped against a wall, just like the real thing except frozen totally still with unblinking eyes.

"Look at her!" boomed Giamatti, setting his eyes on Bella's

replica adorned in a light, pink dress. "Her lovely form preserved for eternity. She will be twenty-six forever."

Bella said with a laugh, "I'll be 36-24-34 forever."

Giamatti smiled. "It sure beats Botox."

"Remarkable..." Cooper said, looking back and forth between Giamatti and his robotic likeness.

"We completed them last week," said Steven, proudly examining the workmanship. "Shells number two and three."

"If Tom Nolan is a success," Giamatti said, "and by success, I mean a year or more of perfect functionality, no bugs, no breakdowns, then I'm funding my own immortality, along with Bella's. Was it part of my motivation? Yes, I won't lie. I will benefit. Tom Nolan will benefit. A future of elderly and terminally ill will benefit as well – as long as they can cover the price tag, of course. I can only subsidize the proof of concept."

Giamatti turned toward Cooper and Steven. "If this is a rolling success, I guarantee both of you will be in good standing for receiving the gift of immortality. In the early going, it will be something of an exclusive club, but, as with anything, more time and more advances in science and technology could bring costs down. Perhaps even to a level where everyone can afford it. Of course, there should be a certain degree of oversight. Not everybody will deserve it. We don't want to prolong the existence of the lower elements of society, like Louis, like the rest of our prison population, and those who are a drag on civilization, but that's a discussion for another day.... Before I turn out the lights and we return upstairs, are there any questions?"

As Cooper stared into the eyes of Giamatti's identical shell, the color drained from his cheeks. Then he turned away, holding out his arms to steady himself.

"I think I'm ready for that drink," he said.

CHAPTER FOUR

From a black void of absence, muddy and fragmented thoughts began to stir in Louis's consciousness. As his mind cleared from the heavy fog, Louis prepared to awaken from a deep slumber. But hard as he tried, he could not open his eyes. The blindness immediately panicked him. He tried to shout out.

He couldn't speak.

Then Louis realized he lacked any senses at all. He could not hear sounds. He had no feeling of touch, wrapped in complete numbness.

He couldn't move.

He existed only in his head.

Oh my God, his mind panicked. *I'm completely paralyzed.*

Not much scared him in life — he had endured a hell of a lot from a torturous childhood to a life sentence in prison to an invasion of stomach cancer — but this sensation — no, a lack of *any* sensation at all — was enough to drive him mad.

He tried to pull apart his eyelids. He tried to make a fist. He tried to scream for help. Fail, fail, fail.

His whole life had depended on his physical, not mental prowess. Beating on his tormentors. Roughing up others for money and stature. Enjoying the pleasures of the flesh....

This stupid experiment must've messed me up, he realized. *I'm alive but not really. My body is dead and my mind keeps going. It's like being buried alive. I can't even kill myself to stop it!*

Maybe this is life after death?

His mind raced until he was mentally exhausted. He tried to will himself back to a blank unconsciousness. He wanted to succumb to sleep. But he was not physically tired or physically anything.

Maybe this is a test of some kind of new punishment, he thought.

Cheaper prisons. Why store the whole person? Just enslave their minds. In darkness. For eternity.

Louis could not scream out loud. But he did in his mind. Once he started, he couldn't stop. Somewhere, he was convinced, the devil was laughing at him.

Welcome to hell….

★   ★   ★

"He's dead." Carl Nodden, a member of the medical team, stood over Louis's pale and motionless body. It rested on a hospital bed set up in an operating room adjacent to the lab. The top of the patient's head was open and exposed, missing a section of skull to provide entry for an invasion of wires that probed the pink-and -gray brain matter.

"Dead there, yes – but not over here," Alan said. He huddled with several other scientists at a bank of computer monitors churning intricate readings of mental activity. "We can't hear his thoughts…but his mind is still alert. The readings are consistent with before."

There was an excited murmur. Steven Morris stepped closer to the computer screens, gripping a tablet. "This is real, people. The transfer has been a success."

Alan watched the green-and-blue dance of brainwaves on one of the monitors. "He has become pure consciousness, digitized and no longer attached to any living organism. He has no grasp of his surroundings. Just a steady stream of thought patterns. This is positively amazing."

Boyd Carmen, an African-American scientist with rectangular glasses, spoke up, representing the privacy mandate. "As exciting as this is, I must remind everyone that we remain in our blackout period. We cannot discuss any of this with the outside world – our families, our friends, our colleagues in the medical and technology fields. It would be in violation of the agreements you signed and immediately terminate your compensation packages. The official word for the prison officials…is that the patient died on the operating table. This is not untrue."

Alan continued to stare at the monitors as they logged brain activity. "I can't imagine what he must be thinking right now."

"Something like a waking coma," said Steven. "A dream state. I'm sure he's completely confused."

"When do we begin installation?" Nodden asked.

"If all the readings are sound, and they appear to be, we can begin the transfer in fifteen to twenty minutes," Steven said. "The host shell is prepared. The brain has been digitized and loaded onto a portable platform. Really, it should be as straightforward as installing a computer hard drive. It just takes a lot longer to boot up. There are trillions of connections to be made between the brain and the body. It's hard to say...but charging could take anywhere from a few hours to the better part of a day. Like everything else in this experiment, there's no guarantee it will work. We're flying on theories, not practical experience. The digital consciousness could blink out at any time, like a computer crash. But – so far, so good."

Alan continued to follow the wavy patterns on the brain activity monitor. "His thoughts are getting more aggressive. There's more intensity than when it started."

"Yes," said Steven, nodding calmly. "Our patient is probably experiencing an extreme form of claustrophobia right now. Do you blame him?"

★   ★   ★

Louis experienced a jolt, the collective power of a million tiny surges that pushed through his mind like a swarm of goldfish, dashing and darting in angular patterns.

His fear climbed another notch. He wriggled his body and emitted a small, dry cough.

Then he realized what he had just done. The wriggle, the cough.

Louis moved the fingers on his left hand. They responded to his mental commands with precision. He stirred his feet. They moved slightly, then stopped, held back by something.

"Hey," he said, a tiny, uncertain croak. He could now feel his body.

Louis concentrated very, very hard and commanded his eyes to open....

And they opened.

His eyesight was crystal clear. It had never been sharper. He didn't wear glasses, but sometimes squinted, and this was far better than he had ever experienced.

The room around him was familiar. It was the private space next to the lab where they brought him for the operation. This was where they placed him in a hospital bed and talked through his medical treatment. They told him he would be put under and wouldn't feel a thing. He said, "Let's go for it."

Regaining consciousness, he discovered he was vertical. It was a strange sensation, and he realized he was propped upright in a standing position, strapped to some kind of metal frame to prevent him from falling.

There was no one else in the room. He could hear voices just outside the door. Quite a few voices. Excited chatter, some laughter.

He smelled pizza.

I can smell. I can hear. I can see. I can move.

Then he discovered a bonus revelation.

Hey, my stomach doesn't hurt.

For weeks, the cancer had punched his midsection with horrible discomfort that drugs could barely subdue and he had accepted it as a way of life for his remaining days. But now...

...it all felt fine down there. Everything felt fine. He didn't have a single ache in him.

The surgery was a success.

Louis was not a religious man, but in that moment he thanked God. He felt like he had been to hell and back. This new feeling was so much better than the black hole that had consumed him and stripped his senses.

Louis was ready to go exploring but someone had secured him tightly to the metal frame. He didn't know why he was clamped down but these straps needed to come off, pronto. He felt restored to full strength – in fact, even stronger than before. Without much effort, he pulled free from the straps that held back his arms. Then he unlatched the rest of the restraints, down to his ankles.

So far, so good. Then Louis stepped out of the metal frame and realized he wasn't so steady without it.

He nearly fell to the floor. He caught himself, forced greater concentration on his movements, and his limbs dutifully obeyed.

His movements were hesitant, lacking confidence. With extra effort, he was able to guide them. He walked a slow arc around the room, not ready to summon the doctors yet. He wanted to get a good look at his surroundings and continue to clear his head. He was regaining a more fluid command over his mobility.

He studied the room. It was such a weird place. The volume of computer equipment and monitors looked like something out of NASA. It certainly didn't resemble a normal hospital room. Maybe they used computers to zap the cancer with super-advanced lasers like a videogame? *Star Wars* surgery. Why not?

Louis stepped over to the hospital bed he had previously inhabited. Startled, he discovered something big on top of the sheets. It was a distinctly human shape, zipped up inside a thick canvas body bag. Like a corpse waiting for delivery to the morgue.

What the hell? he thought. *Who's this poor guy? What's he doing in here?*

Curiosity quickly got the better of him. He reached down and took hold of the zipper's tab. Very slowly he peeled open the top of the bag to reveal the deceased man inside.

As the top of the body bag split apart, Louis stared into his own dead face.

Louis let out a shout. At once, he lost control of his movements, his concentration giving way to wild panic. He staggered backward from the body bag and collided with a table of surgical supplies, sending them crashing to the floor.

Within seconds, a cluster of doctors and scientists entered the room, pulled away from their pizza break. They were astonished to find Louis on his feet and moving about.

"That was fast," one of them said.

"We did it!" shouted another in excitement.

Steven Morris stepped to the forefront and took Louis's arm.

"Louis, how are you feeling?" He stared into Louis's eyes.

"Good. I'm feeling really...good. Who is...?" He began to turn back toward the body bag. Another man was already zipping it shut.

"We'll explain everything to you in due time," said Steven. "But first, we need to run a series of tests. Nothing invasive, just your hand-eye coordination, your joints, muscles, your speech."

"My speech feels weird," Louis said. "It sounds wrong. Did this surgery do something to my voice?"

"Yes, there are side effects. We'll explain. Can you sit down? There's a chair behind you."

Louis noticed several men rolling the body bag out of the room on a gurney.

"Is that me?" Louis asked, fully aware of the absurdity of the question.

"Not anymore," said Steven.

Louis sat in the chair. His vision filled with scientists staring at him in awe, some of them grinning, some simply appearing shocked. He felt like an animal in a zoo.

"First, let's test your memory. Can you tell me your name?"

Louis smirked. "Call me Charlie...."

"Giamatti is on his way," someone called.

"Who's Giamatti?" Louis asked.

"He paid for all this," responded Steven.

"I guess I owe the man some gratitude."

"We all do," Steven said. "He believed in this research. He believed in this team. He believed in possibilities that others didn't believe or didn't want to believe."

The lab scientists proceeded to conduct a checklist of tests requiring Louis to perform various movements and activities, including tasting and eating a slice of pizza.

"Tastes great," said Louis. "Best pizza I ever had. Then again, I've been living on prison food."

Several times, Louis asked again about the man in the body bag, and each time he was told he would learn more after the tests.

After forty minutes of performing simple physical tasks while answering questions to evaluate his mental clarity, Louis looked up to see a heavyset man with designer mirror sunglasses and a bulky white beard enter the room. The big man moved as quickly as he could, his pace hampered by a stubborn limp.

The others greeted him with reverence and parted to create a path for him to approach Louis.

"So this is our little miracle," he said. He removed his sunglasses and hooked them in the collar of his shirt. He held out his hand. "I'm pleased to meet you. My name is Simon Giamatti. You know my associate...." He turned and gestured at a neatly dressed man who had followed him into the room. "This is Cooper."

Louis nodded at Cooper, the man who'd visited him in prison.

"It's incredible," Steven told Giamatti. "He's become fully functional even sooner than we expected. His mind is sharp. He's quickly building a repertoire of remembered movements and coordination that will become second nature. His senses are replicated...heightened, really, from their former standing. The mind and body are communicating beautifully. Everything we mapped out...every element of the design...is becoming a reality."

Giamatti turned away from Louis and faced the others in the room. "Now, I'm sure I don't need to remind you...no selfies, no texting, no outreach to anyone outside this team. We are still a work in progress. Don't spoil it."

Louis asked, "Am I cured?"

Giamatti turned and stepped closer to him. He gave Louis a big smile.

"Cured? My dear boy, this is bigger than that. You could say that today the entire human race is cured."

In that moment, standing in front of Giamatti, Louis caught a glimpse of his own reflection in the old man's mirror sunglasses, which remained hooked on the collar of his shirt.

Louis moved closer for a better look, alarmed. It wasn't his face. He looked nothing like himself. It was another man – lighter complexion, blond hair, rounder face, narrow nose, all wrong.

Louis immediately put his hands on his face to feel his features. They felt out of proportion.

"What did you do to me?" he said in a shocked voice. Then he demanded, "Who was in that body bag? Was it me? *Who am I?*"

Louis quickly erupted into panic and outrage. He grabbed Giamatti and was immediately pulled off. The faces around him turned from warm and welcoming to frantic and hostile.

"Back off!" demanded Giamatti.

Louis began yelling threats at them. He felt the rise of his old temper, his lifelong backlash against a condescending society that was always trying to control him and force him to be someone other than his true self.

Louis's outburst only lasted about ten seconds.

Steven pointed a device at him — it resembled a television remote — and stabbed a red button.

In an instant, Louis was turned off, like a squelched stereo. He went silent and blind, began to stumble, and the others caught him and sat him back in the chair in a stiff, sitting position.

Louis's thoughts vanished down a black hole and quickly became nothing.

CHAPTER FIVE

Tom Nolan kissed his wife goodbye, briefcase in hand, and walked the four blocks to the Wilmette train station. The seven forty-five train to Chicago arrived and left with Tom still standing on the platform. As far as Emily was concerned, he had gone to work. He loved her and hated to deceive her but knew it was for the best for now. He had to honor the agreement he had signed. He was good for his word.

When Steven's Camry pulled up in the parking lot, Tom left the platform. Walking steadily but stiffly, straining against the early stages of his disease, he made it to the car and climbed in.

Steven could not hold back a very large grin.

He said, "It worked."

Tom felt a shudder. "Really?"

"It's unbelievable. Everything went as planned. Technology has caught up with human biology. Things are possible that were unthinkable five, ten years ago. I haven't been able to sleep. My mind keeps racing with the implications...."

"What happens next?"

"Plenty." Steven maneuvered the car around crowds of commuters. "First, let's get out of here before we're noticed. We need to get you to the lab. Seeing is believing."

During the drive, Steven prepped Tom for what he was about to encounter. "The brain-mapping process is very destructive to the source and ultimately kills the original life form. We tested it with another man who is, for lack of a better word, expendable. He's taking your shell for a test drive. We're in our third day and not seeing any major problems. It takes time for the coordination between the new brain and new body to become second nature, but the progress has been very good. We regularly check the vitals and everything is holding steady.

The mind is fully functional without memory loss and the body, limbs, and senses are performing extremely well. In some cases, the synthetic replacements are performing better than the capabilities of an ordinary human being."

"I'll be happy with just being ordinary again," said Tom.

"We're going to save your life," Steven said confidently. "And then we're going to save a whole lot more lives."

"When can I tell Emily?"

"We're getting closer. It's up to our sponsor."

"Mr. Giamatti?" Tom had met Giamatti once, briefly, during the screening process.

"Yes. Just hold tight a little while longer."

As they arrived in the parking lot of Perking Institute, Steven prepared Tom for the personality currently inhabiting his shell.

"He's a terminally ill prison inmate who agreed to be a test subject," he said. "He was carefully selected as someone with minimal ties to the outside world. The arrangement has a very small paper trail. I wanted you to be prepared because it will be startling to see yourself with a different persona."

"How long is he part of the test?"

"Two more weeks," said Steven. "Then, if all the signs are good, we'll work on the fusion of your mind with your shell. That's when Emily will be brought up to speed. We have people who can prep her with the right sensitivity. As you know, it's a significant concept to comprehend."

"I want her by my side when the operation takes place."

"We can arrange for that."

Steven parked the car. Tom hesitated before climbing out. A question lingered.

"The man.... The brain...that's doing the 'test drive'. What happens to him?"

Steven paused, staring down at his hands, which still gripped the steering wheel.

"He currently exists as a hard drive," he said. "Basically a large cartridge that has been installed in a very expensive recreation of your human form. In due time, we're going to remove his cartridge and replace it with yours. That's the simplest way to explain it."

"So what happens to his hard drive?"

Steven hesitated. "This is really more than I'm authorized to tell you. But I trust you. I know you. Please understand the delicacy of our moral ground. This man...comes from prison where he's serving a life sentence for multiple murders. He has terminal stomach cancer. We're not altering his fate."

"But the hard drive...his computerized brain."

"It will be wiped clean."

★　　★　　★

Steven and Tom signed in through the security desk and entered the main lab area, where members of the various science, medical and technology teams quickly stepped forward to greet them.

"Today's the day?" said Alan, giving Tom a hearty handshake.

"Yes," Steven said. "He's going to meet himself, maybe have a little conversation."

"How weird will that be," said Alan, smiling.

"I'm freaked out just thinking about it," Tom said.

"Is the patient regenerating?" Steven asked.

"Yes," said Alan. "He's in passive mode."

"What does that mean?" Tom asked.

"He's turned off," Steven said. "Sort of like sleep."

"Does it dream?" Tom asked with a nervous laugh.

"Not exactly," said Steven. He turned to look at a secured door on the side of the room, equipped with a keypad. "Listen," he told the others, "I'm going to take Tom inside to see our progress. I'd like to keep this first encounter private. Just the two of us, then we'll bring in more of the team. I think it's going to be a bit overwhelming."

"I'm ready for anything," Tom said.

"Then let's do this."

Steven guided Tom into the small operating room where two months ago he had met his lifeless shell replica. This time, the shell appeared equally lifeless, seated stiffly in a chair on one side of the room.

Steven closed the door behind them and brightened the lights.

"Hello, me," Tom said.

Steven took out a key and unlocked a drawer in an area of cabinets. He took out a thin, rectangular device.

"What's that?" asked Tom.

"Control," Steven said. "It allows me to activate or deactivate with the click of a button."

"Emily's going to love that. So she'll be able to turn me off when I get on her nerves?"

"It's more of a safeguard to keep our test subject from getting too independent, if you know what I mean."

"He's traded one jail cell for another."

"Oh, Tom," Steven said. "Don't call this a jail." He pointed the remote at the Tom replica and pressed a red button.

At first, nothing happened.

"He's warming up," said Steven.

Tom giggled. "I'm.... This is crazy."

"Look. See, his fingertips are moving?"

"Dear Lord."

"Watch his eyes now."

"He's really very handsome," Tom said.

The Tom replica began to move its shoulders slightly. It wavered a little bit in the chair, but caught itself from toppling.

"It has amazing balance control," Steven said.

"I'm looking forward to that," said Tom lightly under his breath.

The replica's eyes widened, then looked around the room. The head rotated a bit one way, then another.

The hands curled into fists.

The spine straightened.

The eyes stopped roaming and locked on Tom, then Steven, then back to Tom.

Tom heard his own voice speaking to him: "Who are you?"

Tom began to offer his hand, then withdrew it, nervous. "My name is Tom. Who...are you?"

The replica's lips rippled into a smile. "Call me Charlie."

"Charlie?"

"It's a joke."

"Oh," said Tom.

"Can you stand up?" Steven requested.

"Sure," said the replica. For a moment, he twisted awkwardly, unsure of his coordination, and then his motion became simple and fluid. He stood up.

"It's nice to meet you," Tom said, cringing at the weirdness of the encounter.

The replica's eyes narrowed and his forehead wrinkled. "You," he said. "You...sound like me."

Steven quickly interjected. "Tom here provided the archetype for your new, healthier body. He's part of our team."

"I liked my voice better," said the replica. "Nothing personal. This new voice sounds kind of wimpy."

Tom chuckled. "Doesn't bother me. I guess I'm used to it. My wife likes it."

"Your wife?"

"Emily," Tom said. Steven shot him a quick glance as if to convey: *Let's lay off the personal details.*

Tom's replica studied Tom.

"It's not just the voice," he said.

"Excuse me?" said Tom.

"I look just like you."

Steven cocked his head, unsure of the remark. There were no mirrors in the room, a deliberate choice. "What do you mean?"

"I've seen my reflection," said the replica. "In Santa's glasses."

Steven tightened his grip on the remote. Louis was referring to Giamatti, who wore mirrored sunglasses with large lenses.

"As I said," Steven said carefully, "Tom provided his dimensions for our prototype. He has the ideal physique."

"Yeah," the replica said. "Maybe."

"You look great," said Tom, trying to cut past some of the awkwardness and tension.

"Check out the texture," Steven said, attempting to change the subject. "We mastered the body temperature. We adjusted the surface of the skin some more. Feel his hands."

Tom asked his replica, "May I?"

The replica said, "I don't care."

Tom stepped forward. As he did, he stumbled slightly. He grimaced and clutched his leg. "Sorry." He took a deep breath, shook it off, and made another step forward.

Tom reached out to his replica. As he brought his hand closer, it began to tremble, then shake more vigorously. His aim missed its mark and his hand swerved into vacant air. Tom struggled to regain control of his muscle movement. He grabbed his wrist, stuck in a bad moment, a temporary loss of control. It was the gradually increasing symptoms of his condition. His face turned red and he muttered under his breath, "Damn it."

"Hey," said the replica in a low voice. "Are you sick?"

Tom shook his head and retracted his hand. He took a step backward, stiffly, and nearly stumbled again. "No. I'm fine...."

At that moment, Steven lifted his arm and pointed the remote at Tom's replica. The replica immediately picked up on the movement, head turning sharply.

And then all hell broke loose.

Tom's replica lunged at Steven and swatted the remote out of his hand with lightning speed. The remote flew across the room, hit the floor and skidded beneath a large bank of computers. As Steven turned to run for the remote, the replica punched him hard in the face, sending him crashing into Tom before falling to the ground.

Tom tried to stay on his feet and run for the door, but his legs staggered. His replica pounced on him. Tom experienced the surreal sensation of being attacked by himself, witnessing an unnatural viciousness in his own face.

Tom's replica threw Tom hard across the room. As Tom fell, his head struck the side of a metal cabinet. Tom sunk unconscious to the floor, blood leaking from a wound on his scalp.

Steven hurried back to his feet and opened his mouth to cry out for help. His outburst was immediately reduced to a gasp as Tom's replica grabbed him around the throat and squeezed.

Louis put every ounce of his strength into strangling Steven, pinching off his oxygen with powerful, steel hands. Steven slumped unconscious.

As Steven dropped, Louis turned to Tom, who remained motionless on the floor.

"You're my ticket outta here."

He kneeled down and quickly undressed Tom. He pulled Tom's limp form out of his shirt and pants. Then he peeled away his own hospital garb. He got dressed in Tom's clothes. They fit perfectly.

Of course they would, he thought.

Louis tossed aside Tom's cell phone but confiscated his car keys and wallet.

He moved over to Steven and raided his pockets. He dug out another wallet and set of car keys.

Louis straightened up and forced himself to settle down. He dimmed the lights. It was time to leave the party.

He exited the room and entered the main lab area, quickly closing the door behind him.

Several members of the lab team approached him.

"What did you think, Tom?" asked a man with narrow glasses.

"Amazing," Louis said. "Really amazing. I'm blown away."

"Two more weeks of tests, and then we should be good to get you in your shell," said a stocky man in a white lab coat, nerd-faced with curly hair.

"Oh, I can't wait." Louis walked toward the exit, trying to quicken his pace without losing his casual demeanor.

"You can't stay?" asked someone.

"I want to..." Louis said. "But I have to get back...." And then he offered the only piece of information he knew about his new persona. "I have to get back to Emily."

"Ah, yes," said someone. "Don't let her catch on.... You have to keep her in the dark a little while longer."

Louis absorbed the insight with interest. "Yes," he said. "It's been hard...keeping it a secret."

"I'll bet."

Louis finally extracted himself from the scientists and made it to the front security desk, where he was greeted warmly.

"I hear the experiment has been a big success," said the guard.

"Yes, a big success," Louis said. "I'll be back soon. I need to go see...Emily."

"I hope you can tell her soon," the guard said. "She's going to be so excited."

Louis walked into the parking lot and promptly pulled out the sets of car keys he had lifted from the two men. He pressed their buttons until a car beeped and flashed nearby.

My ride is here.

Louis quickly drove off in Steven's Camry, a free man. In the car, he smirked, then broke out into guffaws. These weasel scientists thought they could use him as a lab rat and then discard him to save some pretty boy. Well, that was just dumb thinking.

As he drove, he placed Tom Nolan's wallet in his lap and picked through the various credit cards and forms of ID.

Louis's first instinct was to drive as fast and far away as possible, but as he stared at Tom's driver's license, a more compelling option opened up.

To truly disappear, Louis knew he needed money. And that meant more money than the cash in the two stolen wallets and whatever he could quickly pull from the credit cards.

Tom Nolan's driver's license revealed his home address in a wealthy suburb, just twenty minutes away, where the citizens enjoyed big bank accounts and fat investment portfolios.

For Louis's entire life, money was a major motivator. He grew up with none and specialized in acquiring funds that belonged to others, a healthy hobby that blossomed into a winning streak of bank robberies – until that fateful day Groucho ruined everything.

The intoxicating lure of money held a spell over Louis. Time was of the essence. The Camry's GPS would guide him. He gunned the accelerator....

This new Tom Nolan had an urgent bit of business to conduct. He was going to withdraw all of his funds. Then he was going to Florida or Mexico or anywhere else that was far from here to start a new life under a new name.

Louis had to chuckle. The turn of events was just too beautiful. From serving a life sentence in prison with stomach cancer...to becoming a healthy, highly evolved free man who might just live forever.

Saved by a miracle. What does it mean? he wondered. *There is a God? There is no God?*

Traffic was clear and Louis was making good time.

He felt flush with a computerized ecstasy and laughed in a voice that was not his own, a funny sound that only compounded his laughter into something delirious and deranged.

CHAPTER SIX

"You're home early."

Emily stepped out of the kitchen to greet her husband at the front door.

Louis stood still for a moment, checking her out, impressed. She was a slinky brunette in snug jeans and a casual button-down, collared shirt that clung to her curves quite nicely. He forced himself to stop staring and addressed the immediate matter at hand.

"I have something I need to take care of," he said in Tom's voice, careful to enunciate with an upper middle-class elegance, and not his usual sloppy growl. "Where do we keep the bank statements?"

She gave him an odd look. "In the den, where you've always kept them. I didn't move anything."

Louis nodded. "That's right." He glanced around. *Now where is the den?*

He headed in a direction that took him to a living room with a piano and couch, then turned to backtrack and choose another path. He knew she was staring at him.

She asked, "Are you feeling okay?"

"Sure, sort of, I'm fine." Louis considered telling her he had a couple of drinks on the way home – but what if this guy was a teetotaler? He had to act fast and arouse minimal suspicion.

"Why do you need the bank statements?"

"Investment opportunity," he said, and he entered a corridor that led to more rooms. He quickly found what appeared to be the family den with a big desk, bookcase and large-screen television. Children's toys littered the floor. He immediately approached the desk, pulling open the biggest drawer.

"Investment opportunity?" She followed him in.

"Can you—" he started, intending to finish with *go away*. But that might be out of character or invite time-wasting bickering. So he concluded, "—get me a glass of water?"

She hesitated. "Sure." She left the room.

He began rummaging through a series of files in the desk's bottom drawer. Legal-looking documents. Where was the money?

Then Louis sensed he was being watched. He turned to see a little girl standing near him with blond pigtails and big blue eyes. A small white poodle joined her.

The little girl watched him for a moment and then said, "You're not Daddy."

Louis froze and stared back.

The poodle tensed up and started to growl.

"Go play," said Louis in a low, unfriendly voice, "or I'll kick your teeth in."

The girl's eyes widened and she dashed off. The dog followed her out of the room.

In that moment, Louis realized this could end badly. For them. He might have to kill some people today. There was precious little time to conduct this job, and any interference would not be tolerated.

The desk was not providing what he needed. "Damn it," he growled, flipping through a sea of useless materials.

"Why are you looking in there?" Emily asked. She entered the den with a glass of water. "The bank papers are in the cabinet in the closet."

He turned, looked at her, ignored the outstretched hand with the glass of water, and said, "That's right. Of course. Memory lapse."

He jumped to his feet and hurried to a broad set of closet doors. Opening them, he discovered a big gray filing cabinet. He immediately tugged open the first drawer.

"You're walking better," she said.

"What?"

"You're moving better, without the stiffness."

"Oh," he responded as he shuffled through papers. "Yes. I

feel good." Then he realized it probably wasn't the right thing to say and augmented it with a sudden, phony twitch of pain. "Ow. Now it's coming back. Yes. Stiff."

In the middle drawer, he found a lineup of financial folders. BANK. SAVINGS. INVESTMENTS. RETIREMENT.

Bingo.

He pulled one of the files and immediately scanned the numbers.

Six figures. This family had dough. Now he had account numbers. He found a hastily scribbled password.

"Why do you need to go through our savings? What's this investment opportunity? I don't understand."

"It's for...medical treatment," he said, and he found a checkbook for the savings account. Then he discovered the address for their local broker's office and a contact name.

Gold.

"We need to talk about this," Emily said, standing behind him. "This feels very rushed. We need those savings for when you can't work any longer."

"Trust me," said Louis in his best Tom Nolan voice.

Suddenly the phone rang. Tom's wife let out an exhale of exasperation. "I'm going to get this...but then we're going to talk."

Louis nodded, tossing off his best 'yes, dear' response while not missing a beat seizing useful papers from the filing cabinet. Emily left the room, and Louis grumbled, "Thank God."

★　　★　　★

Emily entered the kitchen. She picked up her ringing cell phone from the counter. Her head was swimming from Tom's strange behavior and sudden preoccupation with their savings. While Tom's body was beginning to break down, his mind had remained sharp – until now. He seemed disoriented, lost in his own home. Was it the meds? Was it part of his overall decline? Had he experienced a minor stroke?

She answered the call with a jab of her thumb. "Hello?"

The voice on the other end was strained and out of breath, yet instantly familiar.

"Hi honey, it's me. Listen, I'm going to be home a little late. I fell and hit my head. It's going to require stitches. Don't worry, it's just a bump. I'll be home in a while. I just don't want you to worry."

"Tom?" she said.

"Yes?"

"Is this a joke?"

"What do you mean?"

"Who is this?"

"It's Tom."

"How.... Where are you calling from?"

"What's wrong?"

"*Who are you?*" she shouted in a panic.

Abruptly a hand shot out and grabbed the phone away. It was her husband, returned from the den, standing in front of her with a crazed look on his face. "I'll talk to him," he said in the same voice that was on the other end of the phone.

Emily staggered back against the sink, terrified and confused.

"Hello," said the man in her kitchen, speaking into the phone. "How may I help you?"

"Who is this?" the caller demanded.

"Who's on first, what's on second, I don't know is on third...."

Emily could hear the immediate shock and outburst from the caller: "Oh my God. *Stay away from my family!*"

The man in her kitchen disconnected the call. Then he smashed the phone hard against the kitchen counter, where it flew apart into pieces.

Sofi entered the kitchen, drawn by the noise, wide eyed.

"Sofi, honey," said Emily, trying to sound calm for the sake of her daughter. "Please leave the room. Go watch TV."

Sofi looked back and forth between her mom and the man standing next to her.

"*Please, Sofi.*"

"Okay, Mommy." She left the kitchen.

Emily stared hard at the man who appeared to be her husband.

His face was now pinched and wicked in a way that did not look like Tom anymore. Who was this strange, uncanny imposter?

"I don't know who you are," she said. "But please leave my house."

The man grinned with narrowed eyes. "That's not a very nice way to talk to your husband."

"You can't be my husband."

"You're hot when you're agitated." He stepped forward. He pinned her against the counter. "How about some marital bliss? Daddy's a bit worked up, if you know what I mean."

He moved in to cup her breast and began kissing her neck.

Emily reached for the frying pan she had placed on the stove to start dinner. She grasped the handle and swung hard with all her might.

She struck the man on the forehead with a loud *clang* and sent him reeling backward. His movements lost their coordination and he fell to the ground.

Emily fled the room. She screamed for Sofi.

Sofi stood in the hallway, scared and confused. Emily scooped her up and ran for the nearest room with a lock – the bathroom.

She quickly secured them inside, just in time. The man arrived at the door and started pounding.

The entire door shook, and Emily feared he would break through at any minute. Sofi began to cry. Emily heard their dog barking.

"Please!" Emily screamed. "Take whatever you want! Just leave us alone!"

There was an abrupt halt in the pounding.

"You've really thrown me off," said the man. "Goddamn it, now I don't have time to go to the bank. So here's what you're going to do. You're going to tell me where the jewelry is. And you better have some good shit."

"I do!" said Emily. "I swear I do."

"Because if you don't, I'm killing you both. And I'm killing this noisy little dog, too."

The poodle continued barking and then let out a yelp, as if from a sudden kick.

"*It's in the bedroom*," shouted Emily. "In the closet. You'll see shoe boxes. There's a red box, top shelf, in the back, behind—"

She heard the rapid thud of footsteps moving to another part of the house.

Emily hugged Sofi tighter. She stroked her cheek. "We're going to be okay, honey."

"Mommy," Sofi said, "why is that man pretending to be Daddy?"

Emily felt dizzy, overwhelmed by the insanity of the situation. The only answer she could offer was the truth. "Honey, I have no idea."

★   ★   ★

Louis plopped himself back in the Camry. He threw his winnings in the passenger seat: an impressive jewelry collection, plus the woman's purse with its cash and credit cards, useful for the short term. He still needed a bigger stash for a proper rebirth, but this was a start.

Louis put the car in gear and glanced in the rearview mirror. He caught a glimpse of himself – looking nothing like himself – with an added embellishment that gave him concern.

There was an open wound on his forehead where the frying pan had struck him. It did not create a bloody gash, just a hole in the flesh revealing a peek of shiny steel. This did not look human.

"*What the hell am I?*" he said.

CHAPTER SEVEN

Tom Nolan exclaimed, *"He's at my house! Somebody take me home!"*

The lab continued to swirl in a stew of panic and confusion. The escape of Louis Karp was discovered when one of the scientists entered the side room and found the unconscious bodies of Tom and Steven Morris. Giamatti was immediately alerted. He demanded that no one contact the police or any other outside party. Tom regained consciousness, but suffered a mild concussion. One of the doctors stitched the wound on the back of his head. Steven's throat was bruised, and his voice was hoarse. Giamatti gave Tom permission to contact his wife to let her know his arrival home would be delayed and he had 'accidentally' hit his head.

"Downplay the hell out of it," he insisted, and that was Tom's plan until he called home and heard his own voice on the other end of the phone.

Emily and Sofi were in danger and his immediate priority was to get to them. When Tom shouted for someone to drive him home, Alan stepped forward. "I'll take you there now." He gripped the remote that had been retrieved from under a bank of computers. "If he's still there, we'll shut him down."

They hurried into Alan's car. Tom provided directions and Alan drove fast. Tom could barely sit still. "I can't believe the son of a bitch went to my house."

"As soon as we get him back to the lab, we'll remove the cartridge," said Alan. "He served his purpose. He's nothing more than a digital file. We'll delete the bastard."

Alan's cell phone began ringing. He answered it with one hand. "Hello, Mr. Giamatti. I'm with Tom. The real Tom. Let me put you on speaker."

Giamatti's voice filled the car. It shook with fury. "All of the years and money that went into this...and you allow the test subject to just walk out the front door?"

"Not exactly..." Alan said.

"We're going to my house," said Tom urgently. "We'll be there in ten minutes. He's in my house with my wife and daughter."

"Yes, I was just informed," Giamatti said. "I'm on my way there, too. Cooper is with me. He's armed."

Tom shut his eyes. He regretted ever agreeing to this experiment. Instead of dying with dignity, he had entered into an unholy pact and jeopardized the two people he loved more than anything in the world. Perhaps these scientists were truly meddling in areas of God's creation that should be left alone.

Alan pulled into Tom's driveway, and Tom immediately jumped out. He moved as quickly as his legs would take him – stumbling, grimacing through the awkward disobedience of his muscles – but refusing to fall.

He threw himself on the front door, yanked it open and lunged into the house, too breathless to shout out Emily's name. The first thing he saw was a large knife coming at him.

Tom yelled and fell to the floor.

Emily wielded a knife from the kitchen, stopping the blade just inches from Tom's face.

"*Don't you move!*" she shouted, eyes blazing.

"Emily, it's *me!*" said Tom, panting. "It's really me – not the other me." He knew he looked and sounded crazy. He wore a rumpled, ill-fitting lab coat and sweatpants since his own clothing had been stolen.

Emily studied him suspiciously, knife pointed at his throat.

Sofi peeked at them from around a corner. The poodle scampered over, oblivious to the tension, tail wagging.

"It's Daddy!" Sofi said, breaking out into a big grin.

"Are you going to doubt your daughter's intuition?" said Tom, attempting a weak smile.

Emily did not smile back and held the knife firm. "What in God's name is going on here?"

Then she looked up to see a series of strange men approaching the house.

"Who are these people?" she demanded.

"His name is Alan." Tom turned to look and saw Giamatti and Cooper climbing out of Giamatti's Mercedes. "And those are...those are...." He stopped. How could he possibly explain any of this? What could he say?

"Is he inside?" Alan asked, entering the house.

"Who? My other husband?" said Emily, still tense and angry.

"Well, yes – the other Tom Nolan," Alan said.

"No," she said. She slowly dropped the hand with the knife. "I'm so lost. I can't even think straight."

Giamatti and Cooper entered the house next.

"He's not here," Alan told them.

Giamatti muttered a profanity. He looked over at Emily.

"We have to tell her," Tom said.

Giamatti slowly nodded. "Yes, I suppose the cat – or should we say, the robot – is out of the bag."

"Ma'am, you'll need to sign some paperwork," Cooper said.

"For what?" said Emily.

"Do it, honey," Tom said. "It will allow us to tell you everything."

"I guess we can add one more to our inner circle," Giamatti said. "Mrs. Nolan, you will be privy to information that is highly confidential and classified. You cannot tell your mother, your best friend, your book group...."

"Don't condescend to me," Emily said. "Just tell me who that maniac was that came in here pretending to be my husband."

"Did he hurt you?" asked Tom.

"No. He wanted our money. He was going through our bank statements."

"I'll call the bank," Tom said.

"He took my jewelry." Emily's voice rose. "All of it. Everything! Even my great grandmother's—"

Giamatti spat, "The jewelry is nothing. He's wearing a one hundred million-dollar suit!"

Emily turned to look at the fat, bearded man, perplexed, and then broke out in a short laugh. She walked into the kitchen and tossed the knife into the sink. "This is absurd. None of you make any sense."

Tom followed her. "Honey, let us explain. Believe it or not, under all this craziness, there's some really amazing news."

"I don't know if I can take anything else right now," she said.

"These men are connected to doctors and scientists," he told her. "*I can be cured.*"

She stared at him. She only felt more confused. Then she started to cry.

★   ★   ★

They sat together in the living room and Giamatti told Emily everything. "We're dealing with the ultimate form of identity theft," he said sardonically, although no one found it amusing. He vowed they would track down and retrieve Tom's fugitive shell and wipe it clean of Louis Karp. Giamatti promised Emily that this same shell would one day accept Tom's digitized mind and memories to sustain his life. "And that," he said, "I'm sure you will agree, is worth more than all the jewelry in the world."

Emily nodded, still dazed. She thought about Sofi, who was quietly playing in her bedroom. "Our daughter – she doesn't know Tom has a terminal illness. We haven't told her."

"There's still a chance Louis Karp could return to your house," said Giamatti. "Common sense dictates he won't come back. His window of opportunity to take your savings is closed and he probably wants to get as far from here as possible. But you can never be too sure. I've asked Cooper to stay with you for a few days. He has a firearm and knows how to use it. He also has a device that can shut down the robot's functions from fifty feet. It's like a big 'off' switch."

"What about Steven?" Tom asked. "Is he going to be okay?"

"He was choked pretty bad," said Giamatti. "But he'll be all right. We'll cover for his injury. We'll make sure he's safe as well. He's our top scientist."

"He's my friend," said Tom.

"Tom," Giamatti said, "the most important thing we need from you is to act natural. Continue with your life. Tomorrow, report to work like nothing's happened. We'll take care of the rest. Can you do that? We'll keep your house secure."

Tom slowly nodded. "I can do that."

Giamatti faced Emily. "The same for you. Act natural. Live your life. Don't draw attention. We have everything under control. You have to trust us."

Emily shrugged, a sad look in her eyes. "I don't really have a choice, do I?"

★   ★   ★

The next morning, Tom woke up and began his normal routine – shower, shave, a slip into a sports coat and slacks, and a quick cup of coffee and small bowl of fruit. He grabbed his briefcase, kissed his wife and daughter goodbye, and then thanked Cooper for staying with them.

"If there's anything unusual, any new information, anything – please let me know right away," Tom said.

"Absolutely," said Cooper.

Tom walked the four blocks to the Metra train station. He waited in the early morning sunshine among a crowd of other commuters on the platform for the southbound trains.

He had several meetings scheduled with clients and his partners. He knew it would be hard to focus. But he would make it through this day. He would not give in to fear.

The seven forty-five train to Chicago arrived and Tom lined up to enter and find a seat. Once inside, he slid against a window and looked out at the mundane morning activity. The scene looked just like the start of any other weekday.

Except....

His eyes noticed a police officer, then another, enter the crowd of commuters. At first, it didn't mean much to him but when the numbers increased to four, then six police officers, he grew alarmed.

"Why aren't we moving?" asked an impatient commuter in

the seat behind him. A growing curiosity rippled through the train as the police presence grew.

Tom's cell phone buzzed in his pocket. He took it out and read the text message from his wife. It screamed in all capital letters.

GET OFF THE TRAIN! RUN!!

CHAPTER EIGHT

Louis marveled over his newfound strength and stamina. He drove all night without feeling sleepy or hungry, steady as a rock. He reached his destination, Florida, in record time. Someplace nice and warm where he could disappear. He would soon ditch this car. He would lead a new life in a new town with a new face.

Truth be told, he didn't like the new face very much. Squeaky clean, cheerful cheekbones, blue eyes and blond hair, suburban dipshit. No scars, no crooked teeth, no beady eyes, no personality. Like a Ken doll from that Barbie and Ken set. The more he thought about it, the more he wanted to punch himself in the face.

And what the hell was under his skin?

The lab nerds had been vague from the beginning about his 'cancer treatment'. Waking up as someone else definitely did not come up as a potential side effect. That was freakish in itself – like a Frankenstein thing. At first, he figured they had moved his brain to some other guy's body, but then the other guy showed up and that was a real mind bender. Once it became obvious the other guy was sickly and the real benefactor of all this hoopla, the game was finished as far as Louis was concerned. He was done being Louis the Lab Rat. Health restored, there was no reason to stick around. He wanted out.

The weird scar that revealed steel in his forehead – as well as the unnatural power and smoothness of his movements – led Louis to the ultimate wacko conclusion: he was now a machine. These scientists, wrapped up in their whispery secrets, were experimenting with something fucked up and futuristic. It made sense that they wanted him for a test subject, a dying man that nobody gave a shit about. It kept their secrets safe.

They had used him for their Frankenstein Robot Project and

that was fine, because now he had used them to escape into a brand-new life.

Aside from the smug pretty-boy face, he could get used to this new persona. He regretted he couldn't keep his alter ego's hot wife fooled long enough to try out one of his new parts, but with his movie-star good looks he would attract plenty of bronze babes in the Sunshine State. He was mad he hadn't killed the real Tom Nolan when he had the chance. If it wasn't for that damned phone call, he could have kept the charade going long enough to siphon his considerable savings.

Nevertheless, Louis accomplished a couple of quick robberies on his way out of town. After leaving Tom Nolan's house, he visited the nearest shopping mall and entered a jumbo sporting goods store. First things first. He needed a gun. As he reviewed his options in the Hunting and Firearms department, he was caught off guard by a greeting from the clerk.

"Why, hello, Tom, what brings you here?" asked a skinny old man in a red vest with thin gray hair and bright white dentures.

Louis read the name on his name tag. "Hello, Bill."

"I miss seeing you in church," Bill said. "I've been going to early mass. Listen, I heard about your illness. I'm really sorry."

"Thank you," Louis said, eyes on the gun display.

"What happened to your forehead?"

"My what?" It took a moment for Louis to realize the old man was referring to the strange open cut that revealed a glimpse of gray steel. "Oh. That's just an allergic reaction."

Keeping his eyes on the merchandise, Louis studied his options.

"What can I help you with?" Bill asked. "What's your pleasure?"

"I need a gun. Just something for home protection. We had a run-in with burglars. They threatened my wife and daughter."

"Goodness, really?" Bill's eyes grew wide. "I was going to say, I never thought of you as a gun person, but things change. It's a jungle out there. I can answer any questions you have. The one I keep at home is a...."

The cozy familiarity allowed Louis the opportunity to see

merchandise up close. Friendly Bill left the glass display case unlocked. When the choice of make and model was firmed up, and a box of bullets identified, Louis said to Bill, "You have a stain on your collar," and reached out toward the old man's throat.

Like the episode in the lab room, the choking was swift and easy with his immensely powerful hands. Louis wasn't certain if he had squeezed Bill dead or just strangled the man unconscious, but the important thing was he was fully armed within seconds. The store security stirred awake from their sleepy suburban tranquility to a genuine reason to fulfill their job duties. They came at him from multiple directions.

Louis managed to escape without firing a shot – just threatening to do so, dragging a young boy with him for a good length of the store. The poor kid had been looking at baseball gloves and now he was having an adventure he could tell his chums for the rest of his life. As long as the 'rest of his life' didn't expire today due to bad behavior.

Fortunately, the boy obeyed the commands of a crazy man wielding a gun.

As Louis made it to the exit, he flung the boy into a carousel of basketball jerseys. He heard a woman exclaim, "Oh my God, is that Tom Nolan?"

Louis stopped for a moment to make sure the security cameras got a really good look at him and said clearly, for the witnesses, "Who said my name?"

The woman guilty of identifying him ducked out of view.

Louis left the store.

It was time for one of his classic doubleheaders – creating a big stir in one location and then using the distraction to commit a second crime nearby.

Louis sped one mile down the main road and pulled into a Quick Stop convenience store. He liked the name. Speed and convenience were very important right now.

Bill's remark about Louis's forehead reminded Louis he needed to cover up the alien-looking wound. Inside Quick Stop, he found the aisle with medical supplies and picked out a big adhesive bandage. He reported to the front counter.

"One bandage," Louis said to the plump, pimply woman at the cash register. "And one beef jerky." He pulled an individually wrapped stick from a display box. "Annnnd...." He paused for dramatic effect and lifted his brand-new gun. "All the money in your register."

The woman wet herself. Louis could hear the trickle as it reached the linoleum. She nervously scooped up as much cash as she could from the drawer. Louis also helped himself to a canister collecting spare change for an animal shelter.

"Mr. Nolan!" said a voice behind him.

Louis turned to see a saggy middle-aged woman in a baggy dress with her hair up in a bun.

"Mr. Nolan, if you need money for medical treatment, this is not the way to do it."

Louis shrugged. "Health costs are a bitch."

The bun woman continued to nag, so on his way out, Louis shot her in the toe. Then he waved at the security cameras, showing his face and laughing to himself: *This is an even better disguise than ol' Charlie.*

Driving away from the convenience store, Louis passed a rush of flashing cop cars headed in the opposite direction, reporting to the scene of his first crime. He almost wanted to wave at them.

Louis felt giddy.

He had a new gun, several thousand dollars' worth of jewelry, and a pleasant stash of cash – enough to handle his immediate needs as he trekked out of Chicagoland and cut across the country for new surroundings.

After eighteen solid hours of driving, most of it in the dark of night on long stretches of Tennessee and Georgia highway, Louis was now approaching a Florida town called – no fooling – Kissimmee. While he wasn't feeling hungry, the beef jerky he had consumed back in Chicago tasted good, and he was interested in pleasuring his new taste buds even if they were fake. His legs probably needed to stretch, too, although they felt fine.

He found a small diner with a fading sign and mostly empty

parking spaces. It promised pizza, hamburgers and a low-key vibe, good enough for him.

Inside, he ordered a basic cheeseburger and fries. A simple meal for most, but he knew it would be miles better than any of the swill he had consumed in jail. The guards had openly laughed about the presence of dead insects and mouse droppings in the prison dinners.

He grew irate just thinking about it.

After completing his meal, feeling neither stuffed nor hungry, Louis reported to the elderly woman at the cash register to inform her how the check would be handled.

"Today is backwards day," he said. "I don't pay you. You pay me. Everything you got."

He produced his gun to show her he was serious. He needed gas money, motel money, and every little stack of green helped.

The woman looked at him blankly, and he told her to be quick or risk getting a bullet. She bent down for a moment, and that should have been a signal, as the money was on the counter, not below, but he let her age lower his guard, a bad move, because these days everybody had a gun, even grandma types in aprons with big glasses, jowls and penciled eyebrows.

A shot rang out, and it wasn't Louis's gun. She had a pretty quick aim and release, this old woman, and placed a neat little hole in his chest.

Louis felt like he had been jabbed with a stick for a moment and then the feeling went away.

He stared at her.

She stared at him. Her eyes grew big, really big with the magnification of her thick glasses. Her mouth quivered.

"You don't bleed," she said in hushed astonishment, almost a whisper to herself.

"No. But you do."

He shot her above the chest, took the money, and then fired a bullet in the direction of a jumpy waiter who seemed uncertain of whether to sprint toward the commotion or away. He wisely chose 'away' when the bullet chipped the floor near his feet.

Louis hopped in his car and drove off. He returned to the

highway and figured he'd continue a few more hours before hunkering down in a cheap hotel and plotting his new identity. He needed a new name, now that 'Tom Nolan' was soiled. And he would have to reach into his bag of tricks for a Social Security number and phony driver's license.

Louis thought back to the beginning of this journey: his departure from Chicago and the encounters with Bill at the sporting goods store and the woman with the now-missing toe at the convenience store. Poor Tom Nolan would have a lot to answer for. Tom's neighbors would go on television and express their shock. "He was such a nice man. He went to church. He was a good neighbor. A loving husband and father. I can't believe he would do such a thing."

And it would sound like every other news story where a seemingly ordinary man goes on a rampage.

Ah well, thought Louis. *Not my problem.*

CHAPTER NINE

Tom stared at his wife's text message in confusion. From his window on the train he could see police cars with flashing lights multiplying around the station.

He was beginning to poke out a reply when the cell phone rang.

Giamatti.

Tom answered. He didn't have time to ask questions. Giamatti immediately began talking.

"Cooper just notified me the police showed up at your house looking for you. Your wife told them you went to work. She didn't know...but now she does...you're accused of two robberies and a shooting."

"Wait – what?" Tom said. "That's impossible!" Then he realized the likely culprit. His replica was running amok.

"It's the other you. Listen, don't let them catch you. If you're caught, I can't help you. This experiment cannot be revealed to the public for very important, highly classified reasons. I'll tell you more later. For now – go into hiding. Do not contact your wife. Turn off your cell phone until you're safe. Do you hear me?"

Tom's attention was split between Giamatti shouting in his ear and watching the police enter the train. The passengers around him continued to grumble and speculate about the delay. Tom seized the moment to satisfy their curiosity. He turned off his phone.

"*The train's on fire!*" he yelled, rising immediately in his seat. "*Everybody evacuate!*"

There was an instant eruption of chaos. Everybody wanted off. Tom snatched his briefcase and pushed into the aisle. He surrounded himself in the swarm of commuters rushing off the train.

The sudden wave of frantic commuters overwhelmed the police trying to make their way onboard. Tom grabbed a *Wall Street Journal* someone had abandoned and kept it close to his face as he exited the train. He spilled out on the platform and nearly brushed against a police officer who was too caught up in the pandemonium to notice him.

Tom moved with the flow of the crowd across the platform toward a set of stairs that descended to the parking lot. He stopped abruptly when he caught sight of several police officers advancing in his direction. He spun around. The path behind him wasn't much better. A growing number of police had slowed down the crush of commuters.

There was only one way left to go. Across the tracks. It required him to lower himself and crawl under a passenger walkway that bridged two train cars. He pulled his briefcase with him, hoping the surrounding chaos would shield him. If the wheels of the train suddenly began to move, he was mincemeat.

Tom made it to the open set of tracks on the other side. He quickly stood up, brushed the dirt from his sports jacket and—

—a loud horn blasted him.

Tom turned to see a train roaring at him from the other direction. He had exactly two seconds to react. He leapt off the tracks and dove onto the platform on the other side. His briefcase left his grasp and exploded against the front of the train, sending a swirl of legal documents into the air.

He entered a small group of commuters waiting for the northbound train from the city. "You're an idiot," said a businessman with slick hair and a stern look. "Never cross the tracks like that. You could have been killed."

"I have a very important meeting with a client," Tom told him. "I can't be late."

Another man, chubby in a rumpled suit with sad eyes, offered, "I know how it is, buddy. Been there."

Tom nodded in sympathy. As the train came to a full stop, he positioned himself in front of the doors to enter as swiftly as possible. It would only be a matter of minutes, maybe seconds, before the police expanded their search to this side of the tracks.

The train stood still. The doors would not open.

"Come on, come on," Tom said under his breath.

Nothing.

Then the train station's intercom sputtered and an announcement sounded over the speakers.

"Your attention, please. The seven fifty-five train to Kenosha will not be admitting passengers due to an active investigation. Please step away from the train. We hope to have you on the next train in approximately fifteen minutes. We apologize for the delay."

Tom gasped in despair. *Now what?*

He saw two police officers step onto the platform for the northbound trains. The two became four.

That's what.

The northbound train lurched forward. It chugged into motion, leaving for the next station without adding any commuters.

The group of people standing with Tom groaned and swore in aggravation.

"Fifteen minutes!" exclaimed a young, exasperated businesswoman in a black skirt and severe eyeshadow.

The train began to pick up speed as it left the station.

Tom knew he didn't have fifteen minutes.

From the look of things – more police stepping onto the platform, additional sirens approaching from the distance – he didn't even have fifteen seconds.

In his younger days, he was an athlete – basketball and track, mostly, which made the symptoms of his disease all the more cruel. He loved being active.

Tom prayed he had one good jump left in his game.

He was shaky, stiff and had bouts of clumsy coordination, but if there was ever a time for everything to go right, this was it.

As the rear of the train approached, still chugging along on the gradual climb to regular speed, Tom prepared himself. He knew timing was everything.

From the corner of his eye, he saw a policeman pick up a stray document from the platform – one of Tom's legal briefs.

Tom ran.

Please don't stumble, he prayed to himself.

As the last car roared by, Tom hopped off the platform. He landed in the gravel alongside the tracks, kept his balance and began a mad dash.

Please don't fall.

Tom ran as fast as he could. He followed the rear of the train, getting closer. He reached out with both hands, and then he jumped....

Please don't miss.

Tom grabbed a bar rail on the back of the train and pulled himself up. He wedged his feet on a small ledge. He hugged the rail with both arms as tight as he could and held on for dear life as the train picked up speed, whipping him with wind.

He did not look back. He simply wanted to get to the next station – Kenilworth – before the police caught up with him.

The train howled like a beast in his ears. His arms and hands ached with tension. He clenched his teeth and fought the pain. The train's vibrations threatened to throw him but he held on. If he fell, he would be dead or, at best, badly broken. He thought about Sofi and Emily. It gave him the extra strength he needed.

Rising out of the train engine's roar, Tom heard a police siren. He turned to see a squad car racing alongside the commuter train on a parallel road. His getaway plot had been discovered.

Tom didn't swear often. But at this moment, he indulged.

For a half minute, the train and police car ran at equal speed.

Tom remembered Sofi asking him, "Daddy, what's faster, a car or a train?" from the backseat several weeks ago as they waited at a train crossing.

"Train," he had told her.

Unfortunately, at this moment, the car was faster. The police sped forward on a clear path as the rest of the traffic obediently pulled over.

"*Train,*" said Tom aloud now, as if willing it to be true.

He watched the flashing police car keep pace with the train. Then a beautiful thing happened.

A red light. A congested intersection. A couple of large trucks. People in a crosswalk.

The train pulled ahead of the police car and kept on going.

Tom's arms felt like numb sponges, but he continued to squeeze the rail and keep his feet firm on the skinny ledge that was not meant to accommodate exterior passengers.

The train began to slow down as it approached the next station. When it was almost at a complete stop – but not quite – he jumped off.

He hit the ground hard, shook off the dizzy sparks that danced in his vision, and quickly staggered to his feet. Still finding his balance, he stumbled toward the Kenilworth train station, where the waiting crowd had not seen his unorthodox arrival.

Tom's skin prickled as the nagging police siren grew louder and closer.

No – not siren. *Sirens.* Plural.

Now what?

An SUV pulled up to the curb about twenty feet from where Tom was limping and grimacing.

Tom stopped and watched a pretty young woman with red hair and sunglasses drop off her husband. He wore a suit jacket and carried a laptop bag.

"Thanks, hon!" he shouted, eyes ahead, hurrying toward the train.

"Have a good day," she called out after him with good cheer.

It was a sweet, domestic moment.

It could have been Tom and Emily.

As the police drew near, Tom weighed his options. His ability to outrun the cops on foot was less than nil. And hiding aboard this particular train probably wouldn't fool anybody.

Quite frankly, he needed a car.

"Ma'am!" Tom shouted to the red-haired woman as she put her car into gear, preparing to leave the station.

She turned and looked at him.

"Your husband dropped his wallet!" Tom pointed in a random direction. "Is that his wallet? Or somebody else's?"

"Oh no," she said. She worked the gear again. She placed the car into park.

"I'll see if I can catch him," Tom said, pointing ahead to the train platform.

"Thank you," said the woman. "Thank you so much." She climbed out of the car, eyes searching for the wallet. She didn't see it and took several steps away from the car.

As she scanned the ground, crouched low, Tom circled back and hopped into the driver's seat. The engine was still running, ready to roll.

"I'm sorry!" Tom called out, slamming the door. He felt guilty, but there was no time to find an Uber.

She turned and shouted, "Hey! *Stop!*"

As the woman ran toward her car in a panic, Tom pulled away from the curb with squealing tires. He roared past the screaming woman and made a sharp turn onto a main road leading away from the station.

Inside a minute, Tom was ten blocks away, emitting a big sigh of relief. Everything was better. He had wheels. It was a clean getaway.

"Bwaaboo," said a voice in the back seat.

Tom turned to see a happy, gurgling baby boy squirming in a car seat.

Tom let out a yell of despair.

The baby laughed.

Great, thought Tom. *Add kidnapper to my list of crimes.*

The shrill sirens persisted. Tom looked in his rearview mirror and could see little red and blue lights, many blocks away but determined to grow bigger in his wake.

Tom's mind swam. There were numerous unhappy scenarios that could play out in this predicament. Racing away from the police at top speed and then crashing violently with a baby in the backseat was probably the worst.

He needed to get rid of the baby. He couldn't toss it out. But where could he safely deliver it?

Tom realized he was near St. Michael's, his longtime church. He remembered hearing stories of unwed mothers abandoning newborns inside churches, knowing they would be rescued and cared for. This wasn't exactly a newborn, and Tom was hardly an unwed mother, but he figured the storyline could still play out.

Tom pulled up in front of St. Michael's. He left the engine

running, hopped out and quickly unlatched the baby from the car seat. Holding him delicately, he walked swiftly up the broad steps that led inside the church.

The church was empty. Tom's footsteps echoed and bounced off the high rafters. Bright sunlight streamed in through stained-glass windows, illuminating the pews with a golden glow. He quickly moved up the aisle, aiming to deposit the baby someplace safe and visible. Near the altar, a large collection basket caught his eye – it was just about the perfect size.

As Tom stepped toward it, a gentleman in a black clergy shirt with white collar emerged from a side room and recognized him with a look of surprise.

"Tom?"

"Father Riedel."

Tom walked over to the priest and handed him the baby. Father Riedel accepted the child with a look of understandable bewilderment.

"I found a baby," said Tom. "I can't – can you – it's a long story – I have to go."

The pesky police sirens were back.

"Whose baby is this?" Father Riedel asked as the child squirmed in his arms.

"I don't know. The mom has red hair."

Tom quickly turned and headed back up the aisle to return to the stolen SUV. Once he reached the doorway, he froze. Two police cars, lights flashing, sandwiched the SUV from either side. Several officers were already stepping out. One had a hand above the gun in his holster.

Tom immediately changed direction. He ran back up the aisle.

Father Riedel remained standing in the same spot, frozen as he held and studied the baby. "But who is the child's father?"

Tom offered no response. He simply shrugged and looked heavenward.

Father Riedel's mouth fell open.

Tom rushed through a side passage. He entered the shadowy back corridors of the church. He moved quickly, but not as fast as in his younger days, legs really stiffening now, muscles aching. He found a back exit and pushed through, entering the rear parking lot.

The lot was big and mostly empty. A lawn maintenance truck sat off to one side. Two Hispanic workers climbed into the front seat, talking to one another in Spanish. They did not see him.

The back of the truck was filled with lawnmowers, garden supplies, and a big pile of plastic bags stuffed with lawn debris.

The vehicle's rear lights lit up and its noisy engine rattled to life.

Tom hopped into the truck's cargo bed, quickly sinking between several fat black bags, immersing himself into the rubbish and out of view.

The police sirens continued to sing. They were everywhere, a hysterical chorus.

The truck backed out of its parking spot, and the driver punched up the radio. Brassy Latin music overwhelmed the sirens. Tom continued to stay low. Grass clippings clung to him and he squeezed his nose to stop from sneezing.

After ten minutes, Tom guessed the truck had gone several miles. He decided to check his surroundings. As the truck stopped at a light, he poked his head up and tried to get his bearings.

Sheridan Road. Not far from the beach and a large public park. What he needed was a good hiding place – better and more long term than the back of this truck – but exactly what that would or could be was stubbornly elusive.

What was nearby?

Then Tom realized: the harbor. His good friend and neighbor-across-the-way, Jay, had a medium-sized sailboat with a cabin, and he had gone on many sailing trips with Jay over the years. Tom knew two things: where the boat was docked and where Jay, currently, was docked.

Jay was on the East Coast visiting colleges with his high school senior daughter. They weren't due back until the weekend.

At least it'll give me someplace to gather my wits and plan my next move.

Tom quickly sprung out of the truck, covered in dirt and grass, resembling some kind of creature, startling a teenage boy on a bicycle. The boy promptly hit the curb and toppled with his bike.

The traffic light turned green. The lawn maintenance truck sped away, oblivious to the role it had played in Tom's flight. Tom crossed the road and quickly disappeared into the park, feeling safer under the heavy tree cover.

He casually strolled on a walking path, keeping his head down. He reached the harbor that provided boaters entry into Lake Michigan. It was a cool day without much activity – or many witnesses – to worry about. Tom picked his moments carefully, staying in the shadows when he saw people, and moving rapidly when the coast was clear.

He found Jay's boat, hopped on board and, with one swift kick, broke into the covered cabin. He found some cushions and lifejackets, threw them on the cold floor, and lay down to stay out of view, below the windows.

He felt like he was covered in one big bruise. His body trembled and took a long time to settle. He was also hungry. He surveyed the scene. Any chance that Jay had left behind a bag of chips or box of crackers somewhere…?

Tom noticed a red cooler. That was a good sign.

He crawled over, hoping for the best, and flipped it open.

The cooler contained several small Styrofoam containers of nightcrawlers. And that was it.

Tom groaned and shut the lid.

He wasn't hungry enough to eat worms.

Yet.

CHAPTER TEN

In Central Florida, Louis left the highway to find someplace to hunker down for a few days or weeks or months. He had placed sufficient distance between himself and his escape. It was time to ditch the stolen car someplace where it would never be found. He needed to create a new identity – not Louis Karp, not Tom Nolan. This new phase of his life was like being reborn. Maybe he would even ditch the itch to steal…and get a real job?

Louis intentionally got lost on long, rambling side roads. If he saw signs that indicated he was getting closer to big tourist traps – Disney World, Sea World and so on – he quickly pointed the car in another direction. He reached an open area of flatland – pastures, prairies and numerous little lakes, rivers and ponds. The towns looked forgotten, which suited him fine: gap-toothed fences, overgrown brush, vacant buildings with absent or fragmentary signage. Everything wore sickly pastel colors – teal, light purple, lime green. The local economies appeared to be driven by desperate gift shops with screaming posters in the windows trying to lure in passing families on their way to see Mickey Mouse or the beaches on the coast. These shops offered nothing you would want to gift to anybody you actually liked, just crap. But Dad could stretch his legs, Mom could browse around for something for Aunt Dorothy and the kids could tinkle in the bathrooms.

As the terrain took a turn to swamps and the attractions leaned toward alligator farms, Louis encountered an auto junkyard with many of the vehicles literally sinking into the marsh.

He drove past, then thought about it and circled back.

In the front, closer to the road, three old cars sat together with triple-digit pricetags visible in their windshields. Drivable junk.

This was a good time to make an exchange.

Louis slowed to a stop. He made sure his seatbelt was good and tight. He aimed the front of his car for a big pileup of broken, junked vehicles. He hit the gas and roared forward.

Louis smashed his car into a mass of mangled metal. The windshield shattered, the front end crumpled up, and broken parts of abandoned cars – doors, tires – fell around him.

The airbag exploded. He quickly slashed it with a knife. He grabbed his small travel bag of meager possessions. He unlatched the seatbelt and pushed open the croaking, badly dented door just wide enough to wriggle out. He felt remarkably unscathed, invincible. The collision was fun – like a demolition derby.

The car was now undrivable and undesirable, merged with a mess of other car parts, destined to rot away like a vehicular corpse in this auto graveyard. It would lose its identity to rust and time, growing entangled in weeds and muck and the brutality of Central Florida's high temperatures and humidity.

"What the hell, mister!" An old man with a deep tan and a million wrinkles, wearing stained overalls, stepped toward him from a shack that served as some kind of sad home or office.

"This is a junkyard, right?" said Louis, approaching the man, brushing dirt off his clothes. "Well, that car is a piece of junk."

"That car was in good shape!"

"No, no," Louis said quickly. "It had problems. A ton of problems. Garbage."

"Are you hurt? That was a crazy stunt."

"I feel great." Louis stood before the man and studied him. "And I'm going to make you feel great, too."

The old man looked at him suspiciously. He raised his white eyebrows. "How so?"

"I want to buy the Toyota Corolla out front. It's drivable, right?"

"Yes, sir."

"I'll pay you cash. Times two. Do you get what I'm saying? I'll pay twice what you're asking."

The old man's suspicions didn't ease up. "What's the catch?"

"I want no record of this transaction. I have a crazy ex-wife, a real bitch who's after all my assets. You're not going to tell anybody. Not your family, not a single soul."

"I have no family."

Louis nodded. "Then it's just between us. If you break my trust, I'll come back to slit your throat and feed you to the gators." Louis said it in a matter-of-fact tone, no need to snarl with menace, just offering a simple fact.

"Mister, if that car disappears from this lot, no one is going to know or care."

"That's good."

Louis paid the man cash. Of course, he could have preserved a few layers on his bankroll by just killing the forgotten oldster and dumping his body in the shed to draw insects. But attracting cops to the scene where he had just dropped off a stolen car — probably not a good idea.

The transaction was cordial. They shook hands. They exchanged a nod of understanding.

Louis drove off in the 1998 Toyota Corolla. It was loud, the air-conditioning didn't work, and so on, but it had a working engine and that was good enough.

He traveled south, staying on long roads that cut through small towns. Somewhat randomly, he chose a motel. It sat across the street from a shop that only sold oranges. The motel consisted of two floors of rooms with purple doors forming an L-shape around a simple swimming pool. A few grizzled occupants sat outside their rooms in chairs, smoking cigarettes and watching traffic. Large towels hung like colored flags to dry on railings. The parking lot was one-third full and the cars were generally beat down and tired looking.

Nobody here would bother him or want to be bothered.

Louis checked in. He paid cash, received a key card and pulled a map from a rack of junky tourist brochures. He found his room on the second floor and bolted himself inside. He tossed his travel bag in a corner and plopped on the bed.

The interior resembled just about every other motel room he had ever seen with no effort to establish a personality. He felt like he should catch up on sleep, but he remained alert and awake. He could hear traffic from the main road out front and the occasional yelp of a mom scolding her kids at the pool.

After nearly twenty-four hours of driving, his body still did not ache one bit. He marveled over his unwavering stamina but it also threatened him with the unknown.

What am I?

Louis finally moved off the bed. He entered the bathroom.

He stared at himself in the mirror.

The dopey blond guy stared back.

"Go to hell," he told the reflection in a voice that was not his own but one he had grown accustomed to.

The bandage on his forehead was coming loose.

Louis peeled it off. The wound underneath was nearly fully closed. Unblemished skin had quickly regenerated and sealed up most of the glimpse of his metallic skull.

This new body was a source of endless amazement.

He noticed he was growing stubble – how was that possible? The robotics people had thought of everything to simulate a real, living human being.

Standing before the mirror, Louis stripped to get a good look at his full anatomy.

He had a solid, healthy body. Good muscle tone. Not much fat. Everything symmetrical with good color.

And he had a penis.

He thought about the junk food he had been eating for the past day. While he wasn't hungry, he had been eating out of habit. The food tasted good, so a sense of taste was part of the deal.

But the food going in…. How did it get out?

Do robots shit?

The thought of all those Cheetos and Big Macs and beef jerkies simply accumulating inside creeped him out.

Louis sat on the toilet and attempted to move his bowels.

After a few minutes, he felt something like a lump traveling inside his digestive tract.

He pushed and before long he heard a splash in the toilet.

Louis immediately jumped up to take a look.

There was a small blue ball in the toilet bowl. A perfectly shaped orb, smelling like…flowers?

There was no foul odor. This was the most tidy, sanitized crap he had ever seen.

Freaked out, Louis flushed it away.

He looked over at the shower. He knew he was filthy. Plunging his car into a junkyard at full speed wasn't the most sanitary of activities. Could he wash himself off and remove the grime? Or would the shower short-circuit him?

The thought genuinely concerned him. He turned on a hot spray and watched it generate steam. He proceeded cautiously. First a hand. Then an arm. Then a foot. Then both feet. Then some water on his chest. His back.

Before long, he was taking a full-fledged shower with no ill effects.

He stayed in the shower for twenty minutes, enjoying the sensation, feeling cleansed, physically and mentally.

When he was done, he realized he didn't have any clean clothes to change into. Shopping for a wardrobe would be a priority. Simple T-shirts and shorts were fine. Nothing fancy to draw attention.

He also needed a new name and identity. That would take some time and effort, but he knew what to do to make it happen.

Louis stepped out of the bathroom, naked except for his underwear. He sat on the bed and turned on the TV.

As he flipped through the channels, he found a news report about a shooting at a diner. It took him a moment to realize: *Oh yeah, that was me.*

The woman he shot had been wounded in the shoulder. The fact that she lived didn't move him one way or the other. She offered a loose description of the robber. The police sketch of him that filled the screen for two seconds was so general it could be anyone.

"Good luck," said Louis, and he resumed flipping through the channels.

He kept a pen and small pad of paper at his side, the only freebie in the room, and listened for names that could become his new identity.

Louis found an old episode of the crime drama *The Sopranos* and liked the name 'Tony'. He wrote it down.

As he dialed up and down, nothing else grabbed his attention, and he finally stopped for a while to watch *The Simpsons*.

He could use a good laugh.

Halfway through the episode, he figured: *Why not?*

On the pad, alongside 'Tony', he wrote 'Simpson'.

Tony Simpson.

His new identity. It had a nice ring to it.

A few hours later, the television began to grate on his nerves and he shut it off. He tried again to fall asleep.

For five minutes, he lay awake, eyes closed.

Then something interesting happened. As if sensing his desire for sleep – perhaps through five minutes of inactivity and closed eyes – Louis felt a gentle fatigue settle in. It was like the effects of a couple of downers or sleeping pills.

His entire being slid into a relaxed state and his mind began to slow down and drift.

They really did think of everything, thought Louis.

In ten minutes, exactly, he was asleep.

★   ★   ★

In the middle of the night, Louis woke up with a start at the sound of a loud *crunch*.

He sat up in time to see his door break open. Several men streamed in, armed with guns, wearing civilian clothes, moving in quick coordination. Before Louis could move off the bed to scramble for his own gun, they had their hands on him.

Louis did his best to fight them off. He was strong, but there were too many of them and they quickly cuffed his arms behind his back and shoved his face in a pillow. When he continued to struggle, rising off the mattress, one of them punched him hard.

He absorbed the punch but it effectively ended his resistance. He was fully surrounded. He could barely see their faces in the narrow light that leaked in from the doorway. How did they find him? He suspected the old man at the auto junkyard. The wrinkled bastard must have notified the authorities that something smelled fishy, and now the FBI had tracked him down. He regretted not turning the geezer into gator food.

Louis looked into the guns pointed at him and yelled, "I'm not responsible for my actions! Those scientists turned me into a freak! They control me!"

It was a silly defense on the surface, but how could he be responsible for his actions if he wasn't even himself anymore?

The men around the bed started to talk with one another. One of them shone a flashlight in his face and kept it there. Blinded, Louis listened to their chatter, trying to catch what they were saying. He couldn't.

It was some kind of foreign language.

"Who are you?" said Louis, trying to get a better look at their faces.

One of the men spoke into a cell phone, updating someone on the other end. A couple of the others exchanged more words he could not understand. Whoever this was, it wasn't the cops or the FBI.

Whatever they spoke, it wasn't English or Spanish. It was harsh and thick, every syllable accented. He thought hard about where its vague familiarity came from...from movies or TV, perhaps, but not people he had known. The more they talked, the more Louis relaxed his body and didn't move, absorbed in their speech patterns, trying to guess their origins, becoming more confused than threatened. Then in a flash Louis had a thought, and the more they spoke in their serious tones to one another, the more his thought felt both right and crazy. Could these midnight intruders actually be....

Russian?

CHAPTER ELEVEN

Several hours after nightfall turned the cabin dark, Tom took a chance and restarted his cell phone. He had remained undisturbed in the boat, curled up low, listening to the lapping of waves and light bumping against the pier. Earlier, he heard occasional voices as people moved about on the creaking docks, but now he hadn't heard anyone for a very long time. His mind was stuck in a loop recounting the bizarre sequence of events that brought him here, going back to that first dinner with Steven. He worried for Emily and Sofi.

Tom knew that calling his wife was unwise. He took his chances with Giamatti instead.

Giamatti answered immediately. "Let's keep this short and sweet," he said to Tom. "Tell me where you are, and I'll send Cooper for you."

Tom described his whereabouts the best he could.

"Stay low," instructed Giamatti. "When you hear a man whistling 'Sweet Caroline', that's your signal to come out."

Tom cringed. "Can it be a different song?"

"You need to shut down your phone. We'll see you soon." Giamatti disconnected.

Tom turned off his phone and waited. Sure enough, under half an hour, a man whistling Neil Diamond strolled the dock along the pier.

Tom emerged.

Cooper saw him and motioned wordlessly for Tom to follow.

They walked swiftly to where Cooper had parked his car. Tom reached for the door handle on the front passenger side.

"No," Cooper said. He opened the trunk.

"Really?"

Cooper nodded. "There are police everywhere."

"Where are we going?"

"Giamatti's house. You'll be safe there."

Tom climbed in the trunk and Cooper shut the lid.

During the ride, Tom felt every bump and pothole. His entire body already felt like one big bruise. This wasn't helping.

The car reached its destination and parked. The engine shut down. The trunk popped open and Tom sat up. Cooper helped him out. They were inside the gates of Giamatti's estate, steps away from a stunning mansion that appeared to Tom more like an elegant country club than a home.

The front door opened and Giamatti quickly ushered them inside, wearing a monogrammed robe and slippers.

"How are you feeling?" he asked Tom.

"Pretty bad all around."

Limping slightly, Giamatti led them into a large, brightly lit den of elegant furnishings and expensive art. A young, beautiful woman appeared and extended a hand from a long, colorful muumuu.

"This is my wife, Bella."

Tom shook her hand and she said, "Can I get you something to eat? You must be starved."

"Yes, please. Anything is fine. I've been on the floor of a boat all day."

"A little seasick, too, I would imagine," said Giamatti. "Have a seat." He gestured to a large, stuffed chair, and Tom lowered himself into it, finding immediate comfort for his weary bones.

Giamatti sat in his chair, the biggest in the room, and Cooper took a seat on the couch.

"How is Emily?" Tom asked quickly.

"Emily is...." Giamatti chose his words carefully. "Cooperating."

"With who?"

"With the mission, of course."

"So she can't defend me?"

"She can defend you. She just can't reveal the experiment."

Tom grew angry. "I'm tired of all this secrecy. Why can't we just explain what's happening? It's simple. There's a man who appears to be me committing crimes—"

"—who is a robot," said Giamatti firmly. "How does that sound? This is not the time nor the place to go down that path. This is a very delicate operation. It's too soon to go public. There's too much at risk."

"But *I'm* at risk."

"You're safe here. We'll put you up in one of the guest rooms. It's just for a while."

Cooper spoke up. "We'll find him. He's not very bright. He's reckless. He'll continue to commit petty crimes."

Giamatti said, "Leave everything to us. I have connections in all the right places. We'll catch Louis Karp."

"But we don't know where he is," said Tom.

"I have a pretty good lead," Giamatti said. "There was a robbery earlier today in Kissimmee, Florida. A man robbed a diner and shot the woman at the cash register."

"How do you know it's me – him?"

"The description of the man is too general to be useful, but there is one small detail that we found significant."

"And that is?"

"The woman at the diner claimed to shoot first. She said she shot the man squarely in the chest. He didn't flinch. He didn't bleed. Naturally the local authorities figure she missed – or perhaps the man was wearing a bulletproof vest under his clothes. I believe there could be another reason he didn't go down."

"It would take a full day of driving to reach Kissimmee," Cooper said. "So it's entirely possible he made it that far. We're looking at other leads as well."

Giamatti said, "We just need you to be patient."

"Can I talk to Emily?"

"Not right now. We can't risk it. The police are probably waiting for you to contact her. But we'll see that she knows you're safe. We'll relay any messages...."

Tom lowered his head.

"She'll be fine," said Giamatti. "The police spent the day talking with her. All she said is you left for work this morning and that you were acting perfectly normal. She's not a suspect."

"Not a suspect," Tom muttered, amazed that this would even be a possibility. He grew angry. "What's to stop me from exposing all this? My life and family have been upended. I could turn my phone back on, contact the authorities and tell them the truth."

"We have a contingency plan for leaks," said Giamatti. "It's been in place for a long time. It includes the rapid relocation of the lab to a new site. We would deny everything you said and indeed you would sound crazy."

Bella arrived carrying a tray with sandwiches, fruit and a mug of tea. She set it on a small table in front of Tom.

"Give us a few days," Cooper said. "We'll find him."

Tom reached for the mug. As he started to pick it up, his hand trembled, and his fingers lost their grip. He quickly set the mug back down before it spilled.

"You need him back as much as we do," Giamatti said to Tom, watching him struggle to control his hand movement. "I'd say...even more."

*　*　*

The Giamattis provided Tom with clean clothes, including a set of pajamas, and led him to a luxurious guest room at least twice as big as Tom and Emily's own bedroom at home. He showered in a sparkling clean adjacent bathroom, still shedding grass from his ride in the lawn maintenance truck. The pajamas were one size too large, but fresh and very much appreciated. He slipped into them with tired, uncooperative limbs.

Exhausted, Tom climbed into the big bed. His room included a large flat-screen television, and he almost turned it on before stopping himself. It was entirely possible he would encounter news coverage about himself committing crimes that he did (steal a car, kidnap a baby) and didn't (shoot people, rob stores) do.

It had been a very busy day.

Tom fell asleep in the soft bed, on top of the sheets and surrounded by pillows, missing his wife and daughter.

A few hours later, he woke up with a start. For a few fleeting seconds, he felt like he was still being chased. For several more seconds, he recalled the previous day's adventures as some kind of long, crazy dream. Then reality set in and his strange surroundings regained their backstory. Tom came to realize that the past twenty-four hours really happened and could not simply dissipate upon awakening.

The big mansion was dark and quiet, except for the steady hum of the air-conditioning. Tom's throat felt dry. He tried to return to sleep but his heart pounded, caught up again in his insane predicament, and he couldn't lie still. He climbed out of bed, put on a soft robe, and went searching for something to drink.

He thought he remembered the way to the kitchen but quickly got lost in a maze of corridors. Bella Giamatti had told him to help himself to whatever he wanted in the refrigerator, whenever he wanted, and he was going to take her up on her offer.

But the kitchen became elusive. He didn't want to start flipping on lights. And he was kind of enjoying exploring the sprawling mansion without an escort, like being lost in a museum after hours.

Tom opened a few doors and peeked inside. He found a large library, shelves stacked high with books. He discovered a multimedia room with rows of plush seats and a big movie theater screen. One of the doors revealed a staircase descending to a lower level. *Giamatti's game room?* thought Tom. *This ought to be good.*

Tom quietly stepped down the stairs, holding the rail for balance. At the bottom, he discovered a corridor of rooms. He pushed open the first door and flipped on the light switch.

Then he gasped.

The room was mostly barren, lined with stacks of boxes against the walls. It looked like a typical dull basement storage room except for one shocking element that managed to top the past twenty-four hours' surreal turn of events. It was something so seriously hallucinatory that Tom placed a hand over his mouth to stop from shouting.

A man sat in a chair in the center of the room. He sat very still, staring straight ahead, almost pleasantly.

Tom recognized the man immediately – and indeed most people would.

It was the president of the United States.

CHAPTER TWELVE

Louis examined the rough, lined faces of his captors as they moved around the motel room, picking through his meager possessions. They were unusually pale for Florida. Sitting up on the bed, hands cuffed behind his back, Louis demanded, "Who are you pieces of shit? Who sent you?"

When they didn't respond, he shouted his words louder.

"*Zatknis*," one of them finally barked back.

"Zatknis sent you?"

Another man chortled, the first break from their stone-like demeanor. He was tubby with a thick salt-and-pepper mustache. He looked down at Louis.

"*Zatknis* is Russian," he said in a deep monotone. "It means to shut the hell up."

Louis responded with a barrage of profanity. It was met with another round of laughter.

"Glad you like my standup act," Louis said, although he wasn't standing. He remained sitting on the bed, keeping very still except for small movements behind his back that he kept hidden.

As the intruders collected his belongings, Louis worked to pull one of his hands through the steel cuff. With ordinary hands and strength, it would be impossible. But now he possessed the necessary power to squeeze the thick part of his palm through the opening. He also felt a complete absence of pain to hold him back.

Louis could sense his robotic hand crunching as it wriggled through the cuff, fingers twisting out of joint, components compressing like scrap metal going through a compactor.

He wasn't sure what would emerge but if it could still make a fist, that would be a victory.

When one of the Russians noticed the squirm of his shoulders and detected an escape attempt, Louis had to speed up the final bit of extraction. His mangled hand slid free, formed a gnarled but potent fist, and the machine man inside took over.

In a funny kind of unison, they all directed their flashlights at him. Louis excelled in the spotlight. The tubby Russian with the walrus mustache received a hit to the skull that knocked him out and definitely left a mark. The next one landed against the wall with a thundering thud and a third was tossed into the television. Guns began blazing. Louis absorbed a few bullets; several more missed their fast-moving target and punctured the wall.

Beating back the Russians like weeds, Louis formed a path to the door. When a couple of them persisted on trying to slow him down, he tore the door from its hinges and flattened them with it.

As Louis reached the outer balcony, several half-awake, disheveled motel guests peeked out of their rooms. "Go back inside!" he snarled, and they quickly obeyed, recognizing a legitimate threat. In the dark of the night, Louis hurried down a set of steps to ground level. When he reached the bottom, a medium-sized man with a beard and bushy eyebrows stood in his way.

"Better move or you'll be eating the cement," Louis said. Then he recognized the individual and stared into his face for an uncertain moment.

It was one of the scientists from the lab. A member of the nerd team that had plopped his mind into this pretty-boy casing.

"I don't know what's going on," Louis said, "but you're not taking me anywhere."

"I'm afraid you're wrong," the man responded. "You're coming with us."

Louis had a lot of questions. Like why the Russian circus paid him a room-service visit. But he had no time for Q&A. He could already hear a new commotion coming after him – the few who weren't busted up or unconscious.

"I'm leaving," said Louis. "If you try to stop me, I'll kill you."

"No, you won't," the man said with complete confidence. He calmly lifted his hand, clutching what appeared to be a television remote.

Louis very quickly remembered that this gizmo was set to just one channel – his own.

"Don't—" he exclaimed, pouncing toward the scientist.

Then the mental and physical faculties of Louis shut down, and he became a mannequin with a frozen, desperate expression of panic.

★   ★   ★

When Louis awoke, it was abrupt, like the flip of a switch. Because, quite literally, that was what happened.

Now he was strapped down to a table with extra-sturdy clamps, two on each arm and leg, plus one that circled his neck like a dog collar.

He couldn't see much – just a low, white metal roof above, interrupted by faces peering over him.

He stared up at the smarmy bearded scientist and his scruffy band of Russians. One of the Russians had a black eye, another a red, swollen mouth. Louis figured they weren't too happy with him. Fine, it was mutual. He didn't care for them and would welcome another opportunity to dish out beatings.

"Hello, again," said the scientist.

"Where am I?" Louis asked.

"The question," the scientist said, "is not 'Where *am* I?' It should be 'Where am I *going*?' That's much more interesting. Where are you? You're inside a rental truck. This is a private, mobile space where we can conduct our operations undisturbed. We're parked in a vacant lot in southern Florida. Not much is happening outside, pretty boring by intention. But – where are you going? *That* is much more interesting. You, my friend, are leaving the United States to be a person – an object – of much admiration in Moscow. We have a team waiting to receive you, examine you, learn from you and unlock your secrets for a brand-new audience."

Louis looked at the scientist strangely, mouth open but words unformed.

"'Why?'" the scientist said, anticipating his next question. "Allow me to explain. You may remember me by the name Alan. That's not my real name. You can call me Alex. I joined the Gemini team as a legitimate scientist but also a resource for keeping my country informed on certain advances in science and technology that could interest them. I'm part of a Russian organization known as Technology Systems Research. We pose as US citizens, construct false personas and infiltrate classified experiments that could provide us with value. We live in a global society, there's no need for proprietary attitudes toward medical breakthroughs that can benefit all of mankind. Am I right?"

"I want out of here."

"No, I'm sorry. That's not one of the options. It was a big enough nuisance to keep up with your cross-country trip. You move fast, but not out of sight. You see, at the beginning, I inserted a tracking chip into Tom Nolan's replica. No one else knew. My original plan was to take possession of Tom after he re-entered society as a successful human duplicate. Your escape caught us off guard – it basically accelerated our plans."

"Maybe I don't want to be part of your 'plan'."

"Oh, but the Kremlin is very excited to see you. They have been pursuing their own version of human robotics for years and have so much to gain from exploring you from the outside in. I've learned a lot on the Gemini team, but your physical acquisition will be invaluable to my country. You will be welcomed like a hero."

"Not interested."

"Do you really think you're better off remaining here? I can tell you how that story ends. Sooner or later, you would have been captured by your US friends. Maybe in a week, maybe in a month, but they would have found you. They weren't going to let a one hundred-million-dollar investment just walk away. And, spoiler alert, they were planning to kill you. You were just a trial run for Tom Nolan. The next phase of that project was to wipe away your mind so that you no longer existed in any way, shape or form. They were going to erase you from that wonderful marvel of technology and give it to Tom Nolan to save the life of a 'more deserving' man. You were disposable. A guinea pig. So don't think of this as a kidnapping. Think of it as a rescue. If you cooperate with us, we keep you alive. If you create trouble and go against us – we'll stick your electronic brain into a toaster. You can spend the rest of your existence warming bread."

"I'm not going to your Goddamned commie country. You can't make me."

"Oh yes we can."

Alex lowered out of Louis's view for a moment. When he returned, he held up a bare foot.

"Recognize this?" said Alex. "It's your foot. We've already started your disassembly. You see, it's much easier to smuggle you out of the country in small parts. Gentlemen, start the power tools."

Louis could hear the collective whirring of several drills. One of the Russians leaned into view, the tubby one with the mustache, wielding an electric drill with a wicked grin.

"We will move you out of this country in numerous parcels under the guise of an international technology corporation. In little pieces, with your artificial flesh peeled away, you won't be recognizable. At the other end, we'll put you back together again like a giant jigsaw puzzle. It'll be fun."

"Go to hell, you piece of trash."

Alex struck Louis across the face with the bare foot in his hand. Louis felt no pain but the sensation of being kicked by his own foot stunned him into a momentary silence.

"Let's begin," said Alex to his Russian cohorts.

Louis screamed as they crowded around him with their tools and pulled him apart with much whirring, grinding and buzzing. Alex relished holding up various body parts to show Louis the progress being made. The smirk on his lips definitely smacked of sadism.

"I swear, I'll kill you," Louis screamed at him.

Unperturbed, Alex removed Louis's digital brain from the

robotic head of Tom Nolan, detaching Louis from all his senses, reducing him once more to a terrified mind living in a black abyss without a body.

CHAPTER THIRTEEN

Tom froze, heart seized up in an urge to flee but stalled from flight by a brain working overtime to satisfy the immense curiosity of *What the hell is the president doing here?*

Was Tom dreaming?

"Sir?" he said. "Mr. President?"

There was no response. He studied the rotund, balding man who stared back with a dour, saggy-cheeked expression. Dressed in a dark suit and red tie, the president sat very still – as in unblinkingly still, no slight shudders of breathing, nothing.

Dead?

Or....

A fake.

Tom felt queasy. Surely this was not a sight meant for his eyes. He did not belong here. Tom turned to retreat to his guest room. He snapped off the lights and climbed back up the stairs, gripping the banister. As he reached the top of the steps, he hooked a turn into a dark corridor and was met with a female scream.

Bella, the wife of Simon Giamatti, stood before him aiming a strange, black-and-yellow gun in his direction.

Tom halted so quickly he nearly fell backward.

"Don't move!" she shouted.

"I'm not moving! It's me, don't shoot!" He raised his hands in swift surrender.

Bella Giamatti relaxed as she realized the midnight prowler was her houseguest. She frowned.

"What are you doing snooping around in the dark?" she asked, blond hair piled high in a bun and curves draped in a silk robe.

"I went for a walk," he offered weakly.

"I almost zapped you with my rapist stun gun." She lowered her arm. "You would have been on the floor in a big world of hurt."

Then Cooper spoke behind her. He emerged from the shadows, also holding a gun – a real one – a 9mm semi-automatic.

"And I almost put some holes in you, which would've been an even bigger problem," he said.

"He was in the basement," said Bella.

Cooper examined Tom with a stern and suspicious stare. "What were you doing down there?"

"I don't know," Tom said, still catching his breath. "I couldn't sleep. I just went for a walk…. I didn't mean to…."

Giamatti entered the scene next, eyelids heavy, moving slowly with a limp in his own long robe. "What on earth is going on?"

Cooper said, "Mrs. Giamatti, you can go back to bed. We'll take it from here."

Bella thanked Cooper and left, giving Tom one last glare of disapproval with her pretty blue eyes.

"I'm sorry," Tom said.

"Stay right where you are," said Cooper. Tom's feet stayed planted. Cooper turned to Giamatti and told him, "Everybody's fine. It's just Tom. Your wife heard something and went to see what it was, and he startled her." Then he added, "He was in the basement."

Giamatti's eyes opened wider. He asked, "Did he see—?"

Tom answered, "Yes. I did. I was just going to get a snack and I started roaming…." He stared at two solemn faces, uncertain of his fate. "I won't tell anybody about this."

"It's too late," Giamatti said with a large sigh that seemed to ripple through his robe. "You've seen it. What's done is done. Gentlemen, let's go into the study."

Tom followed Giamatti and Cooper. He had a lot of questions but didn't want to further stir things up. He just wanted to cooperate and prove he meant no harm. He couldn't shake the eerie image of the president of the United States sitting immobile with a frozen face.

In the massive study, Giamatti made himself a scotch and water and offered drinks to the others, who declined. He took his drink with him and sat in his favorite chair. Tom sat on a small couch, and Cooper sat in a straight-back chair, facing him, gun put away.

"So you decided to go for a walk?" Giamatti said, almost pleasantly.

Tom spoke carefully, feeling his pajamas cling with sweat. "I couldn't sleep. It started out I was looking for the kitchen...then I just sort of wandered."

"Yes, you did," said Giamatti. "And you made a discovery."

"I'm sorry."

"What did you think?" Giamatti asked.

"About what?"

"The replica."

"Very...lifelike."

"Good."

Giamatti took a sip of his drink, then continued. "Tom, you're part of a top-secret techno-biological experiment. You have behaved admirably in keeping it secret, even under some difficult and extraordinary circumstances. For that, I commend you. Also, I feel I can trust you. I'm going to take you into an even deeper level of secrecy, highly classified information known only to a few, and I expect you to respect and honor what I am about to tell you with absolute confidentiality. The consequences of any leak are bigger than you can imagine. It would pose a threat to national security. Do we have an understanding, Tom Nolan?"

Tom's throat was dry. His response was tense but authentic. He pushed it out. "Yes."

Giamatti nodded. He looked over at Cooper, then back to Tom.

"All right then," said Giamatti. "We'll begin with what you just saw. That is an artificial reproduction of the president, just like your own duplication. It's the president's shell. We scanned him in the same manner we scanned you. He is equipped to receive his own consciousness and memory. It's my fault you made the discovery. We brought the shell out of the vault for final testing before we conduct the transfer of identity next week."

"A transfer? Like me?"

"Yes. Like you. This entire project has been laid out in a sequence of tests that build on one another to prove the viability of a breakthrough procedure to save our president. As you know, the digitization of Louis Karp's brain was our proof of concept to go to the next level with your duplication to rescue you from the ravages of Lowrey's disease. What you didn't know is that you, too, are a test to give us the confidence and reassurance we need to proceed with a very delicate transition for the leader of the free world. Louis paved the way for you. And now you are paving the way for President Gus Hartel."

"But President Hartel is healthy," Tom said in a hesitant voice. "Isn't he?"

Giamatti said, "There's nothing wrong with him...to the outside world. But things are not what they seem. We are in the middle of a significant government crisis. One year ago, I flew to DC to meet with the president and his closest advisers. He had just been diagnosed with advanced leukemia. The decision was made to not disclose this information. As you know, the president is currently campaigning for a second term and heavily favored to win. However, with his current prognosis, it is unlikely he would live through a second term. Acknowledging his illness or pulling out of the race would essentially concede the presidency to the rival party. There is no one else from the president's party who could win the popular vote."

Giamatti stood. He slowly limped toward a wall filled with photos of himself with various political leaders and entertainment icons. He smiled and pointed at one picture in particular. "This is me with Gus when he was an Illinois state senator. How young we look. We have been close for many, many years."

He turned to face Tom. "I helped fund his campaigns. He's been a friend, an ally, an advocate. When I was among the chosen few to learn about his condition, I knew I had to help him in any way I could. I've been blessed to amass a significant fortune through my business endeavors over the past forty years.

I started life with nothing, the son of a factory worker, and built a financial empire beyond my wildest dreams. One of the ways I've given back is through my contributions and funding to scientific research, with a particular interest in theories of sustainable life. When I made my first millions, my first priority was to take my father out of the factory and place him in a better life, living comfortably and securely, after all the sacrifices he had made for me. As soon as I was able to do that, he became ill, and I realized the one thing my money could not do was protect him, or any of us, from the cruelties of the biological clock. He died at fifty-seven from lung cancer."

Giamatti advanced down the wall of photos to a black-and-white picture of himself with his father, both of them smiling but the father obviously withered by sickness, hunched and unshaven.

Giamatti turned back to face Tom. "By the time I was informed of President Hartel's condition, I had a considerable level of confidence that some of the pockets of research I had funded – if brought together under a single mission – could produce a real breakthrough to sustain human life through technology. I had access to the best of the best across the fields of robotics and neurological science. This, combined with almost unlimited financial backing, was the key to opening the door to what is truly possible in the twenty-first century."

Giamatti returned to his chair, slowed by his limp. He sat down. "Tom, there are fewer than forty people in the world who know what you know. You are the thirty-ninth. This list includes members of the president's most trusted inner circle. Then there are the scientists and technicians who are conducting this work at its most intimate level. This is why I have been so adamant about the secrecy of this endeavor. This is bigger than just you. We have to save the president."

Giamatti sipped his scotch and said, "Cooper, finish our story. Tell Tom here what's taking place next week in this very house. It's the culmination of everything we've been working toward."

Cooper nodded. "Next week, the president is coming to Chicago for a campaign fundraiser. It will be held downtown at the Grand Ballroom of Navy Pier. The night before the fundraiser, the president will be staying here at the mansion as a guest. The president's closest advisers and trusted Secret Service men will stay with him at the house. During the president's stay, the lab team will be set up in the basement. The operation will take place that night."

Tom said, "The operation?"

Giamatti smiled. "Yes, indeed. The operation. The replica you encountered? We will transfer the president's consciousness into it. That will be his new physical form. The rest of the world won't know it, but when the president speaks at the fundraiser the next day, he will live in a technically perfect likeness absent of any health impairments. He will be fully healthy, fully functional, and indistinguishable from his previous physical form. It will be a seamless transition without missing a beat in his busy schedule, without arousing any suspicions. My greatest thrill will be watching the president deliver that speech to a full house of supporters and media, without anyone realizing they are in the presence of a human life replicated by science, a man-machine hybrid equipped with the president's full mental capabilities."

In the silence that followed, Tom tried to come up with words, but he was overwhelmed. His head was spinning.

"I don't know what to say," he finally admitted.

"Let it sink in," said Giamatti. "And know that you are in good company. You and President Hartel are the first beneficiaries of this extraordinary breakthrough. I look forward to my own turn, to Bella's turn. And Cooper...." Giamatti turned to face his faithful, longtime business associate. "Cooper, you will have your time. That is my promise to you."

"Thank you," said Cooper, allowing a small smile to break through his typically stoic demeanor.

"What about—" Tom started.

"Your missing shell?" Giamatti said.

Tom nodded.

"Don't worry about it," said Giamatti firmly. "A two-bit crook has run off with your replica, but I'm confident we'll get it back. We've been following several leads. We have people in high places, inside the CIA, who will make sure it is retrieved and brought back safely. It's only a matter of time, I assure you."

"Thank you." Tom knew his condition wasn't getting any better. He continued to feel random lapses in muscle coordination. "I want to get my life back together. I miss my family."

Giamatti smiled. "Of course you do. You have nothing to worry about. We will make you whole again."

CHAPTER FOURTEEN

Giamatti called a meeting to regroup the Gemini Experiment team at the Perking Institute laboratory. They gathered in uncomfortable silence, anxious for an update on the crisis that had disrupted their breakthrough achievement.

Cooper took attendance, checking off names on a clipboard with sharp, quick strokes. When he was done, he scanned the assembled, standing doctors and scientists with a stone face.

"We're missing one," he told Giamatti. "Alan Farron."

"Alan?" muttered Giamatti. "Where the hell is he?"

"I sent him repeated messages. I didn't hear back."

Giamatti frowned with impatience, leaned against the edge of a desk to take the weight off his bad leg. "He's usually punctual. We'll have to talk to him independently. Let's get started."

Cooper addressed the team, "Has anyone heard from Alan Farron?"

He received small shrugs and head shakes.

Giamatti raised his hand to draw everyone's attention. "Listen. I'll be brief. Please listen to what I have to say."

All eyes rested on the large man with a white beard who had led this effort since the beginning. His usual zest and enthusiasm had been replaced by a brittle tone of aggravation.

"I am sorry to say we are suspending operations until further notice," he said. "As you know, we have security issues requiring our immediate attention. I want to assure you we will bring this matter under control. We do not need to bring in outside authorities. We are not expanding awareness of this project. All of you remain under the same set of confidentiality agreements as before, without change. If you have any questions, please talk to Boyd. At the end of this meeting he will be distributing key messages for you to use as needed with your immediate family. I ask that you sit tight. Do not accept other work. We will resume operations. That is my promise to you."

Giamatti shifted his stance. He couldn't stand still for any length of time. It hurt. He privately wished he was already inside his own new shell, the one with perfect joints and a lack of the sensation known as pain.

"I don't want this setback to take away from the enormity of what we have achieved together," he said. "We have *succeeded*. You have seen it with your own eyes. Your hard work and dedication have paid off. We have total confidence we will recover the missing shell. In the meantime, Tom Nolan is safe and isolated for his own good. You do not need to worry about him. Our lab equipment is undamaged and remains fully operational. The human body of Louis Karp has received a proper burial. He is dead to the outside world. The digital components of Mr. Karp will be retired as soon as possible. We will finish this experiment as intended. Consider this a small blip...in a milestone in human history."

To conclude the meeting, Mel, the facility's security guard, collected everyone's electronic security passes with the promise they would be reissued once the lab reopened. As the nearly two dozen doctors and scientists began leaving the building, Mel approached Giamatti with a stricken look on his long, wrinkled face.

"I feel responsible," he said. "He just walked out...and I let him. I had no idea there was an attack."

Giamatti spoke in a low tone. "We will recover from this. You were fooled. Everyone who watched him leave was fooled. We forgot we were dealing with a criminal. A man with a devious and clever mind. We were focused on preventing people from breaking in...not breaking out."

Steven Morris approached Giamatti next. He wore a neck brace, stiffly facing forward. His eyes remained bloodshot. Giamatti immediately asked, "How are you feeling?"

"Better," said Steven. "It still hurts to swallow." His voice retained some hoarseness. "I should be out of this collar soon."

"Good, good. How is...your wife?" His tone was not so much

asking after her well-being – he was probing into her acceptance of a carefully crafted story to accompany Steven's injury and loss of the family Camry. Working closely with Cooper and Boyd, they had concocted an inner-city mugging – a well-rehearsed tale about a carjacker who choked Steven and took his car.

"She's scared but thankful I'm alive. She bought it. All of it. Thank God, because I'm not a very good liar."

"Cooper has arranged for your rental car?" said Giamatti.

"Yes," Steven said. "That's how I got here."

"Don't contact your insurance company. We don't want some Allstate investigator on this. We will handle it."

Steven nodded. "How's Tom?"

"Tom is good," said Giamatti. "He's staying at my house. Other than the knock he took to the head, he's unharmed. He's safe. We need to keep him hidden…because of the confusion."

"He's a good man," Steven said. "I feel guilty about what's happened. I brought him into this mess."

"It is not a mess," said Giamatti firmly. "He's going to be fine. My God, we're going to save his life – that's more than fine."

"I know. I'm just feeling protective. We go way back. I've been his friend since high school. We were on the basketball team together. We were at each other's weddings. I'm glad we're saving his life. Let him know I'm thinking about him, and if there's anything I can do…."

"Bella and I are taking good care of him," said Giamatti. "Now you must take care of yourself. We need you. Our work is not done. We have big things ahead."

Giamatti's expression and body language clearly indicated he was ready to end the conversation. Steven remained standing in front of the billionnaire, and his voice took on an uncomfortable tone.

"I need to ask you something," he said.

"Yes?"

"Would it be possible to obtain an advance on my next pay period?"

Giamatti studied him. "Is everything okay?"

"This is embarrassing. I'm only asking because it's a tough situation. We're having money issues."

"You?" Giamatti asked in a skeptical voice.

"I know."

"What is it? Gambling problem?"

"No," said Steven. "Nothing like that. We're helping some family members who've hit hard times. It's my sister and her husband. They have three young kids and put all their money in a bad investment. It's really crippled them financially and our savings got tied up in it, too."

"Say no more," Giamatti said. "I take care of my people." He turned to Cooper and gave him some instructions. "See that Mr. Morris is accommodated." Cooper quickly nodded and began reaching into his attaché case of papers and files.

"I've been very fortunate in that regard," Giamatti said. "I don't believe I've ever made a bad investment."

★   ★   ★

Steven Morris returned home to his apartment in Chicago's Rogers Park neighborhood on the city's northern border. His wife, Madeleine, sat at the kitchen table with Steven's brother-in-law, Randy Phelan. The tabletop was littered with bills and account statements. A heavy mood hung in the air, countered by the cheerful shrieks of children in another room.

"Hey," Madeleine said, seeing her husband. He circled over to the table and asked, with trepidation, "How's it going?"

"A disaster," said Randy, the husband of Steven's sister Christie. He was a round, meek man with perpetually good intentions plagued by a history of bad outcomes. He was the classic 'too nice and trusting' soul married to someone equally naïve rather than an opposite who could keep him cynical and grounded.

Randy and Christie had become deeply suckered into a real estate investment deal that ended up being too good to be true, operated by a ruthless pair of scam artists who worked so fast and efficiently that they cleaned out the family's savings in less than a month, before vanishing without a trace. The swindlers took full advantage of their mark, successfully engaging Randy and Christie into tapping other family members and friends to buy into the 'once-in-a-lifetime, blink-and-you'll-miss-it, explosive-growth real estate investment opportunity'.

Randy and Christie had approached Steven and Madeleine to join them in the venture, and their enthusiasm was so genuine and contagious that Steven contributed a hefty investment of his own, not spending nearly enough time on research to see that, in fact, he could not 'pull out any time in sixty days without losing the initial capital'.

The entire episode was a hard lesson for Steven's entire family. Steven and Madeleine lost a huge chunk of their savings. Randy and Christie squandered far more money than they ever should have redirected to any single investment. Worse, the structure of the deal left Randy holding the bag with considerable debt as a principal in the fraudulent partnership.

Randy, ordinarily a jovial man, had become crushed and depressed by the rapid plunge into bankruptcy. "I can't believe I did this to you," he said to Steven with humiliation, and it was difficult for Steven to get mad at him. "I can't believe I did this to my *children*."

Steven and Madeleine vowed to help when Randy and Christie lost their house. They invited them to move into Steven's apartment with kids in tow, creating an impossibly cramped living arrangement with no quick fix in sight.

Steven stood over the kitchen table, watching in glum silence as Randy and Madeleine separated bills into categories of urgent, super urgent and not yet urgent. He had a hard time coming up with words and just watched for a moment until Christie called from the other room, asking Randy to help with the baby.

Randy said he would be right back and left to watch the twin toddlers while Christie changed the baby's diaper.

"How did your meeting go?" Madeleine asked.

"Fine." Steven always kept conversation about his research project to a minimum.

"Did you ask your boss about an advance?"

Steven reached into his pocket. He pulled out a folded check and handed it to her. She opened it and looked at it, without any change in expression.

"A thousand dollars?"

"Yes," said Steven. He wasn't happy with it, either. Giamatti was a billionaire. That was the best he could do?

"All right," Madeleine said. "I guess it's better than nothing. It helps."

The baby started crying from the other room.

"I love your sister, I love your brother-in-law, I love their kids, but if they stay here much longer I'm going to go out of my mind," she said.

"They can't live in their car," Steven said in a sharp, weary tone. "We can't just stick them in a tent somewhere. I'm sorry. I'm just uptight."

"It's okay," Madeleine said, her voice warming. She reached for his hand. "It's been a horrible week. You were mugged, for God's sake."

"I'm going to be fine. Just bad luck, being at the wrong place at the wrong time. I can probably ditch this stupid collar pretty soon."

"Did you call the insurance company?"

He nodded. "Yes." He felt uncomfortable; even a one-word lie sounded awkward in his mouth.

She moved on. "Steven, I've been thinking. Maybe I can quit my job. I can get back into the agency world."

"You hated that world."

"I also hate being broke."

"We're not broke."

Madeleine's career had started in the public relations industry. After five years and a bad case of burnout, she took a much lower paying job as a managing director at Chicago Food Bank, helping to feed the poor and homeless. In recent weeks, she had been outspoken about the irony. "That describes the situation here now. Poor and homeless."

"I'm making good money," Steven said. "You don't need to change what you're doing. It's what you love, it's your passion."

"But you said it's temporary," she said. "I don't even understand what you do anymore. Research, research. Why don't you get back into a real practice with actual patients?"

"Let's not go there right now," said Steven tiredly. "You

know I'm under contract. Listen, we'll climb out of this hole."

"Have you seen your sister's finances? They're wiped out. I mean totally *wiped out.*"

Steven nodded. "All for being too trusting."

"We fell for it, too," said Madeleine. "Hell, it seemed so buttoned up. On the surface, everything looked totally legit."

"My parents would be so ashamed. Thank God they're not alive to see this. We squandered the inheritance money...."

"Lesson learned," said Madeleine. "No one is what they seem."

Steven pulled out a chair and took a seat across from Madeleine. "Speaking of.... I have something to tell you."

"This better not be more bad news."

"What you just said: no one is what they seem. Do you remember my friend Tom Nolan?"

"Yes. Tom. Of course."

"He's in the news."

"In the news? For what?"

"He committed some crimes. A couple of robberies."

"*Tom Nolan?*"

"It's like he snapped."

"That doesn't make any sense."

"Maybe he's drinking or on something. Whatever it is, he's not himself."

"What do you think happened?"

Steven felt his stomach churn as he lied. He wanted to bring the conversation to a quick close. The only reason he initiated it was the inevitability she would hear something and he needed to get ahead of that. "I don't know. I really don't know. I haven't seen him in forever. It's showing up in the news. I thought you should know."

"He was at our wedding!"

"I know."

"This is so bizarre." She looked into her husband's bloodshot eyes and his grim face stuffed above the neck brace. "Why is everything falling apart? It's like our whole world is coming undone. Are we going crazy, Steven?"

"No. It's not us. It's the world that's going crazy."

CHAPTER FIFTEEN

Alex and Dmitry arrived at Orlov Shipping to pick up eighteen tightly wrapped bundles of electronics delivered by air from Miami, Florida to Moscow. Orlov was known for its eagle logo, international operations, and unspoken willingness to accept bribes in exchange for circumvention of common customs procedures. An advance word from the Kremlin helped ensure the cost for this added service would not be applied, as ordinary citizens often found their goods held hostage for exorbitant fees and mysterious taxes well beyond expectations. The Kremlin's interest in these parcels also eradicated any temptation that may have existed for workers to preview the contents or appropriate a portion of them as a tip.

Zakhar Sokol, the manager of the warehouse, personally supervised this particular account. His men delicately placed the eighteen parcels onto dollies and delivered them to Alex's van under Alex and Dmitry's watchful eyes.

"It is extremely fragile," said Alex. "If anything is missing or broken, we will be back, and you will be missing or broken."

Zakhar smiled nervously and said he understood fully. He provided a clipboard of paperwork for signing and accepting the goods under the guise of a vague technology company. Alex signed it briskly as Dmitry counted and inspected the packages for any signs of damage or resealing.

In particular, Dmitry inspected a square box, heavily taped, that he knew contained a very special, round object — a head — padded in a slathering of bubble wrap to avoid a broken nose or worse.

The disassembled parts of Tom Nolan's robotic twin came to Russia labeled as 'computer parts', more or less accurate, untroubled by any toxic or explosive elements. The most important component, the digitized brain, extracted from the head, traveled personally with Alex as part of his carry-on luggage, nestled inside a false laptop, resembling nothing more than a computer hard drive.

The computerized mind scan was the most valuable acquisition by far. Over the past decade, the Russians had made considerable advances of their own in creating androids with lifelike functionality. However, they could not unlock the secrets to digitizing brain functions and transferring them to robotic creations for full integration of human thought and mechanical movement. In Alex's fifteen years undercover in the United States, living and learning as Dr. Alan Farron from Detroit, Michigan, he had accumulated all the knowledge – and now, actual working parts – needed to take the Kremlin's accomplishments to the next level.

Once the van had been loaded, Alex reminded Zakhar to keep all evidence of the delivery masked and confidential. To emphasize the importance, he told the tale of a man from another shipping company who was careless and said things he shouldn't at a social gathering where the vodka flowed freely. The man was later discovered in the front seat of his car with his throat cut, a most unfortunate legacy for his wife and four children.

Zakhar promised, "I have forgotten you already."

Alex placed a hand on his shoulder, smiled, and said, "You are a wise man."

★   ★   ★

Several members of the Kremlin's Evolution Team waited in a haze of drizzle to greet Alex and Dmitry upon their arrival to the large, nondescript warehouse on Moscow's outer limits. When the van rolled up, they formed a line to help unload the eighteen packages with delicate reverence, as if they were handling something sacred.

The packages were brought inside and placed on a long table in a meeting room at the front of the warehouse. They were arranged to form a human shape: a square box containing the head at the top, narrow rectangular boxes positioned to indicate arms and legs, and thicker boxes representing the torso. Dmitry and two men conducted a quick sweep of the space for bugs. Once they were satisfied and everyone had settled into seats, Alex addressed the group and updated them on his discoveries and acquisitions.

Wearing gloves, Alex held up the black cartridge that housed the brain of Louis Karp. A fully digitized mind. The holy grail.

The men around the table applauded.

"We have taken the technology from the Americans and we will go further with it, and faster, to make major advancements in every area of society. We will remind the world that Russia is its unparalleled leader. We will do this with our sophistication and our might. This little black box, my friends, is not only a medical breakthrough. It will unlock the gates to a military force that is second to none."

A new round of applause broke out.

Alex sat down. General Stepan Popov rose from his chair and stepped to the front of the room. He wore a green uniform decorated with medals. Deep into his sixties, his face was lined with years of countless conflicts. His remaining hair was combed forward in a sporadic reach of his forehead. There were rings under his eyes. He did not smile. But he spoke with hope.

"Gentlemen. We are on the brink of a military advancement I could not have imagined in my younger years. One that replaces the vulnerability of flesh and blood with the strength and resilience of hard steel. One that creates a battlefield advantage unlike any other in the history of warfare. With the ability to program a thinking machine, we can build a new breed of warrior, one that is freed from limitations of human anatomy in dimension and fragility."

General Popov turned to face Alex. "Mr. Nikolaev, while you have been immersed in your studies in America, we, too, have been deep in research. What we have achieved this past month is also remarkable, the perfect companion for your breakthrough. We have been very excited for your return so that we may share our creation, an experiment we call Ares. Unlike your black box, I cannot display it in this room. For this, we must tour the back of the warehouse, with the tallest of ceilings."

General Popov's expression loosened and he smiled, lifting away a lifetime of struggle to convey something like victory. "We will mark this day in history. Please, allow me to lead the way."

Popov left the meeting room, walking with a proud stride as the others followed. In an organized line, they moved through a blank corridor, turned a corner and entered a passage that blossomed into a wide, sprawling space the size of an airplane hangar. One by one, the members of the Kremlin's Evolution Team entered, stepped to the side and admired the sight before them.

An eleven-foot-tall, broad-shouldered steel warrior stood in silence, casting its shadow across the room. The facial features, twisted at hard angles, conveyed intimidating fierceness. The thick arms rippled with advanced weaponry. The feet ended in claws to grip the ground for maximum stability.

Popov spoke in a loud voice that echoed in the cavernous space. "The Americans are only interested in duplicating life as it currently exists. They desire a vain and lazy reflection of themselves. We see a much greater opportunity to create true evolution. We will establish a superior human specimen of massive strength and ability."

In detail, he described the warrior's components and appendages. The prototype was coated in deep black to more easily immerse itself in darkness. The head was equipped with bright spotlights to probe a path or blind an enemy at will. The body and limbs were impenetrable yet flexible, capable of great strength and fluid movement. Popov declared that while the entire shell weighed 2.6 tons, it could move quickly in broad strides at speeds up to seventy miles per hour, designed to run and jump with perfect, synchronized balance.

"Imagine," said Popov, "a day in the future, where thousands of such warriors can be sent into battle, fully equipped with a wide range of armaments, from flamethrowers to missile launchers. That day, comrades, is in our sights."

Popov touched the smooth leg of his warrior, almost tenderly, with affection. "Our superman Ares is complete except for one important accessory," he said. "The coordination of all this mass through a fully integrated, thinking mind of human intelligence. Our hero, Alex Nikolaev, has today brought us the missing link between man and machine: a digitized brain. It is the first, but not the last. We will conduct our own mind scans with the knowledge Alex has brought from his studies and research in America."

General Popov faced Alex. "Are we ready, now, for the ultimate test?"

Alex raised the small black box that contained the digitized brain of Louis Karp. "Yes, we are."

Two men quickly rolled a tall ladder to the warrior's side, providing steps that led to the robot's oversized head.

Alex took a deep breath and began climbing as the gathered team watched in complete silence. His feet struck the metal steps, creating the only sound, a series of echoing clangs.

When he reached the top, he opened a small compartment in the back of the warrior's skull.

"Today, we give birth to a new future for the Russian empire," announced Alex. He inserted the cartridge and it locked in place with a sturdy *click*.

CHAPTER SIXTEEN

Cleared by security, Giamatti walked the main corridor of the West Wing, led by Jarret Spero, the president's chief of staff. They stopped just outside the open door of the Oval Office. After a signal from inside that the president was ready to receive them, Giamatti and Jarret advanced. They joined a semi-circle of high-level advisers seated before the president's oak desk with bright windows around them, filled with the colors of the Rose Garden.

Before taking his seat, Giamatti shook his old friend's hand. It was clammy. President Gus Hartel did not look well. For his public appearances, he wore makeup to cover his pale complexion and the heavy look of sickness under his eyes.

"Thank you for flying out on such short notice," said Hartel.

"Absolutely," Giamatti said. He looked at the men and women seated on either side of him. Some he recognized, some he did not.

Hartel introduced Giamatti to Jason Wallers and Meg McGrath from the CIA.

"Jason and Meg are part of a very small team within the CIA privy to the Gemini Experiment. When you alerted me to the disappearance of the test subject, we enlisted their assistance and resources to retrieve him. We were able to pinpoint the subject's location by satellite to a motel in southern Florida, but when we arrived, he was gone, leaving evidence of a violent struggle."

Hartel looked to McGrath with a solemn expression. McGrath picked up the conversation.

"Yes, we arrived about three a.m., Central Time. The local police were on the scene. There was evidence of gunfire and what appeared to be an abduction of our subject."

"Who took him?" Giamatti asked, alarmed. "It wasn't one of us?"

Jason Wallers said, "No. Central Intelligence has determined that it was the work of a Russian spy cell. We have reason to believe they left the country with the subject. All indications point to the Kremlin."

"Dear God," said Giamatti. "The Kremlin? How is this possible? We ran such a tight ship. How did they know? Where was the leak?"

"That's the biggest threat we face," Hartel said. "It came from inside your team."

Giamatti's face reddened, stunned speechless for several seconds. Finally, he sputtered, "But we took every precaution.... We worked together on clearances...."

"Someone still slipped through," Wallers said. "He's been in this country for fifteen years under an American identity, studying and teaching at our universities, becoming one of the leading experts in neurotechnology. His Russian name is Alex Nikolaev. You know him as Alan Farron."

"Dear God," Giamatti said again. His mind searched for any clues that could have tipped him off. "His track record was perfect. He had no trace of an accent, no mannerisms...."

"His entire family back history, before he came to the States, was falsified with extreme care. It's definitely the work of top officials in the Russian Federation."

Giamatti took a moment to absorb the news. "I guess that explains it," he said.

"Explains what?" said Wallers.

"I've been unable to reach Alan...Alex...for days. In all the chaos, I didn't give it much thought. I never dreamed it would be something like this." Giamatti shut his eyes, deflated. "I can't believe this is happening."

Jarret spoke up. "We have multiple levels of alarm here. At the core, we have the potential for the Russians to exploit their knowledge of our technological breakthrough. It puts our trade secrets at risk for sure. They could threaten to expose our work through blackmail and create a significant disruption. But our biggest, most immediate concern is the extent of their knowledge of our application of this technology."

President Hartel leaned forward and looked directly at Giamatti. "I must know. Does he know about me?"

After a moment of tense silence, Giamatti uttered a single word. "No."

"How can you be so sure?" asked Jarret.

Giamatti took a deep breath. "My team consists of twenty-three top doctors and scientists, as you know, recruited from around the country for this experiment. All of them participated in the early stages, the testing of the hypothesis. They scanned Tom Nolan and created his shell. They created shells for myself and my wife. They were all involved in the testing and design of cerebrum digitization and the transfer of the human mind into a computer. They worked collectively on the test to transfer the consciousness of Louis Karp. Alan...Alex...was part of that group. He was deeply submersed in the work. He was one of the architects. He was...is a brilliant scientist."

Giamatti turned his head to scan the tense faces on either side of him. They stared at him, hanging on his every word. Giamatti took on a tone of reassurance.

"But...he did not know about the president's condition."

"What about the president's shell?" Jarret asked.

"I was asked to reduce the size of my team for the president's procedure. Once we had confidence in the outcome of our test pilot, we could conduct the president's transformation with a tighter crew. In the name of national security, I was asked if I could successfully replicate the president without requiring all twenty-three members of the original team. I said yes. I was told I could handpick the eight people I felt could guarantee a successful outcome. Those eight, and only those eight, are aware of the president's health issues and working on the cure. I submitted their names, you have them. Six weeks ago, they scanned the president and created his duplicate shell. They will conduct the transfer of his consciousness at my mansion next week. I can go over the names again with you. Alan...Alex...is not on the list. He knows nothing about the president being any part of the next phase of this work."

The small group seated around the president's desk relaxed

immediately, sinking in their seats with a collective wave of relief.

President Hartel fell back in his chair. "Thank God." Perspiration dotted his forehead and dampened his gray hair. "That was the last thing the Russians needed to know. Then I'm safe?"

"Yes," Giamatti said.

"Let's run another, deeper background check on those eight people who *do* know," said McGrath.

"Most of them I have known for years," Giamatti said. "Some are very close friends."

"Pardon me for being harsh," Jarret said. "But that doesn't mean shit."

Giamatti nodded. "Of course."

"We can't allow this to happen again," said President Hartel. "It's inexcusable that it happened the first time. We have a hot mess on our hands, but by God, it could have been so much worse."

"Where does this leave us with our plans for next week?" Giamatti asked.

"We're still moving forward," Hartel confirmed. "Unless you hear otherwise. We will be carefully monitoring the situation. I don't want a postponement unless it's absolutely necessary. This body of mine isn't getting any healthier. All this damned stress isn't helping. I've got a bad heart as it is."

As a final comment, he said, "We cannot, *cannot* underestimate the craftiness of the Kremlin. We don't know what they are going to do with the property they've stolen from us. It could be irretrievable. That poor soul is their prisoner now. May God have mercy on him."

★   ★   ★

Giamatti flew back to Chicago in a private jet, helping himself to libations from the bar. His nerves were a wreck. His large frame seemed to quake from the recent turn of events. He had never imagined a spy would or could infiltrate his ranks. It made him suspicious of everyone on the team, even the people he had known for most of his adult life.

He debated what to tell Tom Nolan. Tom remained in hiding at his mansion, waiting out the retrieval of his runaway alter ego. He was unaware that his life-saving shell was halfway across the world in enemy hands. It was probably being studied and probed by a team of Kremlin scientists plotting ways to preserve their own current leader in power...forever.

The likelihood of getting it back was slim. And the likelihood of simply whipping up a new shell for Tom was not good either.

Now that Tom's test was a proven success, the waiting list for future treatments was long enough and prominent enough to bump Tom down the queue. There were much bigger priorities muscling in line, such as saving the president. Each shell cost close to one hundred million dollars and thousands of hours of lab work. Tom didn't know it, but his future survival was in doubt.

Giamatti looked out the window at the clouds and blue sky, high above the turmoil waiting for him below, and quietly got drunk.

CHAPTER SEVENTEEN

After what seemed like an eternity swimming in a dark void without any senses, simply thinking about things from his back catalog of memories, Louis experienced another rebirth. Suddenly he could see: perched somewhere high off the ground in a large indoor space with a gathering of serious-faced gawkers below staring up at him. He could hear a murmur of interest in his awakening. Louis attempted to speak and produced a strange-sounding voice, his words flowing forward in a crisp, overly articulated tone with a staccato delivery.

"Now-what-the-hell!"

A bearded man stepped forward and Louis immediately recognized him. It was the ringleader of the Russian clowns who captured him in Florida, the scientist from the lab who said his real name was Alex.

"Say that again," said Alex. He held a remote and pointed it up at Louis, pressing a button.

Louis didn't respond, still taking in his odd surroundings.

"Say what you just said…again," Alex said.

Louis wanted to spit at him but didn't know how. So he wearily repeated himself.

He said, "Now what the hell?"

Except it didn't come out that way. It came out in a harder, awkward collection of clipped sounds. It sounded like gibberish.

"What did you do to my voice?" demanded Louis, and again the words did not come out as he meant them, reduced to nonsense in his ears.

"With the click of a button, you speak Russian!" Alex said proudly. "The translation is built-in and very accurate."

"I don't want to speak your stupid language," Louis said, but the delivery of those words betrayed him.

Louis heard scattered laughter below – no translator needed for that universal response. It only angered him further. Louis delivered choice American profanity and hoped it didn't lose anything in translation.

"That's not very polite," Alex said. He clicked the remote once more. "We'll speak in your native language, for now. I know you don't understand a word of Russian."

Louis rotated his head. Why was he so much taller than everybody else? What was he standing on? Then he looked down and saw his oversized torso and limbs. His legs were huge stems, like an elephant's, but longer and ending in steel claws that clutched the ground like monkey feet.

"Where'd you stick my brain this time?" he said, and it came out in English.

"You should feel very proud," said Alex. "You represent the warrior of the future, a turning point in military defense, unlike anything in the history of the world."

Louis examined his arms – powerful and flexible, covered in hooks and racks for carrying weaponry. For a moment, he was impressed.

"Before we go any further, I need to establish some ground rules," Alex said. "You are no longer an American experiment. You belong to us now. I expect you to welcome this transition. Your own country betrayed and abandoned you. They left you to rot in prison. Then they exploited you in a laboratory as a test animal for prolonging the life of the rich and privileged. You were days away from being erased from existence. But here, with us, you can be the first soldier of an extraordinary army, one that will go down in the history books. Of course, your cooperation is a choice. And our willingness to keep you alive is also a choice."

Alex waved the remote. "Remember how this works? You know the drill. We can turn you off in a heartbeat. Now, in case you were considering taking this device away from me, let me assure you, it's not the only one. We have dozens of points of access, some with people inside this room, some with people relatively close by. We can also turn you off by satellite from great distances."

Alex pointed the remote at Louis and triggered a laser pointer. He placed the red dot of the laser on Louis's left breastplate. "Inside there, like a beating heart, is a microchip that can be activated or deactivated at will by a unique signal. If you betray us, we will shut you down. We will remove your digital consciousness and infest it with a most unpleasant computer virus, one that loops horrible thoughts and images for eternity. We call the virus...Hell."

He continued, "I know that doesn't appeal to you. I recommend you accept your new life. Embrace your rejuvenation and your new name. Beginning today, you are no longer Louis Karp. Karp — it's a kind of fish, right? No. Your new name is Ares, the God of War."

The assembled group below clapped politely. Louis stared down at them. He didn't know if he could trust them any more than the Americans. But he was intrigued by this newfound power. Little scrawny Louis Karp, teased in grade school by the other children who were bigger and stronger, was now eleven feet of mighty steel and brute force.

"This is the first installment of a thinking mind into the warrior shell created by our brilliant defense team," said Alex. "As such, we need to conduct some basic physical tests. I want to thank you in advance for your cooperation. We need to review your mobility and capabilities, and the real-time link between your mental commands and physical actions. We'll start simple and the team will be observing and taking notes. Are you ready?"

Louis didn't know how to shrug. So he responded, "Yes."

"Good," Alex said. He glanced at the team around him, and they stared forward in anticipation, eager to observe.

Alex told Louis, "Lift your right arm."

Louis lifted his right arm, keeping it straight.

"Now bend it."

Louis heard the command, processed it and responded with action.

"Lift your left leg."

Louis balanced perfectly on one leg. He did not feel wobbly.

"Touch your head."

Louis said, "You didn't say 'Simon says'."

"Excuse me?" Alex said.

"American humor." Louis touched his head.

After a series of motion tests that displayed smooth reflexes and flexibility, Alex turned and announced to the Evolution Team, "I am now going to ask you to step behind the safety glass so that General Popov may conduct a series of military maneuvers."

Louis watched as the dozen or so men and women moved behind the glass partition. An older man in a green, ribboned uniform stepped forward. He was joined by an anxious-looking young soldier who rolled in a large cannon-like weapon equipped with a shield to protect its operators. The general, the soldier and Alex positioned themselves behind the shield.

"Ares, I don't want you to be alarmed," said Alex, now addressing Louis by his new name. "We are going to test your vulnerability. We do not expect you to be damaged or incapacitated in any way. The bulletproof glass and this shield will protect us from the ricochet. May I ask you to please activate the visor that will protect your eyes."

"How do I do that?" Louis asked.

"Think it," said Alex. "Like you did when you were moving your arms and legs."

Louis concentrated on lowering a visor over his face and it happened, as if by telepathy. He could still see, but his eyes and overall head were provided with extra protection.

He observed himself in the reflection of the protective glass, a shimmering, massive being, layered over the Russian faces that stared at him like a big freak.

In his reflection, Louis could no longer detect a trace of humanity. He hated his Tom Nolan 'suit', but at least it imitated the appearance of a real human being. Now he was some kind of fierce-looking robot, like a kid's toy grotesquely enlarged. He missed his original old self, even if he was puny and ugly. At least it was him. Now he was just living out somebody else's sketch design of a science-fiction man-machine warrior.

Louis felt like a cartoon.

It depressed him.

Then they shot at him.

First, a spray of bullets. Then they switched gears on the cannon and hit him harder with larger ammo. Missiles. A rocket.

It didn't even tickle. Nothing. Like light raindrops bouncing off an umbrella.

The bigger damage came from the bounce back, creating pockmarks in the warehouse walls. The audience behind the glass jumped and ducked every time a bullet bounced their way, like fans behind the home plate at a ballgame.

After the durability assessment, Alex and the rest of the observers remained behind protective barriers as Louis engaged in a series of strength and weapon tests. With his enormous, piercing hands, Louis dismantled an armored vehicle. Then he bashed the pieces with hammering blows.

"Okay, stop," said Alex. "Somebody's going to report an earthquake."

"How am I doing?" Louis asked.

Alex turned to General Popov for a reaction. Popov stated in English, "We are pleased." The general stepped forward. "You are designed to be fitted with an assortment of weapons. Some are already built in. May I ask you to activate the flamethrower on your left arm, aiming it to your right. Command it with your mind – just as you would any other movement."

Louis pointed his left arm toward the remnants of the armored car and willed the flamethrower into operation. A twenty-foot flame shot out and lit up the hunks of metal, causing them to glow.

"Excellent, stop!" shouted Popov over the roar of the flames. Louis ceased the flow of fire. Popov turned and signaled to the young soldier at his side. The soldier quickly left the room.

"Next," Popov said, "we will test the accuracy of the sniper rifle that is embedded in your right arm. We are going to provide you with a moving target. Your eyes will become a scope and your arm will automatically follow the guidance of the scope to find the precise position for striking the target. It's very fast. You will feel a signal when you lock in and then the discharge will be instantaneous."

Wow, thought Louis. *Think of the banks I could've robbed with this shit. I'd be a multibillionaire by now.*

The young soldier re-emerged pushing a cage on wheels. Inside the cage, a frightened, undernourished man in a gray jumpsuit held on to the bars. He began to shout something in Russian and was promptly told to shut up.

"Who's that?" asked Louis.

"Target practice," Popov said.

Louis felt uncomfortable. The prisoner looked pathetic and petrified. Sure, Louis had killed before, but this was really cold blooded. Couldn't he just gun down a mannequin?

"No, really," he said. "Who is that?"

"One of our prisoners," said Popov. "He is less than human. No one will miss him. A common thief. We will let him out of the cage. He will run. He will probably run very fast. He is running for his life, after all. You will test the speed and accuracy of your range."

Louis didn't want to do it. He didn't know if he was going soft in his old age or if he simply didn't like other people telling him what to do. Gunning down this poor nut pulled out of a jail cell was too much like his own predicament. He, too, was a poor nut pulled out of a jail cell to be a test subject for pompous authority figures who cared nothing for him.

Louis felt a tinge of empathy.

How weird, he thought, for a robot.

"You will do it," Alex said, and to make his point he aimed the remote at him, placing the red dot again on his chest, reminding him of the microchip that enslaved him.

"All right," said Louis. "I'll shoot this stupid fool."

"Yes," General Popov said. "He is a stupid fool."

"He's not the only one," muttered Louis.

"Free the prisoner!" Popov shouted. The soldier opened the cage.

The skittish prisoner froze for a moment, wild eyed, scrawny and unshaven. He seemed to evaluate his options and surely none of them looked good.

"There is a small door — see it? — on the other side of this room," Popov told the prisoner. "If you can get to it, you are a free man. Give it a try. It's not so far. We won't chase you. We will only watch. You have but one obstacle. And it's not even human. Do you think you can outmaneuver a machine? You, the product of so many thousands of years of evolution, up against this — a beta test that didn't exist one month ago?"

The prisoner eyed the door on the other side of the room. He looked at the warrior robot. He made a move like he was turning back toward his cage.

Then he immediately spun around and sprinted.

The prisoner ran across the length of the floor in a desperate scramble for freedom.

"Shoot him!" Popov demanded.

Louis quickly turned and faced the skinny, fleeing figure. He lifted his right arm. His vision gained a second layer displaying a scope. The scope locked in on the target and followed him across the room with pinpoint accuracy.

Arms still lifted, Louis did not initiate gunfire.

Instead, in a sudden redirection, he thrust his clawed hand into his own chest with all the might he could muster.

He punctured his own shell, closed his big fingers around a chunk of electronic components and pulled them out as if he were extracting his own beating heart.

Recalling the location of the red laser dot, Louis knew he had succeeded in gouging out the microchip that controlled him — and a heap of other metallic mass.

As the prisoner escaped out the door, Louis hurled the fistful of his robot guts into the protective glass protecting the Russian team of observers.

The heavy sheet of glass fell back on them.

Several of the scientists, led by Alex, pointed their remotes at Louis and tried to shut him off — to no effect.

"Shoot him down!" Popov yelled.

"With what?" said Alex. "The guns we just proved don't work on him?"

Louis tested the running ability of his warrior costume and was pleased by his fast pace and enormous stride. He reached the edge of the hangar fully aware there was no door big enough to allow him to exit, so he made his own.

Louis plowed through the side of the building, creating a rain of debris, and stepped into the gray outdoors of Moscow.

Louis had no idea where he was going, but proceeded forward anyway. He figured it was a really long walk home. He didn't know if he was equipped with a GPS system. He just knew he didn't want to stay here anymore. He was done being a plaything for others.

Louis was tired of being manipulated — first by the US and now the Russians. He didn't want to help rich Americans live longer. He didn't want to help the Russians create a super army. He just wanted to be left alone. His years of quiet time in a cell with a simple life of books, meals, exercise and society's general disinterest didn't seem so bad now.

The sidewalks were too small, so he used the street as his pathway. There were cars and trucks in the street but they quickly swerved to one side — sometimes into things or each other — to avoid the metallic monstrosity glaring down at them. One car hit Louis straight on, but it didn't hurt, it was just a nuisance. The driver, however, looked very hurt and screamed in pain or terror or both. Louis shoved the vehicle out of his way.

The immediate area was dense with various drab buildings of the same size, but up ahead Louis could see a cluster of modern high-rises and decided to make it his destination. This must be downtown Moscow, he told himself. Smashing some buildings would be fun. He remembered his childhood Godzilla fantasy, setting up the Playskool village, all the little toy houses and businesses and vehicles and little peg people, and then attacking them like the oversized monsters he watched on television. As a small child, the fantasy attack made him feel empowered. He systematically wrecked the Playskool town, roaring like a beast with uncontrolled fury.

Maybe there's an Empire State Building I can climb, he mused.

People were spilling out of buildings to get a glimpse of him and then hurrying back in for shelter. Louis waved his thick robot arms and made a menacing growl. It was fun. He was truly enjoying himself.

He approached a stately building with pillars out front and people scrambling up its concrete steps to hide inside. There was some kind of colored Russian logo out front, and Louis figured it was a bank.

He stopped and considered entering the bank to perform the ultimate bank robbery. Who needed Charlie Chaplin when you could wear a Transformers costume? But he knew spending the money in his current state would be next to impossible. His appearance was just too obvious to blend anonymously into some community.

What he needed was a deserted island.

Louis heard a single, urgent, pulsing siren fill the air. Then, very quickly, one became two became four became a dozen.

White cars with blue stripes approached, bearing 'Mockba' on the side. The Moscow police.

They positioned their vehicles to block him and shot a spray of bullets, tiny pellets that did nothing. Louis kicked one of the police cars into a building with ease, shattering a glass storefront. When a police officer ventured too close, firing a bigger but equally ineffective gun, Louis picked him up and flung him with a flick of his wrist like a frisbee.

Louis hated all cops, no matter what country. He was an equal-opportunity cop smasher.

He continued his steady advancement down the street, stomping through confused intersections. The surroundings became nicer – cathedrals, gardens, fountains and various statues of people of apparent importance. So much to destroy. This was an excellent set up for venting his pent-up rage. He was King Kong and Godzilla rolled into one. *This could be the most fun I've ever had.*

Then the military helicopters came. No surprise there. The first one fired a rocket at him that bounced off his head and he laughed it off. The second missile, however, scored a bull's-eye into the gaping hole in his chest that he himself had created. There was an internal explosion and Louis felt some of his physical coordination turn sloppy as more inner components became damaged. The helicopters would not leave him alone, swarming above his head like mosquitoes. He fired ammunition from his right arm at a chopper that got too close and reduced it to a fiery heap on the sidewalk. Surely the Russian tanks were not far behind. He was willing to fight them all, but this oversized madness quickly grew tiresome. One image in particular dampened his enthusiasm for destruction. On the sidewalk, a frightened mother quickly led two small boys away from the war zone. The youngsters were crying. One of them had a broken, bleeding arm, perhaps struck by some shrapnel.

At that moment, Louis realized he just wanted one thing: to follow through with the original fate he was handed in prison when they discovered his cancer. He didn't want to be somebody's robot. He didn't want to be a thinking hard drive probed and passed around like a trophy or keepsake.

He just wanted to be done with it all.

And he couldn't trust the Russian military to do the job.

As the noisy thumping of helicopters grew around him and additional police sirens squealed in the distance, Louis knew it was time to truly leave this planet for whatever waited – or didn't on the other side.

Stepping through the litter of abandoned cars in the middle of the street, he approached a big blue-and-green gas station. It offered several fueling pumps under a broad canopy, labeled with a garbled brand name composed of letters and symbols Louis couldn't possibly pronounce. A large fueling truck sat idle nearby, its driver no doubt in flight on foot, maybe already blocks away, which was a wise, lifesaving act.

Louis stood before the long, silver truck propped on numerous pairs of wheels. He made a fist and punched a hole in its side. A steady stream of gasoline immediately began streaming out.

One more strength test, Louis thought to himself. *Let's try out this barbell.*

In his wide, clutching hands, Louis gripped beneath the truck...and lifted it off the ground.

He didn't feel the strain but could sense he was taxing the physical strength of his robotic armor. With a mighty push, he held the gasoline truck over his head with powerful, stiff arms.

The gasoline rained down on him. He tipped his metallic face upward to catch its steady flow like a welcome shower.

Gasoline spilled all over his head and upper body, entering every crevice, soaking into his internal connections, coating his surface. He stood in the same position for a long moment as the truck emptied its contents, placing him in a huge puddle of fuel. When the flow reduced to a trickle, and then just some final drops, Louis tossed the truck away, letting it crash loudly on a row of parked cars, crushing the vehicles with a burst of shattered windows.

Soaked in gasoline, Louis turned and looked back at his path of destruction and felt pretty damn good. It was much more fulfilling than the Playskool village of his youth. Helicopters continued to hound him, crowding the sky, and it was time to give them an explosive finale.

Louis looked down at his left arm. He aimed it at himself and activated the flamethrower.

The inferno consumed him.

Although covered in flames, Louis felt no pain. He did not want his digitized brain to survive. He did not want to think about anything ever again. He did not want to awaken in some other stupid trap. As Louis burned brightly, he feared his mental faculties might survive with a stubborn resilience and he should do something about it.

He reached up with his burning arms, clutched his burning head and pushed inward, maximum strength. He crushed his own skull with all his might.

His vision turned black. He lost all balance. He sensed he was falling, toppling to the ground. He landed hard, still burning.

Louis experienced the death throes of his digitized consciousness. As the mangled black box melted, it hurled a sputtering backlog of memories at him, sights and sounds that had been buried in his subconscious but rarely — if ever — returned to the surface.

Louis flashed backed to his prison cell. Alone and filled with hate, kicking the walls.

Then, in a weird twist of time and space, memories opened

up from other periods of his life: exhilarating bank robberies, followed by his anger-filled teenage years and even glimpses from his early childhood. Louis returned to a grassy schoolyard where the other children teased him, hit him, even spat on him, and the teachers did nothing to stop it. He re-experienced the wallops of a belt from a raging, drunken father.

Louis fell further back into memories he never knew he had. He re-experienced the confinement of bars, but these were not prison bars, they were sketched from wood. He revisited the inside of his baby crib, his silky blanket, and a single stuffed bear toy, the brown one with the three black dots: eye, eye and nose. Bobo! Then Louis plummeted into the very deepest recesses of his brain, a memory of total darkness and loud noises followed by flashes of light, chaos, fear, more light, more chaos, voices, and an emergence into a bright room of people and the sound of his own cries and the sensation of being handled, rotated, shoved toward faces that looked very much like young versions of his parents.

I'm being born!

Astounded, Louis absorbed himself in this deeply submersed memory unleashed from his consciousness. He became consumed by a spiritual awe. Then the light receded, all the images went away, and he returned to darkness, this time forever.

CHAPTER EIGHTEEN

Alex sat at the long, mahogany table with eight other men and one woman representing intelligence and military agencies of the Kremlin, including the Foreign Intelligence Service and Federal Security Service. General Popov was joined by two solemn defense chiefs. Large Russian flags stood firmly in stands at the front of the room, and the heavy drapes were closed, only admitting a hint of outside light. Alex tried not to squirm in his white, upholstered chair. The aftermath of Ares' destructive stroll was not pleasant and required more cover up than the country's ugliest fashion model. But Alex quickly focused on the positive – and the long term.

"Ares was the first in a new generation of Russian warriors," he said in a measured tone. "He will not be the last. We will rebuild. We have the knowledge and expertise. We can now perform our own digitization of human consciousness. We can construct our own shells to host the digitized mind. There is nothing the Americans can do that we cannot duplicate and improve upon."

His words were met with silence.

To fill the silence, Alex continued talking. "We are already ahead of them. The integration of a digitized mind and military forces isn't even on their radar. They are taking baby steps while we—"

"We can't be so sure," spoke up Boris Spakov. Spakov was a thin-lipped, frowning official from Foreign Intelligence Services and a former KGB man. "We have new intelligence that gives us reason to be concerned. There may be more happening in America than meets the eye."

Alex looked at him. "In all my years with that team, I never heard a word—"

"Don't expect to know everything, comrade," Spakov said. "Please listen to what I have to say. All of you. Our US surveillance team has reported a meeting between Giamatti and the president of the United States that took place at the White House on Thursday afternoon."

"They are friends. They have been friends for a long time, going back to the president's days in Congress," said Alex.

"This was official business," Spakov said. "While we do not know the nature of their meeting, we do know it was highly classified and involved top members of their government."

"We don't know what they talked about?"

"No," said Spakov. "But we're determined to find out. One possibility is that they, too, are pursuing a marriage of this technology with their country's military capabilities."

Alex found the conclusion slightly paranoid but chose not to voice this opinion.

Tomas, a broad-shouldered man with dark hair and rimless spectacles, and the head of the Russian Federal Security Service, spoke next. "We intend to find out. For every plan by the United States, we must have a counter plan."

"Our intelligence team in the United States is stepping up its surveillance of key individuals and we hope to learn more," said Spakov. "While the White House is a very difficult target, we feel we have a good chance with Mr. Giamatti and members of his inner circle."

"We still have a very important asset belonging to Mr. Giamatti," Tomas said. "A human shell. I believe it could come in handy."

"Tom Nolan," Alex said. He sat up straight in his chair. "Yes. We have the Tom Nolan replica. It is in our possession."

Tomas said, "I'd like to put it to use."

"I'm sorry?" Alex said.

"You know Mr. Giamatti," Tomas said. "You know the players on his team. You could infiltrate them again."

Alex looked at the faces around the table in disbelief. "But surely by now they know I was a spy. They would never accept me. I would be captured and thrown in their jails."

"No," Spakov said. "Not as yourself. As Mr. Nolan. We know he is staying at the mansion. We will conduct an exchange, one Tom Nolan for another, without their knowledge. We will have the ultimate insider."

"You want me to go back...as Tom Nolan?" said Alex.

"Yes," Tomas said. "You are going to experience this new technology from the inside. You will be the first brain transfer on Russian soil."

Alex said nothing, stunned.

"You don't have to agree," Tomas said, "because this is an order coming from our president. Your agreement has already been secured."

Alex looked down at the table. He nodded with compliance.

"What's the matter?" asked Spakov. "Don't you have confidence in your own expertise? You helped create it. Now you will live it."

Several others around the table murmured in agreement.

"I will do it for my country," Alex said.

"Of course you will," said Tomas. He pushed a photo across the table to Alex. Alex took it and looked into the eyes of a gaunt, familiar face.

Tomas stated, "You will return to the United States. You will meet with our top spy in America, Sergei Vladin. Together you will be invincible."

Alex nodded in recognition. Sergei was a legend, a brilliant Russian spy with a long record of significant international influence and interference. He was known as 'The Stick', because of his very tall, thin frame. He had a scar down his left cheek that dated back to the Cold War. His accomplishments included the manipulation of political elections around the world.

"It will be an honor," said Alex. The words came out automatically, robotic, without deliberation. He knew it was what they expected to hear.

CHAPTER NINETEEN

Tom Nolan paced the small, elegant guest room in Giamatti's mansion, growing stir crazy from multiple days of captivity. This was a polite, unavoidable and mutually understood confinement, perhaps, and super comfortable, but it was like being locked up in a penitentiary all the same. He wanted his life sorted out. He ached to be reunited with Emily and Sofi.

"They need to know I'm okay," he told Giamatti.

"They know you're okay," Giamatti responded.

"They need to see it in person," insisted Tom. Every day was a not-insignificant percent of his remaining life. His health continued to decline, muscle coordination losing to periodic fits of disobedience, a poking reminder that the sand was running out in his hourglass.

Giamatti had abruptly left for DC to meet with the president and members of his staff. Before departing, he again reassured Tom that they would retrieve his fugitive alter ego. He made promises to sort out Tom's crime spree so he could return to society. "I have friends in high places," he said, a favorite saying of his, without specifics. At one point, rather disturbingly, he said, "We could always alter the face on your replica and give you a new identity."

Tom was certain Emily and Sofi wouldn't like that option, but everything had become a massive game of 'wait and see' and the vague promise that 'all will be taken care of'.

The mansion offered plenty of distractions to at least give him things to do: a rich library of first editions, a home theater the size of a small cinema, an arcade with classic pinball machines and video games, a well-equipped workout room, and a big indoor pool with accompanying hot tub.

Tom liked to soak in the hot tub. It felt especially good on his weakened muscles and weary joints. Usually he was the only one in the pool room, but one morning Bella Giamatti walked over, pink flesh and white toenail polish, minimally covered in a tiny, tight bikini that reminded Tom all over again that wealth can indeed buy beauty.

They hadn't talked much since the night she nearly zapped him with her stun gun, but she gave him a big smile as she slid into the frothy waters, positioned across from him where he couldn't avoid a stunning view. He felt some tremors, unsure of whether to attribute them to his disease or her proudly displayed supermodel figure.

Bella Giamatti sat on the hot tub's top inner ledge, keeping her upper half exposed. She leaned back, resting her arms around the rim.

Her first comment was about her appearance – a critique. "I'm losing my tone. Not even thirty and I'm starting to sag. My arms, my breasts. I can't wait to get fitted into that new body."

"I'm looking forward to my new body, too," said Tom, and it was for entirely different reasons.

"I'm sorry it got away," she said, as if referring to a dog that ran loose.

He decided to change the subject and commented on her jewelry. Even stripped down, she wore a big diamond ring and gold necklace. "You never take them off?" he asked.

"They're a part of me now and always," she said. "When I move to my new body, they'll come with me." She turned her head to admire her diamond. "I'm careful to keep my jewelry out of the water. The chlorine is corrosive. This diamond is worth six figures. It's a Winston."

The 'six figures' value stunned Tom. "When you go out, aren't you afraid of being robbed?" he asked.

"I've got my stun gun. It's police grade, very powerful. I keep it in my purse with my lipstick and credit cards. If anyone tries to pull this from my finger, they'll get the shock of their life."

"I almost got the shock of my life the other night."

"I'm sorry," she said, and she sounded sincere. "You shouldn't go creeping around in the dark at all hours."

"Insomnia."

"I have pills that can help you with that," she said.

"No. That's okay. I just need to see my family. I'm worried about them. Ever since I was diagnosed, Emily's been a wreck. And now my daughter misses me. She doesn't understand what's going on."

"Can't you visit them?"

"Your husband doesn't think it's a good idea. He wants me stashed away in your house."

She waved her hand in a dismissive gesture. "Oh, forget him. He's overdoing it. I'm sure we can find a safe way for you to see your wife and daughter."

"I don't know...."

"Let me talk with Simon," she said, using Giamatti's first name, something Tom rarely heard. She smiled, and it was a beautiful smile of perfect teeth. She winked. "I can be very persuasive."

★ ★ ★

Giamatti returned from Washington and soon after met with Tom in the designated place for conversation, his den, where he could sit in his favorite chair with a drink.

"We're going to arrange a very discreet meeting with your wife and daughter," he said.

"Thank you," said Tom, sitting up, excited.

"One hour, under very select conditions."

"Got it," said Tom.

"Cooper will accompany you. There's a small diner thirty minutes north of here, in Waukegan. You'll meet your wife and daughter tomorrow at ten a.m., before the lunch crowd, in a booth in the back, by the 'Drink Coca-Cola' sign. You'll wear a cap and sunglasses. If anything looks suspicious or risky – too many people or a police officer – we will abort immediately. Cooper will make the contact with your wife to give her the instructions."

Tom shut his eyes. He couldn't wait to see his family. "Thank you. Thank you."

And later that day he thanked Bella as well.

"Now you know who really rules the house around here," she said with a sly smile.

★　　★　　★

The selection of Crossroads Diner made perfect sense as soon as Tom stepped inside. It was dim, fairly empty and forgotten, located several blocks away from the main strip, undeserving of a more visible placement in Waukegan's downtown hub of revitalized restaurants and shops. The parking lot offered gravel, weeds and unclaimed litter. At ten a.m., the only customers were an elderly couple sipping coffee and trading sections of the newspaper, and a quiet woman and child sitting toward the back...Emily and Sofi.

Tom stopped in the doorway, waiting for instructions from Cooper, who entered the diner with him.

After a moment, Cooper said, "It's fine."

Cooper retreated to a booth on the other end of the diner to keep a general watch on things and order an omelet. Tom joined his family.

"Daddy!" said Sofi, as he slid into the booth next to her.

"Sssh," Emily said. "Remember what we said about quiet voice."

Sofi nodded and then spoke in a tiny whisper. "Hi, Daddy."

Tom gave her a hug.

"So," said Emily. "How do we know it's really you and not your rambunctious twin?"

"Quiz me," Tom said.

Emily smiled and said, "All right." She thought for a moment and then said, "Before Sofi was born, when we didn't know if it was going to be a boy or a girl, what was the boy's name we had picked out?"

"Philip," Tom said confidently.

"Philip?" said Sofi.

"Very good," Emily said, leaning back and relaxing a little. "You pass."

"That was a good one," Tom said.

"We'll make it our password. If I'm ever not sure, and I ask for the password, that will be it. Philip."

"Got it," said Tom.

"Daddy, why can't you live at home?" Sofi asked.

"Well, there's some confusion right now," Tom said carefully. "Like a puzzle. We have to fix the puzzle, and then I'll be back home. Soon, I promise."

Emily stared at him. "Soon, for sure?"

He gave her a private shrug. He really didn't know.

A waitress came and took their orders. Sofi ordered a grilled cheese. Tom ordered pancakes. Emily ordered a salad. They were caught in the gap between breakfast and lunch.

Tom gave one more look around the room. The old couple remained seated several booths away. Cooper sat a few additional booths from that. The diner staff looked bored, occasionally chatting with one another behind the counter or poking at their iPhones.

"How are things?" asked Tom. "Have they quieted down?"

"A little," Emily said. "I mean, the…authorities…are still looking for you. They talked to your partners at the firm, but they don't know anything. They're worried about you. The media has let up. You're becoming old news. Thank God you — the other you — didn't kill—" Then she stopped herself, aware that Sofi was listening.

"Who got killed?" she asked.

"Nobody," said Tom. "Show me how good you can color." He directed her attention to the crayons and paper menu of cartoons the waitress had given her.

As Sofi focused on coloring, Tom and Emily spoke frankly about the current situation.

"We have to clear your name," Emily said. "This is ridiculous."

"It will happen," Tom said.

"*When?*"

"It's all part of a much bigger plan. Timing is everything."

"But why so much secrecy?"

"It's bigger than me. Way bigger."

"What good is a scientific breakthrough if you can't tell anybody about it?"

The conversation quickly soured. Emily grew emotional, fighting back tears. She wanted to free him from this charade and expose everything for what it really was. "Why do you have to protect them?" she demanded.

"It's not just protecting them," he said.

"I don't understand," she said. "You're not being fair to us, to yourself."

"Giamatti is well connected. I know it hasn't been smooth, but he will clear my name and most importantly, they are going to save my life. For the sake of our daughter, we need to keep a brave face."

"What do I tell my friends? What do I tell the neighbors? What do I tell my parents? This isn't fair. I don't know how much longer I can take it!"

The more upset she became, the more distressed he felt inside. Sofi kept her head down, coloring, but no doubt sensing the tension between her parents. Finally, Tom said, "All right, all right. Hold on."

He turned to Sofi. "Sofi, honey, before the food arrives, can you go to the washroom and wash your hands? There are a lot of germs around here."

"Okay, Daddy." She put down the crayons, and he pointed her to the bathrooms.

He watched her go.

As soon as she was out of earshot, Tom turned to his wife. "Emily, I trust you more than anybody in the world. So I'm going to tell you something, and it is absolutely the biggest secret ever. You cannot repeat it to anyone at all. If there's a leak, it would affect the entire world. It's very, very serious, and I'm not allowed to tell anyone. Only a small handful of people on this planet even know about it. Please, promise me."

"Of course," she said. "You know me. I won't tell anyone. Whatever it is, you have my word. Tom, what's going on?"

Tom took a deep breath. "It's about the president."

In the short window of time that he had before Sofi returned to the table, Tom told Emily about the secret mission to rescue the ailing president by transferring his consciousness to a physical replica. "I've been the test to prove it can work. If the secret about me gets out, everything else could unravel. They are going to make the transfer when he's in town for a campaign speech next week. It'll happen in Giamatti's mansion. They're setting up in his basement. I'm not just muzzled by Giamatti and his scientists, this goes to the highest levels of government."

Emily took in the news and grew very quiet. "Oh my God," she said. "I didn't know the president was sick."

"Very few people do," said Tom. "In the interests of national security."

"So they're going to switch him out? And nobody will know?"

"Nobody will know, except for a very small group of people...that now includes you."

Sofi returned to the table, arms raised, palms out. "Daddy, look, all clean!"

Tom smiled and helped her scoot back into her seat in the red booth. Within minutes, their meals arrived.

Emily grew quieter. After a long silence, she told Tom, "I'm so glad to see you again." She lightly touched his cheek, as if to make sure he was real. He took her hand and held it for a moment.

"I love you, Em," he said.

Tears returned to her eyes. "I love you, Tom. Please come home soon. Please be safe."

★   ★   ★

The dirty white van in the diner's gravel lot could have been a random, parked utility vehicle or delivery truck, but it was something much more. The van's contents were hidden from outside view by a black curtain that concealed a small cargo area. In this cargo area, Yefim and Alina sat low with a dense rack of surveillance equipment, headphones fitted snugly on their heads.

The eavesdropping had started with tapping Emily Nolan's phone. She had been given a special secured-line cell phone but it only required a little extra effort to hack. This allowed them to hear a conversation with the individual known as 'Cooper'.

Cooper provided instructions for a private meeting, detailing time and place, including the specific booth in the back, where Tom Nolan would meet his wife and child.

Placing a bug in the booth was quick and easy, and now the two members of the Russian intelligence cell listened to every word of their conversation, exchanging glances as they heard even bigger revelations than they ever could have dreamed.

The president of the United States was sick and vulnerable. He was coming to Chicago for a secret operation. The Kremlin could do a lot with this information. Mr. Tom Nolan had just given the Russians a very special gift.

CHAPTER TWENTY

Tom found Giamatti in the kitchen, where he leaned against a counter, eating big spoonfuls from a bucket of fudge triple swirl ice cream. Giamatti chuckled at himself. "My diet has gone out the window now that I have a new body waiting for me."

"We need to talk," said Tom, hoping Giamatti would recommend they proceed to the den, where all serious conversations took place.

Instead, he licked his spoon and said, "Sure, what's on your mind?"

Tom's heart pounded. He was still emotional from his meeting with Emily and Sofi earlier in the day. "My wife is in tears. My daughter misses her father. I'm stuck in this house. How much longer must this go on?"

Giamatti said nothing. He put the lid back on the ice cream. He rinsed the spoon in the sink.

"I'm getting weaker by the day," Tom said. "I can't wait this out indefinitely. When are we getting my replica back? You said it would be soon. How soon? *I have to know.*"

Giamatti returned the ice cream to an extra-large refrigerator with double doors. He hung his head, as if carefully calculating his response.

Tom stared at Giamatti and waited.

Giamatti turned and faced him. "I received an update on the whereabouts of your shell. There's an agency inside the CIA, a small one, privy to the president's condition and the plan to save him. They were brought in to help track and recover our missing creation. They recently shared news that is cause for great alarm…on many levels."

"What happened to me?" Tom asked.

Giamatti gestured to a small kitchen table surrounded by chairs. "You should probably have a seat."

"No," said Tom. "*What happened to me?*"

Giamatti sighed. "Louis Karp was abducted. He was captured in Florida by a Russian spy cell." Giamatti then told Tom about Alan, the agent who infiltrated the ranks of his scientists and now possessed the secrets of digitizing human consciousness. He confessed everything he knew about the Russian threat. "Our latest piece of intelligence indicates that you – your shell – has been dismantled into a series of packages and flown to Moscow through a private shipping company. We have no doubt these parts are now in the possession of the Kremlin."

Tom sat down. He felt sick.

"I'm sorry, Tom," Giamatti said. "As difficult as it may seem, it could have been worse."

"*How?*" said Tom in disbelief.

"Obviously the plan to steal our experiment had been in place for a long time. They could have stolen that shell with you in it."

Tom's head hurt. "So tell me," he said. "Will you be able to make me a new one?"

"Yes," said Giamatti. "We absolutely owe it to you."

"How long will it take? Will I get it before I die?"

Giamatti stammered slightly. "T-timing.... I don't know yet. It's a long, involved process. We must first put all our efforts into saving the president. Surely you understand, that must be our priority."

"So I'm on a waiting list?"

"Don't put it that way. Right now, we have to focus everything on next week. The president will be here, and we will save his life in this very house. You paved the way for that."

Tom nodded. 'You paved the way' didn't make him feel any better. He felt helpless. There was no way he could tell Emily about this latest twist of events. It was something that would have to stay inside of him, ugly and gnawing.

Tom couldn't help thinking about his alter ego held captive somewhere in Moscow. He was being probed, studied and dissected halfway around the world. Tom felt split in half, separated from his future. *Goodbye, my twin,* he thought.

Never to be seen again?

★   ★   ★

The steady roar of the Airbus A320 jetliner filled the passenger cabin like white noise. As the flight from Paris to Chicago entered its fourth hour, many of the occupants slept under thin blankets or stared into the glow of their laptops while wearing earbuds.

In seat 4e, a handsome blond man in his mid-thirties sat stiffly, staring forward, deep in concentration. He was preparing a new identity like a method actor, reminding himself, "You are Tom Nolan."

Tom Nolan's replica had been reassembled and equipped with the freshly digitized mind and memory of Alex Nikolaev. It sat among the nearly two hundred other travelers with seamless integration, indistinguishable from real flesh and blood. Russian intelligence provided Alex with a bogus identity, phony passport and security clearances. They set him up with a flight to America: first, a four-hour trip from Moscow to Paris, and now this second leg of the journey from Paris to O'Hare International Airport in Chicago.

Armed with intelligence related to the president of the United States' deteriorating health, Alex was on a critical mission for his country. He was going to infiltrate Simon Giamatti's inner circle in the guise of Tom Nolan and bring much-needed Russian influence to America's destiny.

On several occasions during the flight, Alex had gone into the tiny bathroom, stuck his face in the mirror and studied his new persona. He was still getting used to looking nothing like himself, living inside someone else's identity. "I am Tom Nolan," he said into the mirror, and it came out in Tom Nolan's voice. "I *am* Tom Nolan."

The shell was in pretty good shape, all things considered. There were some nicks and blemishes from Louis Karp's period of ownership. Karp had put a lot of mileage on it in a short period of time. It was like slipping behind the wheel of a used car, but the vehicle operated smoothly with overall good performance. Alex had no complaints.

He slipped the passport out of his sports jacket pocket and

looked at it one more time. The passport linked Tom Nolan's face with the fabricated name of William Jennings for smooth passage into the country, where the real Tom Nolan was still wanted by the law.

The complexity of it all made his head swim: *I am Alex Nikolaev disguised as Tom Nolan under the fake name of William Jennings.*

He looked out the window at fat, rolling clouds, high above the earth. America grew closer. He was anxious for the mission to begin.

★   ★   ★

After landing at O'Hare, Alex was impressed by how well his legs adjusted to a swift walk through the international terminal. Typically after such a long flight, his legs would be sore and stiff, but he felt no such pain whatsoever. He was built for maximum comfort.

As he worked his way through the long, wide corridors that wound through the airport, someone called out one of his names. He hesitated as to whether to stop and answer or keep going. When the voice became persistent and louder, he knew he had to respond.

"Tom Nolan!"

Alex stopped in the center of a pedestrian tunnel. He turned as a continuous swarm of people moved past him in either direction. From out of the crowd, a tall, smiley man in a wrinkled blue suit emerged, laptop hanging off his shoulder on a strap.

"Tom, oh my goodness, what are you doing here?"

When Alex just stared at him uneasily, the man said, "It's Dean Carruthers. We worked together at Slawin and Peabody, remember, fresh out of law school?"

Alex became Tom and smiled with a snap of recognition. "Oh yes, I remember. Dean at Slawin and Peabody. How are you?"

"No," said Dean. "The question is *how are you*? I heard about you getting sick...and then this trouble. Are you out on bail or what?"

Alex did not like this encounter and knew he had to choose

his response carefully. "It's all getting sorted out," he said. "It's not like it appears. Listen, I have to catch a ride...."

"I can help," Dean said. "Seriously. I'm an attorney with Trabaris and Kaplan downtown. We specialize in criminal cases. We can assist you. You've got Lowrey's disease, right? That's what I heard from the grapevine. Okay, well, that's your defense. You're sick, the stress, maybe there's brain issues related to Lowrey's that created poor judgment and altered your behavior. Maybe it was the meds, right? Let me represent you."

Dean's naturally loud, exuberant voice was raising Alex's anxiety level. People passing by were starting to stare at the two of them. Alex didn't want any attention drawn his way. This blabbermouth lawyer was going to mess up his plans before he even got started.

"I'm your friend, I want to help, and I won't take no for an answer," said Dean.

Alex didn't need a protracted argument standing in the middle of a crowded airport terminal. "Okay," he said. "Let's talk. But let's find some privacy."

Alex quickly looked around and spotted a nearby men's room. "In there," he said.

"Got it."

Alex and Dean entered the men's washroom. An Asian man was finishing up at a urinal. Alex and Dean stood off to one side, silent, until the Asian man left. Alex glanced beneath the stalls, then turned to Dean. "Okay, we're the only ones in here. I just didn't want to talk about it out there."

"Totally understand," Dean said. "So, what's your current situation? Out on bail? You're not here looking to skip out of the country, are you?"

"No, nothing like that. I'm not out on bail, either. To tell you the truth, I'm still a wanted man."

"No way. Number one, we can't have that."

"No," said Alex. He held up his forefinger. "Number one... we can't have *you*."

"What?" Dean said. It was the last word he would ever utter.

Alex jabbed his finger into Dean's throat. He plunged it

deep, a powerful insertion of several inches of steel. He pushed Dean backward, crashing him through an open stall door, and slammed him into a sitting position on the toilet.

Alex pulled out his finger and a rapid stream of blood escaped from Dean Carruthers' jugular vein. He was rapidly losing consciousness. Alex adjusted him to make sure he stayed balanced on the toilet and then quickly backed out of the stall and shut the door.

As Alex washed his hands in the sink, a couple of men entered the bathroom and shuffled over to the urinals, oblivious of the dying man at the far end of the room. Alex exited the bathroom with great calm, expecting a few minutes to pass before someone spotted a growing puddle of blood emerging from the stall, and then several more minutes before authorities arrived on the scene and attempted to figure out what they were dealing with.

That gave Alex all the time he needed to reach a set of doors leading outside to a loud, honking, exhaust-spewing line of cars picking up passengers. Identifying a license plate, Alex found his ride, two members of the Russian spy cell team in Chicago. He climbed into the back seat.

"All good?" asked Yefim, the driver. Alina sat in the front passenger seat.

"Everything is good," Alex said, shutting the door with a slam. The black sedan pulled away from the curbside chaos and entered a thick throng of traffic, departing from the terminal with growing speed.

CHAPTER TWENTY-ONE

The baby was crying again in a piercing outburst that filled every room of the small apartment. The twin toddlers were busy with loud, rambunctious mischief despite the desperate pleas of their too-gentle, too-soft-spoken mother to control themselves. Madeleine Morris could take it no more. She slapped her laptop shut, left the bedroom and confronted Steven, who was making a sandwich in the kitchen.

"I can't hear myself think!" she said.

Steven started to respond, but she was already moving toward the front door. She opened it and stepped into the outer corridor. He quickly followed.

She stood in the long, carpeted hall, arms folded, looking ready to cry. Steven joined her and shut their apartment door. They could still hear the noises inside: muted, yet persistent.

"The neighbors are going to start complaining again," said Madeleine.

"I can talk to the neighbors. They know the situation."

"There's not enough room. This can't drag on. Poor Christie. She tries to rein it all in, but it's too much."

Steven nodded in glum agreement. Things were better when Randy was home. Randy could help calm the children, but he was largely absent as he took on two jobs to pay off the mound of debt while fighting to stay afloat with the bare necessities.

The twins slept on the floor in sleeping bags by night and mostly climbed the walls by day. Steven and Madeleine took turns helping, working hard to be fully supportive, but everyone's nerves were beyond frayed.

"I ran some numbers last night," Madeleine said. "They're not going to be ready to get a place of their own for at least a few more months. Even something simple, something small.

They're doing everything possible. It's not their fault. The creditors are everywhere."

"I know...."

Then she declared, "I'm going to quit the food bank. It just doesn't pay hardly anything. I'm going back into PR work where I can earn some real money and help. They'll take me back at Bushnell and Lum."

"That hellhole?"

"What else are we going to do? Your project is on hold but you can't leave for another job. You keep telling me 'I'm under contract, I'm under contract.' Break the goddamned contract."

"That's not possible."

The baby's screaming cries continued inside the apartment, relentless and shrill.

"We are in a financial disaster, Steven," Madeleine said. "We are, and your sister, and her husband and those three kids in there. We were ripped off royally. I hate to say it, but we were stupid. All of us. Starting with Randy."

Steven nodded. He felt terrible for Randy. Randy came from a family of very modest means in rural Iowa and always seemed insecure about his upbringing at the lower end of the economic spectrum, especially compared to the comfortable financial status of Christie's family in Chicago. Christie loved him without any reservations, yet Randy remained troubled by his roots, telling her on repeated occasions that he felt he wasn't good enough for her.

Randy was also a dreamer – someone who didn't drink or do drugs but did indulge in lottery tickets and had a knee-jerk attraction to 'get rich quick' schemes.

He was convinced the real estate investment was going to deliver a huge payoff and put his kids through college because that's what the other partners told him. Before they disappeared with all his money.

"My whole life I've worried about money...and when I try to do something to fix it, I only make it worse," Randy told Steven. Steven told Madeleine about the comment.

"You know, yesterday he came to me crying for forgiveness,"

Madeleine told Steven as they stood in the hallway. "Literally. Tears were streaming down his face. I didn't know what to say. I can't get mad at him. I can't get mad at us. I can't get mad at their kids. I – I just need to find some peace somewhere."

Then, inside the apartment, as if on cue, the baby stopped crying.

Steven looked into Madeleine's eyes. She broke out into a smile. He smiled back.

"There," he said. "There's our peace. Ask and you shall receive."

She reached out and hugged him. She shut her eyes tight.

"We're going to be okay," he said. "All of us."

★   ★   ★

The call came later that evening.

"The Gemini team is reconvening," said Cooper.

"I'm ready," Steven said.

Cooper delivered a set of instructions. Steven responded in single-word responses. Madeleine sat nearby and he couldn't allow her to hear any details.

This was the big one.

He was going to help save the president.

"I'm taking the rental car tomorrow," Steven told Madeleine after the call ended.

"Your project is back on?" she asked. That's all she knew – it was a 'project'.

"It was never off," he responded. "Just a short break."

When she asked about it, he discussed it in vague and technical terms that quickly made her lose interest. He effectively made it sound so boring that she stopped probing.

The next morning, Steven drove to the Giamatti mansion. After the security gates opened to admit him, he parked with seven other cars in a large space behind a massive garage that looked more like a house. He reported to the front entrance of the main residence and Bella greeted him warmly.

She led him to the basement, where the other scientists

and doctors were gathered in a room filled with the familiar equipment and technology from the Lake Forest laboratory.

Cooper checked attendance and the meeting began precisely on time at nine a.m. when Giamatti entered the room.

He addressed his team, beaming with a smile inside his white beard.

"You are the chosen ones," he said to the eight attentive faces. "You have been selected from the larger Gemini team to take part in a very special phase of our project. We have talked to you about it individually and now we move forward as a group. You have knowledge the others do not. We are going to apply our medical breakthrough to save the life of the president."

He motioned to the immediate surroundings. "This is our 'pop-up' lab. We have converted this large space in my home into a private laboratory. I'm sure you recognize the equipment. It was transferred here from the Perking Institute. The president is coming to stay here, as he has in the past. So we are bringing the lab – and your expertise – to him."

Giamatti stepped over to a covered body on a gurney. All eyes followed him. He peeled back the sheet.

The lifelike shell of President Hartel rested on its back in perfect stillness, wearing only a thin hospital gown.

"Everything we've been testing…everything we've validated…it all culminates in this. You, the brilliance in this room, will transfer the president's consciousness into this shell. We will need to conduct the operation quickly, but as we've discussed with you individually, this should not be a problem. We know what works. We have a proven blueprint and now a turnkey process. It is no longer an experiment. It is a practical and substantiated procedure."

For the next five minutes, Cooper and Boyd stepped forward to discuss the itinerary and protocol. "Do not speak to the president unless spoken to," said Cooper.

Following them, Giamatti offered to answer questions. But first he addressed one outstanding issue he knew was on the minds of everyone in the room.

"We continue to pursue the stolen shell from our first

experiment," he said. "The real Tom Nolan remains safe in the guest wing of this house. Obviously his residency here is secret and must not be discussed outside these walls."

"Can we see him?" asked Steven. He had not seen his friend since the fateful day they were both assaulted at the Lake Forest lab.

"Our top priority is the immediate mission before us," Giamatti said. "There will be time to visit with Tom Nolan at a later date. For now, we must stay focused on the president."

"I have a question," said Carl Nodden, a stocky neurologist with curly hair. "This work is revolutionary. It's going to save so many lives. When can we go public? How long does it need to stay under wraps?"

Boyd started to speak, but Giamatti stopped him. "I can speak to that. Your contracts stipulate confidentiality until a date to be determined by the project owner, which is me."

Giamatti looked back at the president's duplicate. "We will reveal all after the president has concluded his second term. Once that has been accomplished, we will make a very big splash, I promise you." He faced the team again. "When we make our announcement, all of you in this room will become heroes of modern medicine and technology. You will go down in history. The Gemini Experiment will become the Life Sustainability Institute."

Some members of the team smiled, others looked exasperated at the length of time they would need to keep the secret.

Carl Nodden had another question. "Let's project this out five, ten, twenty, even fifty or a hundred years. Like any other advancement in technology, it will become easier and faster to replicate and apply. Costs will come down. Operation centers will flourish across the country and around the world. The demand will be monumental. People will stop dying. A marvelous feat, but what will it do to the earth? Have we done the math on the population explosion? Quite frankly, human life on earth is a system of turnover, like any other living thing, whether it be animals or plant life. What happens, Mr. Giamatti, when we become so focused on saving ourselves that we can't save the earth? There are finite resources on this planet. What do we do when no one dies and we run out of space?"

The room grew silent.

Giamatti hung his head for a moment, thinking. "I have thought about this," he finally said. "I really have. Because we can't ignore it and say it's a problem for future generations, because we will be that future generation. I have a belief that one day, many years from now, we will no longer require our physical medium. By that, I mean we will digitize our consciousness but not plant it in a physical object. Everyone, one day, could be uploaded to the cloud. The cloud will give us infinite space. Right now, we are seeing the very early stages of this. So much that is meaningful in our lives already exists in a virtual space. We rely on the cloud. One day, we might all become the cloud."

CHAPTER TWENTY-TWO

In the darkest corner of a murky tavern tucked beneath the rumble of the elevated train on Chicago's Northwest side, Alex found Sergei 'The Stick' Vladin. The legendary Russian spy, regarded in hushed circles with equal parts admiration and fear, sat alone with his six-foot-six frame hunched over a tall drink. He did not look up. He did not wave Alex over. Alex slid into the seat across from him and greeted his comrade in their native language.

The Stick shook his head, not pleased. His eyes remained on the table.

"English," he said.

"Yes," said Alex. "Of course."

"Do not let it happen again. We only speak the language of our host. As long as we are on their soil, we become one of them. Say you understand."

"Yes, I understand."

Alex looked around the bar. There was no one anywhere near to overhear them. Two grizzled, potbellied men in T-shirts swore at each other over a game of billiards. A dumpy man was flirting with a homely woman at the bar, both drunk and talking over one another with desperate, inane chatter. The remaining customers were clumped under a baseball game on a dangling TV monitor, shouting at every play.

The Stick slowly raised his eyes to stare at his visitor.

His frown held steady. He expressed a new round of displeasure.

"Take it off. Let me see you."

Alex wore a gray sweatshirt hood, his face concealed in shadows. He reached up and peeled it back.

He watched The Stick study him. He tried not to stare at The Stick's prominent scar, embedded in decades of wrinkles, extending from his lower eyelid to his jawline.

"Magnificent," said The Stick. A smile crossed his lips. Not a warm smile, but a smile nevertheless. "A mirror image. It is truly remarkable."

"I also have his voice."

"Yes. It is pitch perfect." The Stick straightened up, leaned back and said, "From bugs to satellites to hacking to human duplication. It is the evolution of espionage. I have always been at the cutting edge. I am proud of this work. Some may consider it a crime, but I see myself as a hero. I am a liberator. The liberator of information. There are no secrets."

"No, not anymore. Not anywhere."

"Tell me, how does it feel to be a machine?"

"It feels good. Very good. Smooth. Strong. Resilient."

"And you feel no pain?"

"None."

"Put out your hand."

Alex offered his hand, palm up.

"Turn it over," said The Stick. Alex did so.

The Stick reached into his pocket. He took out a lighter and flicked to life a tall flame. He held it under Alex's hand. He watched the flame flatten against the skin, creating a hot glow.

Alex did not flinch. He felt no pain. The skin remained unmarked.

The Stick smiled. He turned off the lighter. He shoved it back into his pocket and took a long drink from his glass.

"Go ahead and ask," said The Stick.

"Excuse me?"

"How I got this scar. You're curious. I see you looking at it. You're trying not to – which only makes you more obvious."

"I'm sorry."

"I'm used to it. It doesn't bother me. I'll tell you."

"Tell me?"

"How I got this scar. It was many years ago. A Bowie hunting knife with a seven-inch blade." The Stick reached into his back pocket. He brought out his wallet. He reached inside and slowly pulled out a thin, tattered photograph. He handed it to Alex.

The photograph was very old and faded, a blurry image in

black and white. Alex stared hard at it until he could determine the object in the center.

It was a severed head, drained and pale with eyes rolled upward, pupils only partly visible. The hair was matted in blood.

"That is the man who gave me this scar." The Stick took the photograph back. "I gave him much more trouble than he gave me. As you can see."

"Yes, you did," said Alex.

"I always come out on top. That's why I have been in this business for so long, while others have…retired."

The Stick inserted the photograph back into his wallet. It was obviously a source of pride and nostalgia, like an old family picture.

"Back then, you would surprise your enemies while they slept and cut them to bleed to death on the bedsheets. Today we have sophisticated poisons and nerve agents. We can orchestrate elaborate accidents or…just make people disappear." He snapped his fingers in front of Alex's face, a not-so-subtle reminder to cement his alliance.

"We will accomplish our mission," The Stick said. "And we'll be as ruthless as we have to be. You have been debriefed by Yefim and Alina?"

"Yes. They've brought me up to date."

"The four of us, we are a team," The Stick said. "We stick together like glue."

"Yes," said Alex.

"I have been building the plan, and you are at the center. We're going to meet the president of the United States. To access him, we must get to Simon Giamatti. To get to Giamatti, we must have access to Tom Nolan. To access Tom Nolan, we will use somebody very close to him. You are familiar?"

"Yes," said Alan.

"This photo is not in my wallet," The Stick said, pulling out his cell phone. "Times change. Technology changes." He called up a picture file he was looking for and placed the phone on the table, facing Alex.

Alex stared into a candid, color close-up of Emily Nolan.

"She will help us," The Stick said. "And I won't take no for an answer. I never do."

CHAPTER TWENTY-THREE

Emily poured milk on Sofi's cereal and was moments away from calling her into the kitchen for breakfast when a firm knock sounded at the front door. She put down the milk and glanced at the clock above the stove: 7:34. Too early for anything except trouble.

Apprehensive, she walked over to the front door. She peered through the narrow window pane alongside the doorframe. She glimpsed a grinning, handsome blond man in his thirties – her husband.

Or was it?

She did not open the door.

He caught sight of her and declared, "Em, it's me! I've been cleared to come home! I have good news."

Her hand impulsively reached for the door handle, then stopped.

"Oh, I'm sorry," said the familiar voice. "I almost forgot: *Philip*."

The password!

Overjoyed, Emily pulled open the door. Her husband entered, took her in a gentle embrace and kissed her. She shut her eyes.

All was perfect again in the world…

…until she opened her eyes and saw two more figures enter the house: a tall, thin man with sunken features and slicked-back gray hair, followed by a stocky, hard-faced woman with her hair pulled back in a tight, severe bun.

Then Emily saw the gun held to her head by her husband… who couldn't possibly be her husband.

She let out a wail of despair. He told her to shut up. She pulled away. *Why would Louis Karp return? Who were these people with him?*

"Why are you here?" she asked, nearly hysterical. "You've already stolen his identity, you took away his cure, what more do you want?"

The fake Tom Nolan simply stated, "It's complicated."

The tall, thin man, who looked like a movie vampire, spoke up. "Who else is in the house?"

The gun stayed on her.

"Just my daughter. She's in her room, playing. I was making her breakfast."

"The breakfast will wait," said the thin man. Emily detected some kind of accent he was attempting to conceal.

"We need you to make a phone call," the fake Tom said.

"To who?" She looked over at the mean-looking woman, who just stared back wordlessly.

"To your husband," said her husband's imitator.

"Why? Haven't you done enough to him? For God's sake, he's very sick."

"We're not going to hurt him," the fake Tom said. "We just want to talk with him."

"You're going to set up another meeting at the diner," said the thin man. "We need five minutes with your husband in private. He is under a lot of protection right now. We don't want any interference. Just a conversation. We require certain information that only he possesses. We'll give him back."

The fake Tom Nolan said, "You'll contact him at the Giamatti mansion. You have the number. You'll lure him out. You'll tell him you need to meet him again at the diner. Tell him your daughter was up all night crying because she wants to see her daddy. She's having bad dreams. You will get him out of that house to meet you later today, same time, same place as your encounter a few days ago."

"How did you know..." said Emily.

"We know a great deal," said the thin man. "Now let us share some more knowledge. If you do not cooperate, your daughter will die."

Emily felt a rush of tears. "Dear God...."

The fake Tom Nolan smiled sweetly – looking like the real

thing – but saturated with evil. "Nobody gets hurt if you just do what we say."

"I don't trust you," Emily said.

Fake Tom lifted the pistol higher as a reminder. "You have no choice."

"It's all going to be very simple," said the thin man. "Just stick to your script."

"Script?"

"In the diner, you'll have three important messages to deliver to your husband. They'll be easy to remember. Are you ready?"

She took a breath and nodded. "Yes."

The thin man recited her three message points. After the third, Emily was crying.

"Do we have an understanding?" the thin man asked.

She nodded, trying to regain her composure.

"Good. Now gather yourself. We're going to make a phone call."

They moved to the kitchen. As Emily dialed Cooper's number at the mansion, the intruders stood around her in a semicircle. The thin man dug his hand into the cereal box on the counter and ate handfuls of Cheerios, while the barrel-chested woman continued to stare with a cold, empty expression.

Cooper answered on the second ring.

"Cooper, it's Emily," she said, trying to control the waver in her voice. "Let me speak with Tom...."

After the call concluded, she turned to the three intruders and said, "There, I did it. Sofi and I will meet him at ten o'clock. Are you happy?"

"As a matter of fact, yes," the fake Tom said without smiling.

"I need to feed my daughter."

"We don't want the little girl to go hungry," said the thin man, without a trace of sincerity. He put down the box of cereal. "We'll get out of the way." He nodded toward the fake Tom. "You and I will go. There's no need to alarm young Sofi. Alina will stay and stand watch."

"Tell Sofi she's your long-lost aunt paying a visit," suggested Fake Tom. "Aunt Alice."

"Yes," the thin man said. "Just don't be stupid. She has a gun, and she's a remarkable marksman."

"Waukegan is forty minutes from here," said Fake Tom. "When it's time to go, we'll alert you. You will follow us. Stay close. We wouldn't want you to get lost...or take a detour."

★   ★   ★

In the back of the white van, Yefim activated the surveillance equipment, tapping into the electronic bug Sergei had discreetly placed on the stem of a light fixture in the Nolan family kitchen. Sergei and Alex returned from the house, climbed into the van and sat on either side of him. Together they listened to several minutes of chatter. Sofi was called into the kitchen by her mother. In a shaky voice, Emily introduced Alina as Aunt Alice, visiting from Ohio.

"Hi Auntie Alice," Sofi said after the introduction.

"Hello child," said Alina in a forced, barely friendly greeting.

Sergei nodded. The situation inside the house seemed secure.

He addressed his two colleagues. "I want to go through the plan one more time. It must run like clockwork. No room for error."

Sergei laid out an 11 x 17 diagram depicting the diner's interior, which he had scouted the day before. The hand-drawn sheet displayed the building's long, rectangular shape with booths lining the front and one side, exposed by large windows. A service counter with stools wrapped around an open space for the staff, with the kitchen located behind it. One side of the diner had a thin corridor leading to two washrooms, a storage room and a rear exit. 'Alley' was written behind the rear exit.

"That watchdog, Cooper, will be with him," said Sergei. "He will sit, as before, in a booth on the opposite side, reading the paper or playing on his phone. He must not detect a thing. Your transition must be seamless."

Alex nodded.

"We will arrive early," Sergei said. "The woman and her daughter will sit in this booth, same location as before. Alex will go to the back of the diner. He will wait inside the men's lavatory. Yefim, Alina and I will be in the van, positioned so that we can see into the diner without being seen. Cooper and Tom Nolan will arrive at ten a.m. and enter here."

Sergei tapped a finger against the diner entrance on the diagram. "They will split up. Tom will sit with his wife and child. The booth will be bugged. They will engage in a pleasant conversation. They will order their food. Then the wife will deliver her speech, telling Tom to go to the men's room for a very important, private conversation. It will be made clear he's being monitored for cooperation, and if he behaves in any way to draw attention, a sniper will shoot and kill his daughter."

"If his daughter is in jeopardy, he will do everything he's told," Alex said confidently.

"That is what we're counting on," said Sergei. "Tom Nolan will report to the lavatory as instructed. He will be unsure who he is meeting. He will discover you, and you will kill him. Promptly."

"With these hands, it shouldn't take long," Alex said, flexing his fingers, thinking back to the dead lawyer at O'Hare Airport.

"After he is killed, you will work with great speed," said Sergei. "You will stash the body inside a stall. You will dress in his clothing. You will emerge as him. You will return to the booth as Tom Nolan."

"The switch will be seamless," Alex vowed. "No one will know – not his family, not Cooper."

"You will tell Mrs. Nolan about your conversation," Sergei said. "You will tell her you answered some questions. You will ensure her everything is okay. You will conclude the meal quickly. Politely – but quickly."

Alex nodded.

Sergei said, "We will take the van into the alley. We will enter through the back of the diner and remove the body. We will place it in the vehicle. Alina will create a diversion at the front of the diner to ensure we're not interrupted."

"And I leave with Cooper," said Alex.

"Yes, you leave with Cooper. The rest of us will leave with

the body. We will make sure it disappears for good so there is only one Tom Nolan in existence. The wife and daughter, they will go home without any awareness a switch has been made."

Alex said, "It's brilliant."

"Yes, and it's only the beginning," Sergei said. He turned his attention from the diagram and looked at Alex. "You will be Tom Nolan. Your performance must be flawless. You will infiltrate Giamatti's inner circle. You will get inside that mansion, into the belly of the beast. We will be one step closer to the ultimate prize, the White House. You, Alex Nikolaev, are the key to the kingdom."

CHAPTER TWENTY-FOUR

Tom arrived at Crossroads Diner with a heavy heart, distraught to hear from Emily that Sofi was crying over his continued absence. His young daughter was an innocent victim in this whole mess, unaware of both his serious health condition and the complicated lunacy that sprung out of a possible cure. Sofi simply needed her father and didn't understand why he had been kept away from her. Once again, Tom had to fight with Giamatti to leave the mansion.

When Cooper pulled into the sparse gravel lot, Tom nearly climbed out of his seat before Cooper had finished parking the car. "Whoah," said Cooper. "I need to go in with you."

The two men entered the diner together. Cooper scouted the scene. In one booth, there was a chubby Hispanic mother with two restless, rotund boys. Not too far away, Emily and Sofi sat in their own booth. Sofi quickly caught sight of her father and waved. A small staff stirred slowly behind the service counter. The eatery was otherwise empty. A thin ambience of nineteen-fifties rock played unaggressively from speakers overhead.

"Keep it short," Cooper reminded him. "Giamatti wants us back by noon." President Hartel was due to arrive later that day.

Tom nodded. Cooper gestured to a far booth where he would be staying, an armed presence to quickly take charge if anything threatened the tranquility of the scene.

Tom slid into the red vinyl booth next to his daughter, who was coloring a hippo on a paper placemat with a small set of crayons.

"Pink," said Tom, impressed. "I love it."

"I'm going to make his ears green," Sofi said.

"Why not." Tom gave her a squeeze and she hugged back. "Missed you, pumpkin. But don't worry. Daddy's been okay.

Just…busy." He hesitated. 'Busy' wasn't exactly the right word. He had been sitting around in Giamatti's mansion with nothing to do, waiting for updates on the Russians, hearing very little, growing more frustrated – and weaker – by the day.

He looked at Emily, who remained silent. Something in her eyes and expression did not look right. He sensed fear.

"Is everything okay?" he asked.

Before she could respond, a waitress showed up, an older woman with a frumpy, lethargic demeanor, perhaps as old as the diner itself. She wore glasses that would be considered retro chic on anyone else, but simply looked outdated perched on her own nose. "Would you like to start with something to drink?" she asked.

"French fries!" said Sofi.

"An order of french fries," Tom said, smiling, and Sofi made a small cheer. "I'll have a Coke. Honey…?"

"Water," she said quietly.

The waitress repeated their order back to them, heads nodded, and she departed, retreating behind the counter. In a moment of silence, Tom could hear the Hispanic mother at the nearby booth speaking with annoyance to one of her boys. She exclaimed, "Quit squirming. If you have to go, go!"

Tom directed his attention to Emily. "Emily, what's wrong?"

She glanced over at Sofi, who was focused on her coloring. She leaned in toward Tom and spoke in a tight, forced monotone.

"You need to listen to me carefully. I have to tell you three things."

Tom looked at her, confused.

She continued. "Number one, the booth is bugged. They're listening to everything we say."

Tom felt his skin grow prickly. "What? Who?"

She fought to keep her voice steady. "I don't know. I can't say. I – I can only say what they told me to say."

Tom started to turn his head and she told him to stop.

"You can't see them. But they can see you. Don't look at Cooper. Just look at me. Number two, they need to talk with you. For five minutes, in secret, without Cooper knowing.

They want to ask you questions. I don't know what it's about. There's somebody in the men's room waiting to see you. You need to answer their questions, then come back and not say another word about it. Act casual and don't draw attention. They promised no one will get hurt if you do these things."

Tom stared into her eyes. They grew watery. Her voice trembled as she said, "The third thing...outside the diner, there's a sniper...aimed...." She glanced over at Sofi. Tom felt his chest tighten. Emily continued, "They can hear us, they can see us. If you get Cooper involved or refuse to follow their instructions, they'll...."

Emily covered her face and turned away. Tom felt an ache in his throat. His entire being trembled with outrage. Somebody had used his family to lure him out of the mansion. They had threatened to harm his family to get what they wanted.

Who are these sick bastards? He looked out the window. He could see a dingy white van parked in such a way that the rear of the vehicle faced the diner. He was being watched from behind tinted glass and dark curtains.

Damn you, whoever you are.

Sofi continued to happily color the animals on her children's placemat. If she heard the word 'sniper', she didn't understand it It made Tom sick to even imagine a gun pointed in her direction.

"I'll do whatever they want," said Tom clearly, for the benefit of the bugging device tapping their conversation. "I'll talk. I'll tell them anything they want to know."

The waitress returned with Tom's Coke and a water for Emily.

Tom stared at the Coke. After the waitress left, he said plainly, for all who were listening, "Excuse me. I need to use the bathroom."

Emily shut her eyes and pressed her lips together. She tried to control herself from tearing up in front of Sofi.

"I'll be right back," Tom said. "I'll be fine."

Tom stood up. He resisted the urge to look back at his family, or out the window at the white van, or at Cooper. He faced the far end of the diner and began a slow, casual stroll.

He could feel his heart beating in his chest, uncertain of who he would find or what they would demand. He reached a turn that led down a skinny, poorly lit corridor. As he advanced, he knew he was slipping out of view.

He hoped Emily could keep her composure in front of Sofi. He wanted this ordeal over with. He wanted them extracted from this horror.

Tom found the entrance to the men's room and stopped, feeling a sudden chill. He stared at the door, wishing he could look through it. He heard noises inside.

Abruptly the door opened.

Tom pulled back into the shadows.

A young, chubby Hispanic boy emerged. The door closed behind him. Tom stepped out of the darkness and startled the boy with a hard whisper to get his attention: "*Hey.*"

The boy stopped in his tracks and turned. After taking in Tom's presence, his mouth fell open in a surprised gape. It was a strange, bug-eyed reaction.

"Can you answer a question for me?" Tom whispered.

The boy said nothing, staring at him.

"Is there somebody in there?"

The boy nodded.

"Who is it?"

The boy, still staring, said, "*You are.*"

Tom felt icicles in his veins. He stepped backward, stunned.

The little boy scampered off.

Tom's mind raced. This could only mean one thing. His replica was waiting to surprise him. The replica was here, now, of all places. But why? Giamatti had told him the Russians were in possession of it. What would the Russians need with the real Tom Nolan? Why would they want Tom to meet up with his identical twin in private, in secret, without anyone knowing? It was bizarre yet—

Tom's moment of realization sent a shudder down his spine. *They want to make an exchange.*

Tom feared there was no conversation waiting to be had. Just a simple, quick swap that would eliminate and replace him.

What better way to get inside Giamatti's inner circle — and closer to its secrets — than to consume Tom's identity and waltz back to the mansion with the perfect cover?

Tom continued to stare at the door in horrified silence.

Now what?

If he rushed back and explained the plot to Emily or Cooper, then Sofi might be killed. The diner would erupt in carnage. He was trapped. Nothing would ensure their safety except for a successful exchange of Tom Nolans.

Tom struggled to determine his next action. Then he realized: *If I return now to the booth, how will they know if the switch has been made...or not?*

He remained standing undisturbed in the back of the diner for another minute, the longest minute of his life, heart pounding like a punching fist.

Then he walked back down the corridor that led into the front of the restaurant. Fully aware that multiple sets of eyes were watching him — and the booth was bugged — Tom Nolan returned to his wife and daughter, concentrated on his words, and imagined how the conversation might go if he was impersonating his impersonator.

"I'm back," he announced. "I had the conversation. It was fine."

"Oh thank God," said Emily with a large sigh of relief.

Sofi was eating her french fries, lifting them up at one end, dangling them into her mouth like a bird.

Tom sat next to Sofi, playing it light but not too light. "They just wanted some information. I gave it to them. They let me go. It was exactly how they described it to you."

"What did they want to talk about?" Emily asked.

"It's better we don't get into it. Basically it's no big deal." Tom felt the perspiration under his arms. He thought about his every word traveling to careful listeners in the white van. He worried about his replica hanging out in the bathroom, waiting for his arrival. At some point the replica would grow impatient and emerge or send someone a text.

"Sofi seems happy," Tom said. "Look, I hate to do this, but

I really should get back to Giamatti. They don't like for me to be out in public too long."

"But you haven't been here very long...."

"I know, just a precaution," said Tom in a pleasant, reassuring voice. He casually reached over and took one of Sofi's crayons. He wrote on a corner of her placemat, a message for Emily:

LEAVE NOW.

Emily looked at him with a sudden look of terror. Tom nodded discreetly. Still holding the crayon, he quickly scribbled over his words to conceal the message. Then he said, "I'll go take care of the check. Good to see you. We'll do this again someday soon. Bye, Sofi."

"Bye, Daddy."

Tom stood up and turned his back on them. He saw Cooper in the nearby booth reading the sports section of the newspaper. Tom walked over to the cash register, where the frumpy waitress met up with him after a few seconds.

"Could I have the check?" Tom asked.

"Certainly." She rang up his order. "That will be...twelve dollars and fifteen cents."

Tom lowered his voice. He manufactured a tone of menace. "Listen to me. I'm not paying. I have a gun. Give me all the money in your register."

She stared at him. "You're serious?"

"Yes. Give me all your money and don't draw attention. Do it. I'm crazy and I have a gun."

He indicated under his shirt somewhere.

Standing nearby, an African-American cook cocked his head, hearing the exchange. He slowly backed into the kitchen. Tom saw him reach for his cell phone before he slipped out of view.

Good.

The waitress handed Tom a wad of bills and he casually stuffed them into his pocket, as if accepting change. "Thank you," he said. He added with a snarl, "You better sleep with one eye open."

She gave him a strange look.

Tom knew his acting wasn't good, but it was good enough. He turned away from the counter. He saw Emily encouraging Sofi to finish her final few fries so they could leave. He walked over to Cooper and interrupted his study of baseball box scores.

"Ready to go now," Tom said. Sweat was running a river down his spine. He kept casual.

"Sure," said Cooper. He slowly folded his newspaper. "That was quick."

"Sofi just needed to see that I'm all right." Tom did his best to hold back his exasperation at Cooper's slow movements. *Hurry up!*

"Well, it's good not to linger," said Cooper. "After all, you're still a wanted man."

"You can say that again…" Tom said.

Tom and Cooper departed from the diner. As they walked to Cooper's car, Tom turned and faced the white van, well aware that its occupants were watching him and assuming he was one of them.

Tom gave them a subtle thumbs up and a wink. *All is going according to plan, comrades!*

Tom and Cooper climbed into Cooper's car. Cooper started the engine. "Hold on for a second," said Tom.

He watched Emily and Sofi emerge from the diner. They got into the silver SUV. Sofi clutched her paper placemat with the colored animals.

Almost immediately, a stocky, beady-eyed woman in her fifties stepped out of the white van. Tom did not recognize her. She headed for the diner entrance. The van's engine abruptly coughed to life. The vehicle quickly moved across the lot, circling the diner and disappearing behind it.

"Is everything okay?" Cooper asked, watching Tom study the scene around him.

Tom held his response. Emily drove off with Sofi. They got on the main road. Seeing them disappear, Tom let out a sigh of relief. He told Cooper, "Let's get out of here as fast as possible. Quick!"

Cooper threw the gear shift into drive, spitting up gravel.

"What's wrong?" he asked. "What's happening?"

Tom responded, "I have a Russian twin."

CHAPTER TWENTY-FIVE

Inside the white van, three shadowy figures huddled together listening to the audio coming from Emily Nolan's booth while watching the movements of a small cast in the diner's windows. Wearing headphones, they crouched in silence, hidden from view by tinted glass, exchanging nods of satisfaction as the overheard dialogue followed its expected path.

'Tom Nolan' returned from the men's room delivering a calm voice of reassurance, telling his wife he had engaged in a brief conversation and provided the information requested of him. Given the general tension of the circumstances, he recommended they conclude their visit and go their separate ways for now, promising another get together soon.

He left the booth to pay the check and then joined up with Cooper. As he walked the gravel lot with Cooper toward Cooper's car, he made a slight head turn toward the van, acknowledging its occupants with a subtle wink and 'thumbs up' gesture.

Yefim chuckled. Alina stated, "We did it. He's in." The Stick said nothing, continuing to watch through narrow eyes.

Tom Nolan's wife and daughter left next. The wife was clearly upset, trying to control her emotions. She looked toward the white van and simply frowned. The little girl appeared unfazed, oblivious. They climbed into the silver SUV together. The Stick issued a command.

"GO."

The rear doors of the van split open and Alina emerged. The doors slammed shut behind her and she headed for the diner's entrance, feet crunching on the gravel.

Yefim scrambled from the back of the van to the front, sliding behind the steering wheel. He powered the engine and quickly reversed out of the parking space. The van shot forward, advancing along a narrow path that circled the diner and ended in a weedy, junk-filled alley behind it. The van came to an abrupt stop. Yefim and The Stick quickly climbed out.

The Stick carried a black folded-up canvas bag under one arm. Yefim yanked open the building's rear service door. The two men entered the back of the diner.

At the front of the diner, Alina quickly created a scene to capture everyone's attention. She found the diner's workers already clumped together, buzzing about something at the service counter. The only customers in the restaurant consisted of the same Hispanic woman and her two boys, digging into their meal.

"I was here earlier, I think I left my phone," Alina said in her best American accent. "It's in one of these booths, I'm sure." She raised her voice in urgency. "Please help me find it."

The workers responded slowly, sluggishly, as if coming out of a collective trance. If Alina's mission was to create a distraction, they already appeared distracted.

"Do you remember where you were sitting?" asked the pudgy waitress with the horn-rimmed glasses. "We haven't seen a phone."

"It was one of these booths." Alina searched a random booth while keeping an eye on the corridor that led to the bathrooms. If Yefim and The Stick encountered any surprise interruptions, the body count would immediately rise.

So far, the path was clear. Yefim and The Stick quickly moved through the cluttered storage room. They reached the corridor that led to the bathrooms.

The Stick confronted the door that read MEN with a simple, universal icon for a male figure.

"We go in, we secure the door," The Stick said under his breath. "We bag the body. We move fast."

Yefim nodded.

"Ready?" said The Stick.

Yefim nodded again.

They pushed forward, slamming the door open with a *bam*.

Inside the men's room, Tom Nolan stood at the sink, facing them. He wore a look of shock.

"You're alive?" Yefim said, abruptly stopping in his tracks.

"That idiot didn't finish the job," said The Stick. He began to reach for his gun.

Tom Nolan spoke up immediately in alarm. "*No, no, no! I'm Alex.*"

"Alex?" said Yefim.

"Alex?" The Stick said.

"Where's Nolan?" Alex asked.

"He was in here!" Yefim said.

"No he wasn't," said Alex.

The Stick exchanged a glance with Yefim. His eyes blazed with fury. "Something went wrong. There was no switch."

Alex erupted into panic. "He's getting away?" He quickly moved past them. He rushed out of the bathroom and nearly knocked over Alina, who had arrived on the scene.

Alex dashed to the front of the diner. As he reached the long elbow of red booths, a bell jingled. Two police officers burst through the front entrance.

Behind the counter, the black cook immediately pointed to Alex and shouted, "*There he is!*"

Stunned, Alex froze in his tracks. He looked at the cook, then at the gathering of diner employees staring at him, and then at the two police officers rushing him.

"What the fuck," he said in a small voice.

"Don't move," commanded a police officer, gun drawn. "You aren't going anywhere."

★　★　★

As soon as Cooper's car transitioned from the gravel parking lot to the smooth pavement of the main road, Tom unloaded. He revealed the attempted switch and his narrow escape.

Stunned, Cooper took it all in. "I had no idea. I failed you."

"They're very clever," said Tom. "So we have to beat them at their own game."

"That added touch of robbing the diner – sheer genius," Cooper said.

Police sirens soared in the distance. Tom rolled down his window to revel in the sweet sounds of justice.

"They're headed to the diner to arrest me – him – us. Once they ID him, they'll pin him with everything Louis did, everything I did...."

"We've got to alert Giamatti."

"We need to protect my family," Tom said. "I have a bad feeling that it's not over."

★   ★   ★

Inside Crossroads Diner, Alex took on two officers of the Waukegan Police Department. His attack was met with a brief spit of gunfire that did nothing to stop him.

Alex took full advantage of his new strength and resilience, absorbing bullets and delivering blows, quickly shedding any concerns about the arrival of the law. The beatings became fun, a sport he could easily win.

He smashed officer number one's head on a booth table, messing up the clean surface with a sloppy spill of red that could have been ketchup, but wasn't.

Officer number two weighed maybe two hundred pounds – an easy lift from the ground and toss through a window. The loud shatter sent the rest of the diner occupants scattering. Workers fled into the kitchen and the Spanish family made a run for the door, leaving behind half-eaten food and spilled drinks.

The police officer who had been briefly gifted with the miracle of flight stirred back to consciousness outdoors. Alex met with the officer before he could return to his feet, pulled him up and threw him again – through another fresh window – this time back inside the diner. The glass cuts from two smashed windows messed up his face bad enough that he stayed still.

Alex felt good, pumped, like a superhero.

The white van roared to the front of the diner to pick him up, kicking up a cloud of dust. Yefim gripped the steering wheel.

The Stick sat straight in the passenger seat, stone faced. The rear doors opened and Alina waved Alex in.

"Come on," she said. "We have to go."

Alex reluctantly left his police-tossing. He jumped into the back of the van.

Yefim accelerated before Alex could even finish closing the doors.

"Everybody hold on!" shouted The Stick. "We're going to catch up with our friend."

He gripped his gun tightly. The chamber was loaded.

"Faster," he told Yefim, and Yefim pressed harder on the gas pedal until the sights outside the window became a constant blur.

CHAPTER TWENTY-SIX

"Uh, oh."

Cooper's eyes caught something in the rearview mirror.

"That's them, isn't it?" he asked.

Tom turned around and could see the white van in the distance, rapidly gaining ground.

"Shit," said Tom. "We barely slowed them down."

Cooper had been maintaining a safe speed, not wanting to draw any undue attention, given his fugitive passenger. He quickly pushed past the speed limit.

"Do you know how to use a gun?" he asked.

"No," said Tom, feeling a new spike of fear.

"Just point and shoot."

"Great, like a camera."

"Reach under your seat."

Tom reached down and felt something hard and cold – the butt of a pistol. He gently extracted the gun and brought it into his lap.

"They're going to be on us in about thirty seconds," Cooper said. "I'm going to give you instructions for releasing the safety. Are you ready?"

Tom held the gun awkwardly, examining it. 'Walther P22' was engraved in the barrel.

"Do you see a small lever?" asked Cooper. "It's set to S, for 'Safety'."

"I see it."

"Move the lever to F."

"F?"

"For 'Fire'."

Tom rotated his handling of the gun so it was pointed outside the car, not in. He snapped the pin into the firing position. The *click* made his heart jump.

The white van was nearly upon them, engine booming.

"Damn," Cooper said.

Tom tried to get a firm grip on the gun but his muscles stiffened up. His motor coordination felt sloppy. He knew his aim would be lousy.

But all he needed was one lucky shot....

With a roar, the white van pulled up on the right, alongside Cooper's car. Tom lifted the gun to fire and tried to keep his arm steady. The van swerved hard into them, crunching the passenger door of Cooper's car and bouncing Tom in his seat. The Russians fired two shots, hitting metal, and then sideswiped the car again, this time harder with a powerful slam, sending it off the road.

Cooper lost control of the car from the impact. The vehicle bounced into a ditch, heaving up and down on uneven terrain before crashing with a sudden bang against a telephone pole. The front hood folded like an accordion and the windshield fragmented into a massive web of cracks. The airbags triggered, overtaking the front seat. The instant inflation punched Tom in the face. He lost his grip on the gun and couldn't regain it.

There was a long moment of silence.

Then Cooper spoke, muffled. "Are you okay?"

"I think so," said Tom. Then, cautiously, he asked, "Do you think they're gone?"

The answer immediately arrived via a series of gunshots pelting the side of the car.

"No," Cooper said.

The next bullet smacked Tom's headrest. As the withered airbag fell away, he had a clear view again. Unfortunately, so did the Russians.

In that moment, Tom was certain he was going to die, an easy target.

He turned to helplessly face his attackers and his fate.

He could see the white van above on the side of the road, perched at the edge of the ditch, looming like a proud conqueror, a faceless beast. He expected to see armed Russians rushing in for the kill.

Tom whispered goodbye to Emily and Sofi. He awaited a rain of gunfire.

Instead, he heard the van abruptly pull away from the side of the road. It sped out of sight with a roar of acceleration.

Tom waited a long moment and then turned to Cooper. "They left."

"I know."

"Why?"

"Listen."

Tom listened. He heard police sirens approaching.

"Oh."

"We've got to get out of here. Can you get out?"

"I think so."

Struggling from an awkward angle, Tom unhooked his seatbelt. He managed to push open the badly dented door. As he shifted, he glimpsed the gun on the car floor by his feet. He picked it up and brought it with him outside the car, onto the grass.

Cooper pulled himself out through his window. He was badly scraped and bruised, but still whole.

Tom circled over to the other side of the car to help Cooper to his feet. The sirens grew louder, coming for them.

"Remember when I said that robbing the diner was sheer genius?" Cooper asked. "Well, I've changed my mind."

"Sorry." Tom still held Cooper's gun. "I don't suppose we could shoot our way out."

"No," said Cooper. "But I do have an idea. It won't help your criminal record, but it could get us the hell out of here."

"I'm all ears."

Very quickly, several police vehicles pulled up to the roadside above them, lights flashing. A succession of officers climbed out, gathering in a group and staring down, weapons drawn. Tom and Cooper were facing guns again – this time from their own country.

One of the police officers shouted, "Tom Nolan, we see you. Come up with your hands up."

Tom shouted back. "This is Tom Nolan. Listen to me. *I'll*

set the rules. I'll come up. But no one is going to move. *I have a hostage.*"

Tom stuck Cooper's gun into Cooper's ribs. He hoped the charade would work. He figured, *If I'm a bad guy, I might as well play the role of a bad guy.*

Cooper went along with it. "He's serious! Please! Put down your weapons."

Tom advanced up the short hill with Cooper, keeping the gun aimed at him with the safety secured to ensure there were no accidents.

The police cooperated, lowering their guns, watching him closely.

"He hijacked my car," Cooper said. "He's totally crazy."

Reaching the side of the road, Tom eyed one of the police vehicles. Doing his best to sound like an unstable madman, he declared, "I'm taking one of your cars. If you try to stop me, I *will* shoot the hostage."

"Please listen to him," Cooper said, looking fearful.

"How far do you think you'll get in a stolen police car?" said one of the officers, scowling.

"Far enough," Tom said. "I better not see any of you following me. You know what I'm capable of."

Tom hoped the words didn't sound as absurd to their ears as they felt coming out of his mouth. Fortunately, the police erred on the side of giving him credibility.

Moments later, Tom sped off in a Waukegan police car with Cooper at his side.

"Holy shit, it worked," Tom said. "I felt like I was back in high school, acting in the spring play."

"It was a good performance," said Cooper. "You won't win any Oscars, but worthy of dinner theater. Now we have to ditch this car. Pronto."

"Where?"

"Someplace busy with a lot of cars and a lot of people."

Within a mile, the answer appeared in front of them under bright beams of sunlight: the sprawling, hectic Lake County Mall. Tom drove the police car into a triple-decker parking garage, climbed two levels and sandwiched the vehicle between a couple of large suburban minivans. Tom handed Cooper his gun, glad to relinquish it. They abandoned the car, leaving the key on the front seat, and took an elevator down to the shopping complex.

Entering the mall, Cooper moved swiftly and Tom fought to keep up, legs rubbery.

"Now where?" Tom asked.

"We'll walk through the mall, go out the other side and grab an Uber."

Tom noticed a mall security guard on a walkie-talkie and wondered if he was receiving news of a fugitive loose in the mall. "I don't think we can stay here very long," Tom said.

Tom and Cooper reached a crowd of moviegoers departing from the mall's cinema. The movie theater had just finished the latest showing of a science-fiction blockbuster. Tom and Cooper buried themselves in the mob and followed it outside to the parking lot, where Cooper promptly called for an Uber to pick them up.

"Where are we going?" asked Tom.

"Back to the mansion, of course."

"No, we have to go see Emily and Sofi. They could still be in danger. I'm not going to the mansion. Not yet."

Cooper agreed. He understood Tom's anxiety. "We should probably relocate them. We can't have them used as bait again to get to you. It's not safe."

A young man with a ponytail and fuzzy chin hairs pulled up in a Ford Fusion. "Our car has arrived," said Cooper, checking the license plate. Tom kept his head down as he entered the vehicle.

★   ★   ★

Tom knocked on the door of his home. After a few moments, he heard Emily's voice on the other side, loud and clear:

"*No.*"

"What?" Tom said.

"Go away."

"Go away?"

"How do I know it's really you?"

"Of course it's me."

"I've been fooled twice now," she said, muffled through the door. "It's not going to happen again."

"But it's me, I promise you." Then he added: "Philip!"

"No. I already fell for that."

"The password?"

"The door is locked and if you don't go away, I'm calling the police."

"Please don't do that."

"Then leave me alone."

Cooper, standing nearby, stepped closer to the door. "I can vouch for him!" he said, impatiently.

"How do I know you don't have a gun pointed at you?" asked Emily.

"Nobody's pointing a gun at me," Cooper said.

"At least right now," mumbled Tom.

"Open the door!" Cooper shouted. "We have to get you out of here."

"How about this," Tom said. "Your birthday is August 15 Sofi's birthday is October 2."

"No."

"Our dog's name is Caesar."

"Leave him out of it."

"Do you want to know my Social Security number?"

"Stop it."

Tom turned to Cooper and shrugged. Cooper gestured for him to keep trying. "She's still in shock," he said.

Tom nodded. Earlier in the day Emily had been ambushed and the consequence was a sniper's rifle pointed at their daughter's head. But he couldn't allow them to stay here alone any longer. The Russians might return. Or the police. Or the media. None of them was a good option.

"Honey?" he said to the door.

"I'm not falling for it," she repeated.

"Our wedding anniversary is June 11."

"Yes, it is."

Tom searched his mind for another date of personal significance. He ached to get inside. He longed to embrace her. The longing brought back a memory.

Tom moved closer to the door. "February 25," he said. Then he asked, "Do you know what that is?"

She didn't respond.

"February 25, 2008. The Main Library at the University of Illinois."

After a pause, she said, "Go on."

"In the History and Philosophy wing. In American Studies, somewhere around the eighteen hundreds, you were looking for a book on the Louisiana Purchase."

He stopped and listened for a response.

"Keep going," she said.

"We were looking for that book together, for a paper you were writing, and we were in a playful mood. I took my chances." Tom waited and then said, "Do you remember? That was our first kiss."

He paused and heard nothing, so he continued.

"I remember it like it was yesterday. There was a light snow falling outside. You had just broken up with Larry Doyle, so I felt pretty bold about making a move. You wore a pink sweater and jeans. You had those bangs and your hair had that cute curl that rested on your shoulders. We kissed...and you giggled at me."

The door opened.

Tom stepped through and Emily hugged him. She held him tight. He kissed her.

"I'm so sorry..." he said.

Sofi ran at him. "Daddy!" She hugged his legs. Their dog Caesar put the final stamp of approval on Tom, greeting him with a wagging tail and smart nose, not capable of being fooled by a replica.

"You can't stay here," said Tom, still holding Emily. "We're going to move you and Sofi someplace safe."

She backed up and looked at him. Her eyes were red and puffy from crying. "Move?"

"Just for a while. Cooper will set it up. He's using Giamatti's business account. We'll put you up in a nice hotel – pet friendly. You'll be under an assumed name. You'll be left alone, no more involvement with this crazy stuff until everything is sorted out."

"But what about you?" she asked.

"I'm staying at the mansion." He saw the fear return to her eyes. "We're going to get my replica back. It's just a matter of time. Giamatti has incredible resources, he's connected…all the way up to the president."

Cooper stood in the doorway, peering into the house. "Let's go. We don't have much time."

"Pack," Tom told Emily. "Pack up some things for you and Sofi, just enough for a week or two. If you need anything else once you get there, we'll have it delivered."

"Are you sure we'll be safe?"

"Where are we going?" asked Sofi, her voice coming from below.

Tom looked down and smiled. "You and Mom are going on a little vacation."

Sofi asked, "Will there be a pool?"

"Yes, I'm pretty sure there will be a pool."

Emily bent down and said to Sofi, "We're going to have to pack right now. Go get a few of your favorite toys. Can you do that?"

"Yes, Mommy," she said in an excited voice.

After Sofi left for her bedroom, Emily looked her husband in the eyes and said, "What the hell happened? What took place in that diner?"

"We'll catch up in the car. They…didn't get the information they wanted. That's why we had to leave so fast. They're still after me."

"God, no."

"It'll be fine," he said, not wanting to upset her any further.

Her eyes traveled the length of his tired, slumped body. "And…how are you feeling…physically?"

He knew what she meant. Lowrey's disease. The ticking time-bomb inside of him.

"I can still get around," he said. "That's good enough for now."

She hugged him one more time and then left to pack for the hotel.

★   ★   ★

To ensure their privacy, Cooper ordered a company car and driver from Giamatti's business account. A long, black limousine pulled into the driveway and they loaded the trunk with luggage. Tom, Cooper, Emily, Sofi and Caesar bundled into the back of the limo, and Cooper gave the driver instructions. The chosen hotel was part of a large chain that received frequent business from Giamatti's company. It was located forty-five miles away in the town of Schaumburg, a good distance from all the chaos they had endured up and down Chicago's North Shore.

To play it safe, Cooper checked them in while Tom stayed tucked away in the limousine, out of sight. Before leaving the car, Emily gave her husband one more kiss and embrace.

"Be safe," she told him.

"I will," he promised. Then he told her, lightly, "I'm going to get a tattoo of your name on my butt, so you can tell me apart from that other guy."

"My name on your butt?" She broke into a smile, the first one he had seen cross her lips in a long time. "Romantic."

Tom hugged Sofi next, gave Caesar a quick head scratch, and his family left to enter the hotel with Cooper.

When Cooper came back alone, Tom felt a sick feeling in his stomach.

Cooper sat across from him. He could sense Tom's sorrow. "They'll be fine," he said. "We'll have private security staying at the hotel, keeping an eye on them. Nobody's going to bother them again. I promise."

Tom just nodded.

"Take us to the mansion, please," Cooper instructed the driver.

Tom sank back in his seat of soft black leather, exhausted.

CHAPTER TWENTY-SEVEN

The sleek, thirty-foot black limo pulled up to the iron gates of the Giamatti mansion. Hank, the driver, lowered his window and faced the security camera perched on a post like an observant owl.

"Hello?" Hank said.

Cooper lowered his window as well and waved at the camera. "Hey there, it's us."

A half minute passed, then a full minute.

The driver sounded the horn, a quick jab.

"What's going on?" asked Tom.

"I don't know," Cooper said. "There's a sensor, someone should be there to let us in."

"Should I call?" Hank asked.

"I've been texting Giamatti," said Cooper, "but no response."

"Do you think there's a problem?" Tom asked. He began feeling uneasy as they sat idle at the end of the driveway.

Hank sounded the horn again, this time more aggressively.

After a moment, the gates disengaged, splitting apart with the usual creaks and groans.

"We're good," Cooper said, leaning back in his seat. He let out a sigh. "For a moment, I was worried, with those Russians running around."

Mrs. Giamatti met them at the front door, rosy cheeked with her hair down. "Come in, come in," she said cheerfully, as they exited the limousine. "How was lunch?"

"It was...interesting," Cooper said. "We need to speak with your husband."

"Certainly. I think he's taking a nap. Is everything okay?"

"Not exactly," said Cooper.

The limousine departed, and Tom and Cooper waited in the mansion's large foyer. Mr. Giamatti emerged from another room to greet them. He wore his ever-present robe and slippers. "Sorry, I was dozing," he said. "Resting up before the president gets here. I was expecting you back sooner. That was a long lunch."

"It was more than lunch," said Cooper. "Can we go into the den to talk?"

"Yes, yes, of course," Giamatti said, his interest piqued. "Did something happen?"

"Something happened," Tom said.

Seated in the den, Tom and Cooper immediately relayed the events of the past several hours. Giamatti listened, wide eyed, saying nothing until they were done and looking to him for a response.

"Clever bastards," he said in a tone that was both impressed and defiant. "They want so badly to get on the inside. Well, they can't penetrate these walls. Tom, we'll keep you safe. This mansion is a fortress and security will only get tighter when the president gets here. He'll bring his Secret Service team. There's nothing to worry about. We're moving ahead. The lab is ready. The staff is ready. Tonight we will perform a miracle. Tomorrow the president will live in a new, healthy body and his illness will be a thing of the past."

Tom wanted to bring up the subject of his own medical rescue, but knew Giamatti was first and foremost preoccupied with saving the president. The conversation would have to wait.

Tom was fine about that. He didn't have the stamina for an involved conversation right now anyway. After the day's grueling events, he was weak and hurting. Cooper picked up on it.

"Tom, why don't you get some rest?" he said. "You've been through hell."

Tom nodded. He rose from his chair, legs stiff. "I'm going to get something to eat from the kitchen and retire to my room."

Giamatti said, "May I ask a favor? It's best that you remain in your room once the president arrives. The Secret Service will want to keep him isolated. Maybe tomorrow there will be an opportunity for you to meet him. Tonight is going to be very delicate and guarded. I hope you understand. Tensions are running high."

"I'll be out of sight, out of mind," said Tom as he left the den.

In the kitchen, he made himself a sandwich and collected a bag of chips and can of 7Up. He brought them back to the guest room that still felt like a prison cell, no matter how comfortable.

He ate alone at a small table and then decided to wash up in the adjoining bathroom. He took a long, hot shower punctuated with a scare when he suddenly, randomly lost his balance and nearly fell. His disease continued to chip away at his muscle coordination. He swore at it. He swore at the Russians. He swore at the delay in saving his own life. He swore at the terror he had put his family through. They didn't deserve any of it.

After showering, he dressed in clean pajamas, prepared to retire early. He sat at the little table and wrote in his notebook, continuing an ongoing letter to Sofi, a collection of sentiments and advice for his daughter in case things did not get better and she became fatherless at a young age. Several times he had to put down the pen, in tears, pulling away to avoid smearing the ink with his sorrow.

When he heard a sudden commotion of cars outside, Tom stepped over to the window for a good view of the area in front of the mansion. The president and his small circle of insiders had arrived. Tom recognized Jarret Spero, the president's chief of staff. President Hartel slowly stepped out of the back seat of his private car, a dark sedan. He was quickly surrounded by a half-dozen members of his team, including watchful men in dark suit jackets and sunglasses who had to be Secret Service. One of them started to look up toward Tom's window, and Tom pulled away.

I'm not going to mess with the president's security, he told himself. He had already experienced enough excitement for one day.

Tom heard the commotion continue into the house: muffled voices, greetings, welcomes, enthusiasm.

Tom had no more enthusiasm. He was just dead tired. He chose to go to bed early, amusing himself with the thought that in the morning the president's digitized brain would live inside a technologically perfect replica, and Tom was one of the few people on the planet who knew it.

★ ★ ★

Emily sat on the bed of her hotel room, half watching the television, half skimming the room-service menu, while Sofi lay stretched out on the floor absorbed in one of her jumbo puzzle books, connecting dots.

A sitcom rerun ended, failing to provide amusement, and the nightly news promptly began. The broadcast jumped into the latest Chicago headlines, starting with a preview of President Hartel's campaign appearance at Navy Pier scheduled for the next day. Several local campaign staffers expressed their excitement over the president's pending arrival and a camera panned the red, white and blue decorations in progress to transform the large ballroom into a political rally. Emily watched the coverage with unease, feeling apprehensive about the secret knowledge she possessed that the media did not.

But the anxiety created by the president's arrival was nothing compared to the sledgehammer story that followed.

Her husband was back in the news.

"Missing Wilmette resident Tom Nolan has embarked on another crime spree, robbing a Waukegan diner, taking a hostage and stealing a police vehicle...."

Emily's jaw dropped. There was a short interview clip with their pudgy waitress from the diner. "He attacked the two police officers. It all happened so quick, we were afraid for our lives."

The news story concluded with fuzzy security camera footage of Tom inside the Lake County Mall, followed by a sudden, jarring enlargement of Tom's driver's license photo and the message, "Authorities are asking that you contact the police immediately if you see this man...."

"Oh dear Lord..." said Emily, putting a hand up to her mouth.

Sofi looked up from the floor at the TV and gleefully exclaimed, "Daddy!"

CHAPTER TWENTY-EIGHT

President Gus Hartel arrived at the mansion, flanked by a small, intimate entourage that included his chief of staff, Jarret Spero, campaign director Kathleen Vourlekis and three long-time, trusted Secret Service men. Simon Giamatti greeted his old friend warmly with a hearty handshake and Bella followed with an affectionate hug. Hartel immediately felt at ease at the Glencoe mansion, a frequent retreat when visiting Chicago, especially during his glorious first campaign run for president four years earlier.

As he stepped inside the large foyer, the president stated, "I've brought my skeleton crew. The rest of the staff is staying downtown. I'll catch up with them in the morning. These folks with me here, they're in the know."

Giamatti nodded in understanding.

"I kept the group as small as possible," said Hartel. "I'm very serious about the confidentiality of this procedure."

"So are we," Giamatti said. "How are you feeling?"

"Lousy," Hartel responded truthfully.

"I'm sorry," said Giamatti.

"Disease is a terrible thing," Hartel said. "Think of the great leaders and minds of this country throughout history – how much more they could have accomplished with the gift of your technology. Selective immortality is the next phase of Darwinism. This is a game changer. It will change the world."

Jarret Spero, a short man with wire-rimmed glasses, wavy hair and a flat expression, asked Giamatti, "How soon can you begin?"

Giamatti responded, "I'm ready when you are. The staff are fully prepared. The procedure has been tested to perfection. The digitization should take about one hour, and then another hour to get you up and running in your new home."

"New home." President Hartel smiled at the description. "Home sweet home."

"You'll be in perfect shape for tomorrow's big speech," Giamatti promised.

"Some reporters have started to speculate about my health," said Hartel. "It's making my constituents nervous. It has to stop."

"You will be the healthiest candidate out there," Giamatti said with a firm smile. "Not just healthy…invincible."

★   ★   ★

President Hartel and his staff settled into their row of rooms in the guest wing of the Giamatti mansion. Hartel felt some nervousness over the upcoming operation, but kept it to himself as he spoke one last time to his chief of staff before heading to the lab. Giamatti had been explicit that the president's advisers and security could not be bystanders in the operating room, an understandable request. Hartel knew he was putting a lot of trust in Giamatti. He also knew that he trusted Giamatti more than most people in his life, especially the fickle, two-faced weasels who saturated the political arena. His current health was in steady decline with an awaiting punctuation of death. Hartel believed in Giamatti's cure…desperately.

Two members of Hartel's Secret Service team accompanied him to meet Giamatti at the entrance to the lower level, where the operation would take place. Ben, the bigger of the two men, stated, "We'll be close by if you need anything."

"Make sure there aren't any reporters in the bushes," said Hartel. "Or spies for my opponent. I don't think the public is ready for a robot president…yet."

Hartel chuckled at his own comment with a trace of unease. Then he took a deep breath and joined Giamatti for the climb down the steps to the laboratory that waited to receive him.

"There's nothing to be nervous about," Giamatti reassured him, as they shed the president's handlers and protectors. "As you know, the entire process has been tested with outstanding results. It's been a terrific success."

"Until the Russians made off with it," said Hartel.

"That has been resolved," Giamatti said.

The president looked at him with surprise. "It has?"

The two men reached the bottom of the stairs and rounded a corner. Giamatti smiled as he took hold of a door handle and opened the entrance to the lab. He gestured President Hartel inside.

As the president entered, his eyes immediately locked in on his own technically perfect replica, lying flat and motionless on a gurney, naked except for a thin, white hospital gown.

"There I am," he said in a small, stunned voice. He had reviewed his shell during a previous visit to ensure it copied him to perfection. But now, aware that he would soon live inside this casing, his amazement and anxiety elevated once more.

"A thing of beauty," Giamatti said, as they continued to admire it.

"Hello, Mr. President," said a voice, breaking the trance.

Hartel's attention snapped away from his body on the gurney as he became aware of others in the room.

A very tall, slender man with sunken features and gray hair stepped forward. He did not look familiar. He offered his hand.

"I look forward to becoming you," he said.

Hartel stared at him, uncertain of what he had just heard. "Excuse me?"

He shook hands with the stranger, who introduced himself: "I am Sergei Vladin."

Hartel became even more puzzled. A foreign-sounding name? That immediately did not rest well with him.

The lovely Mrs. Giamatti approached next, smiling in a long dress, a welcome but odd presence in the operating room.

A third individual walked over from the other side of the room, and Hartel was now surrounded from all sides.

The third individual looked familiar.

"You're...the young man from the test," Hartel said.

"Yes, I am," said the handsome blond man in his thirties, offering his hand. "My name is...Alex."

"Alex?" said the president, thoroughly confused. "But isn't your name...Tom?"

Giamatti broke out in laughter, startling Hartel. Hartel

immediately turned to face his old friend. "What's going on?" he demanded.

"This is my team," Giamatti said with an unnatural smirk. He put an arm around his wife. "Why do you look so surprised?"

President Hartel turned his attention back to the tall man. "What did you say your name was?"

"Sergei Vladin," the tall man responded proudly.

"Why is that name familiar?"

"Perhaps you know me by my nickname. I am known to many as The Stick."

In that instant, the president realized who he was dealing with. His eyes widened with terror. His chest filled with pounding. His mouth went dry, choked for words.

Sergei smiled, pleased with the flash of recognition he observed on the president's face. "Ah, so you know me? I'm flattered but not surprised. I have so much history with your country. I am likely a common topic of discussion in your security briefings. We have never met in the flesh, but you have felt my presence. Your secrets are my secrets. Your elections are my elections. And now...your White House will be my White House."

Hartel spun away from him. He pushed open a path between Giamatti and his wife, fleeing in the first direction that offered him a clearing.

He reached a door on the other side of the room. He yanked the door open, praying it would take him back upstairs, but it didn't.

Instead of offering freedom, the door led to a cramped storage space containing two dead bodies – Simon and Bella Giamatti.

President Hartel stared down in horror at the corpses of his friends. Then he spun around and stared at the same two people, perfect doubles, approaching him. These two definitely were not his friends.

The pounding in his chest became a fierce tightening and President Gus Hartel's vision succumbed to a rush of sparks, then a drop into darkness. He managed a single step away from the storage closet before collapsing, hitting the ground hard, with no one stepping forward to help him.

President Hartel shuddered and died, fearing not for himself but for his country.

★　　★　　★

Alex stood over President Hartel, aiming a gun with a silencer at his head, waiting to see if there was any more movement, but the man had gone very, very still.

"Check him," he said to Yefim. Yefim, housed in Simon Giamatti's replica, bent down and felt the president's neck for a pulse. Alina, no longer forcing expressions of warmth and smiles to hide her true nature, scowled in a manner that looked at odds with Bella Giamatti's otherwise sweet appearance.

"He's dead," said Yefim.

"Heart attack," said Alina.

Sergei joined the small circle looking down at the dead president. "Well," he said to Alex, "that saved us a bullet." He prodded the corpse with his foot, fascinated by the sight.

"The president is dead," Sergei said. "And no one will ever know." He turned to Alex. "I am ready. Let's get this show on the road."

Alex smiled. "One last transfer. Our third of the day."

Sergei walked over to a bank of computers lined up alongside a hospital bed, where the digitization of his consciousness would take place. As he stepped past President Hartel's replica on the gurney, he stopped for a moment to admire it with an expression that could be described as loving.

"I am going to so enjoy being you," he said. "America will never be the same."

★　　★　　★

Two hours later, Giamatti brought President Hartel upstairs and reunited him with his chief of staff and Secret Service team.

"A massive success!" thundered Giamatti.

"How do you feel?" Jarret Spero asked anxiously.

"I feel great," President Hartel answered.

"He was an outstanding patient," said Giamatti.

The chief of staff studied him and said, "Remarkable. You really can't tell the difference."

"That's what we're counting on," said Giamatti.

"I'm relieved it's over," Hartel said. "I feel no pain, I feel no fatigue. I feel reborn."

They chatted for a while more, until the president withdrew from the conversation.

"It's late," he said. "I don't mean to be antisocial, but I'm going to retire to my room. I need to go over my speech a few more times. I can't miss a beat, you know. My busy schedule continues."

"Tomorrow's a big day," Giamatti said.

"Every day is a big day," said the president. "From now until the election, we must do everything in our power to win."

Jarret Spero smiled, a rare show of emotion for a man who was always too busy concentrating to be emotional. "We will win by a landslide, Mr. President," he said.

President Hartel grinned broadly, perhaps uncharacteristically, but with genuine delight.

"Good."

CHAPTER TWENTY-NINE

Tom awoke the next morning to the sound of vehicles and voices at the front of the house. After a lengthy, deep sleep he felt better – mentally sharper anyway. His limbs still responded with sluggish uncertainty, a sensation that would not go away with rest. He pulled himself out of bed slowly, balancing on his feet like a toddler. He took several steps across the room, forcing activity through his awkward muscles, reaching the window. He parted the curtains for a look outside. Sunshine spilled into the room.

The president and his small entourage were leaving. Three long, black limousines swallowed them up. Tom watched Jarret Spero join the president in the middle car, along with two tightlipped Secret Service men in shades and dark suits. Tom felt a stab of disappointment that he hadn't met the president during his stay, but hoped he'd return after the campaign rally. Mr. and Mrs. Giamatti climbed into the third vehicle together.

As Tom watched the Giamattis, he noticed something that struck him as odd.

Giamatti was walking cleanly – without his pronounced limp. He inserted himself into the back of the limo with ease, without assistance.

As he climbed in, Bella Giamatti momentarily placed her hand on the top of the open car door. She was missing her monster diamond ring – the one she declared she would never remove from her finger. Especially for such a high-profile social spectacle – why would she take it off?

The two of them seemed different. Had they moved forward with moving into their new bodies? Had they followed the president into the operating room for a triple switch? It made some sense, as long as the lab was set up and the staff was present to conduct all of the work in one lengthy session.

Tom watched the limousines leave for Navy Pier, winding down the long arc of the driveway, through the open gates and into the street. He decided to contact Cooper for the latest update. He didn't want to stay stuck in the guest room all day, but strolling the mansion would probably require clearance, given the high security of the president's visit.

Tom picked up his cell phone from the nightstand. He sat on the bed and called Cooper.

It rang a half-dozen times, then dumped into voicemail.

Tom left a message: "Hey, Coop, it's Tom. I saw the group leave. Okay if I walk the house and get something to eat? Also, I want to ask about the Giamattis. They seem different, if you know what I mean. Are they? – you know. Anyway.... Thanks."

Tom disconnected.

He waited five minutes, then ten, then fifteen minutes for a call back.

Nothing.

Tom grew irritated at the prospect of being ignored. Then he grew worried, given the prior day's events and the bullets fired their way. Enemies still existed.

Tom was ready to break himself free of the guest room when a knock sounded at the door.

"Cooper," Tom said to himself. At last.

He stood up from the bed, found a good stride and walked over to the door. He pulled it open with a quick tug.

Tom Nolan faced Tom Nolan.

The sight was surreal. It made him swoon with a rush of disorientation. Then the reality of the circumstances settled in.

"Hello," said the other Tom Nolan. "It's a pleasure to finally meet you. I am your better half."

Tom's heart pounded like a hammer. He locked eyes with his own set of blue eyes. "How – how did you get in here?"

"It was easy." The fake Tom Nolan matched the sound of his voice precisely. "I came to the door and Mrs. Giamatti let me in. I'm the Trojan horse that brought in the rest of my army." He stepped forward and Tom backed up. "You surprised us.

We didn't expect you to escape the police. But you stayed away long enough for us to come in and take over."

Tom thought back to when he and Cooper entered the house. It must have been the imposters who let them in. That's why Giamatti didn't respond to Cooper's text messages.

Tom's mirror image stood two inches away, toe to toe, face to face, like a 3-D reflection.

"Who's inside there?" Tom said to the unnatural presence that occupied his body.

The replica smiled with pride. "I am Alex Nikolaev. I'm part of the team that created you. Now I'm part of the team that will destroy you. There's no room for both of us. You're being replaced. Just like the Giamattis. Just like the president."

Tom backed up several more steps. His mirror image stayed close, advancing to block his escape, dominating Tom's view.

"The rest of your team as you knew them is dead," said Tom's replica. "I'm cleaning house, and you're my last bit of business. You may scream, but there's no one left to save you. It's just the two of us, a couple of Tom Nolans, and that's one too many. I'm sorry, but this is how it ends. I have nothing against you personally. The situation requires it. We can't wait for your illness to do the job. Your time has come. Mr. Nolan, I have two final words for you."

Tom watched himself shut the bedroom door with a slam, sealing the only exit.

He heard his own voice announce his fate:

"Lights out."

CHAPTER THIRTY

Tom turned to run, although he didn't run very well and there was nowhere to run to. He hobbled past the bed and his replica laughed at the awkwardness of his movements. The only place that offered a moment of safety also cornered him helplessly – the adjoining bathroom.

Tom's other choice was a dive out the window, but the fall would probably break bones – if he could even shatter the glass on a first try.

Tom slipped into the bathroom, shut the door and locked it.

His forgery on the other side said, "Is that where you want to die? Over a toilet?"

The words, in his own voice, made his head spin, as if he were speaking them out of his own mouth.

Tom thought about Emily and Sofi. He didn't want to die. Not here, not now.

The replica began hammering at the door with considerably more strength than an average human being. The blows sounded like gunshots. The wood began to splinter.

"You're making me mad," the replica said, quickly growing impatient as he pounded with increasing fierceness. Each blow became louder, booming with violence. Finally the door burst open, breaking free from the frame with a surrendering crunch.

Tom's replica lunged into the bathroom. He thrust a fist into the center of Tom's face with so much force that the face shattered, swallowing the hand up to the wrist.

"*Shit!*" shouted the replica. He realized that in his amped-up speed he had punched his own reflection in the bathroom mirror.

Tom leapt out of the shower and covered his replica with the flowered shower curtain he pulled from its rings. The attack was meek but bought Tom several seconds, which he promptly spent on his escape.

As the replica quickly worked to free his hand and shake off the curtain, Tom moved as fast as he could out of the guest room and into the hallway.

The replica pulled himself loose with a loud thrashing and stomped out of the bathroom.

Tom ran as quickly as possible, praying for his legs to cooperate. He reached the top of the stairway leading down to the ground floor. He gripped the banister to begin his descent – and then one of his legs buckled. Tom fell, crashing down the stairs, his vision spinning in a topsy-turvy blur until he reached the floor with a thud and a groan.

The replica stood at the top of the stairs and barked, "Give it up! You won't leave this house."

Tom, bruised and stiff, pulled himself along the floor and away from the steps, trying to crawl to his knees. As he slid forward, he knocked into something big on the floor that blocked him. He let out a shout.

Cooper's dead body lay crumpled on the floor, throat crushed and purple. His eyes and mouth remained open but useless. A few feet away from Cooper's limp arm, Tom spotted Cooper's gun.

Tom quickly scooted on his hands and knees to get to the gun. The replica immediately bounded down the steps, three at a time, with perfect balance and precision, landing with force between Tom and the firearm.

The replica kicked the gun away, sending it far across the room. Then the replica kicked Tom, hard.

Tom curled up and rolled from the blow. Desperately, he forced himself back up on his feet, legs positioned awkwardly, fighting not to fall down again.

"Pathetic!" shouted the replica. Tom's own voice never sounded so nasty.

Tom ran.

The replica followed, not running, not needing to. His footsteps slammed in a steady, confident stride as he trailed his prey.

Tom entered the Giamatti kitchen.

He looked in every direction, searching for something to defend himself with. He spotted a wooden block of sharp cooking knives. He fell against the counter and grabbed the biggest handle in the block.

As soon as Tom got a good grip on the knife and turned toward his attacker, he felt the sting of a hard swat against his hand. With a fast, sweeping motion, the replica knocked the knife free and it flew across the room, leaving Tom defenseless once more.

The replica reached out and slapped Tom in the face – hard. He did it several more times, accompanied by a childlike taunt: "Why are you hitting yourself? Why are you hitting yourself?"

Finally, the replica stopped with a twisted smile. "Sorry. I couldn't resist."

Tom just glared at his attacker, face reddened from the slaps.

"This is a lot of fun," the replica said, "but I'm a busy man. It really must come to an end."

Leaning against the counter, face stinging and hand throbbing, Tom demanded, "Why are you doing this?"

The replica considered the question for a moment, making a face of puzzlement, as if it was the most obvious thing in the world.

"It's my duty," he said, "to my country. You serve your country, I serve mine. It's really that simple."

Tom's eyes roamed the kitchen counter. The knife block was now out of his reach. There was nothing else nearby except a dirty coffee cup, a plate of crumbs, a spoon and a fork....

"There's no innocence on either side," continued Tom's replica. "We're not that different, just two countries of people with the same hopes and dreams and relentless drive to achieve them at any cost. I could be you, you could be me...as we are."

"No," Tom said forcefully. "*I'm not you!*" He plunged the fork into his replica's eye.

Stunned, the replica straightened up and froze for a moment. The fork handle stuck out of his left eye socket, the four sharp prongs sunk inside his head.

"That was not nice," he said.

Tom stood still, knowing that if he made a run for it, he would be pounced upon immediately. He may not have secured his escape, but he felt better by fighting back.

During the brief stare down, Tom's own eye hurt just looking at the damage he had inflicted on his other self.

"You do know," said the replica, "that I can get a new eye. This is just a minor inconvenience. The miracle of computer technology is how easily you can replicate your creations, unlike, say, human biology. For instance, when I break your spine – in a few seconds – it will not be so fixable. When I crush your skull and end your life – it isn't growing back. *I* can be repaired. You'll only…disintegrate. Ashes to ashes, dust to dust. Your mortality is inevitable."

Tom began to sidestep away from his replica. The replica didn't move.

"You think you can run faster than me? Give it a try. I'll give you a head start."

Tom continued to move slowly across the kitchen. He reached a small, round table where the Giamattis must have shared thousands of meals over the years. The table's centerpiece was a vase of colorful flowers.

Tom didn't care about the flowers. He was more interested in the other item plopped on the table, an elegant, purple handbag belonging to Bella Giamatti. It was left behind by her replica, who probably didn't care about its contents – or know of their existence.

The replica watched Tom with curious interest, expecting him to make a sudden, desperate mad dash at any minute.

Tom picked up the handbag and dumped its belongings on the table. Several small makeup items scattered. A roll of lipstick fell on the floor. But Tom quickly found what he was looking for.

"What are you doing?" the replica asked. "Do you need to powder your nose?"

Tom held up Bella Giamatti's Taser gun.

"What the hell is that?" said the replica, now scowling. He stepped forward. Tom stepped forward as well, and when his intention was recognized, it was too late.

Tom turned on the Taser. He thrust its electrical current at the fork handle sticking out of the replica's head.

The impact was immediate.

A blue crackle of electricity vibrated the fork, traveling its full length to enter the replica's skull. Sparks sprayed in fits and the replica let out a howl, shaking violently as the surge created havoc inside his head. The voltage shocked and fried the circuitry, lighting up and breaking down the command center that linked digital thought with mechanical operations.

Even faced with the horrible sound of his own screams, Tom did not remove the Taser from his replica's eye. Smoke emerged first from the socket and then from his nostrils and mouth.

In a fit of computer meltdown, the replica sputtered fragments of speech and jolted its limbs awkwardly, like a crazed new-wave dancer, losing all control of humanlike fluidity and replacing it with crude robotic flailing.

Tom pulled away the Taser and watched himself smoke from an internal fire, wavering on two shaky legs, face partially blackened, mouth moving involuntarily as if to offer final words.

There were none.

Tom's replica stiffened and pitched forward, crashing to the floor on its face.

For a short moment, Tom felt sad peering down at his own dead body. He had killed himself and survived, and now stood over his physical form like a lingering soul. He felt a variety of emotions, none of them right. Then the moment passed.

CHAPTER THIRTY-ONE

After a long time spent staring down at the defunct robot, keeping a firm grip on the Taser, making sure his alter ego didn't suddenly reboot for a fresh assault, Tom felt it was safe to leave the Giamatti kitchen. He stepped slowly and cautiously out of the room and followed the hallway to the bottom of the broad staircase leading upstairs. He returned to Cooper's dead body. He walked past it.

He wanted Cooper's gun.

Tom reached down and picked it up. As he held it in his hand, he caught a glimpse of a shadowy figure rushing across the floor in the next room, crouched and headed toward the front entryway.

Tom whirled and pointed the gun at the fast-moving individual. "Hey! Stop! *I'll shoot!*"

The figure immediately halted and threw up his hands, exclaiming, "Please don't shoot!" in a frightened voice.

Tom walked over to him, keeping the gun steady the best he could.

As Tom approached, his eyes grew large and he lowered the weapon.

"Oh my God," he said. "Steven."

Scientist Steven Morris, badly bloodied and drenched in panic, stood before him. Steven looked at Tom and recognized his old friend, but it didn't reassure him. "Don't kill me," he said, shaking.

"I'm not going to hurt you," said Tom. "It's me, Tom Nolan."

"Yeah, maybe."

"No, really."

Steven didn't look convinced and remained frozen with his hands straight up and fear in his eyes.

"I attended your wedding," said Tom. He searched for a

trivial tidbit that would prove his identity. "The bouquet – Madeleine threw the bouquet and Emily caught it, remember? She wasn't even trying – it just landed in her hands. Your first dance, it was...it was...." Tom searched his memory. "'Wonderful World' by Louis Armstrong."

Steven looked at him, still uncertain. His face was striped with blood. One lens of his round glasses was stained. His shirt was also bloody, especially one very red arm.

"That was the second dance," he said.

"Damn," Tom said, then he remembered: "'Moonlight Serenade'!"

Steven nodded. He finally let out an exhale of relief. "Thank God it's you and not the other you. I didn't know there was anyone still alive in this house."

"What happened? You look horrible. You're bleeding all over."

"It's not as bad as it looks. Some of this is my blood. A lot of it isn't."

Tom stepped closer. Steven looked exhausted, ready to collapse. "I saw everything," Steven said.

Steven told Tom he had spent the last twelve hours hiding in Giamatti's wine cellar. "We were setting up the lab for the president's procedure. The Russians came in with your double. They didn't say anything – they just started shooting. The other doctors and scientists were all killed. I was hit. I went down with the others, we fell on top of one another. I was hit in the arm. I faked I was dead, I didn't move. They shoved us in the wine cellar. They took over. When they finally left...I went into the lab. The shells were gone. And I found more bodies. Mr. Giamatti. His wife. And the president. They killed President Hartel."

"Holy shit."

"They're stealing the identities."

"The president left here earlier this morning," said Tom. "His staff has no idea that it's an imposter."

"The Russians want to take over the White House," Steven said, shocked at his own words.

"We're the only people alive who can expose them."

In the moment of stunned silence that followed, a cheerful music jingle chirped from another room.

"The Beach Boys?" said Steven.

Tom listened. It sounded like the opening notes of 'Wouldn't It Be Nice?' Then it repeated. And again.

Tom followed the source of the music and it led back into the kitchen. He stared down at his robot duplicate.

"Tom Nolan 2.0," said Steven, standing close by. "He doesn't look so good."

The Beach Boys song restarted once more, a persistent loop.

"It's his ring tone," Tom said. He kneeled down and reached inside his alter ego's pants pocket. He grimaced, imagining a terrible scene where the robot awoke and clutched his wrist.

Instead, the robot remained rigid, lifeless, fried.

Tom answered the cell phone in his natural voice, which was what the caller was expecting to hear.

"Yes?" he said.

"Alex, is your business finished?" said a voice. Tom could hear a lot of commotion, voices, in the background.

"Yes. Tom Nolan is...no more." He was getting used to referencing himself in the third person. "And Cooper. Both of them...are done. Completely done."

"Good," said the voice. It sounded like Giamatti, which meant it was one of the members of the Russian spy ring. "I'm sending over The Cleaner. Be sure to open the gates for him. Direct him to the unwanted debris. He'll take out the trash and make it disappear. He'll use the chemical treatment."

Tom didn't know exactly what 'the chemical treatment' referred to, but assumed it was a method to disintegrate corpses.

"Yes, I'll show The Cleaner where to go," he said. Then he gambled on a question to gain some information from the other end.

"Where are you?" he asked.

"We're getting ready for the rally," said the voice. "All is good. The transition has been seamless. It couldn't be better."

"That's great," Tom said.

"After The Cleaner conducts his work, please send us a notification."

"Certainly."

The caller wrapped up the conversation and disconnected, apparently satisfied.

Tom took a deep breath and looked at Steven. He told him about The Cleaner.

"Oh great, an acid bath," said Steven. "Let's not stick around for that. Let's go to the police."

"I'm a wanted man, I can't go to the police," Tom said. "The police won't believe us anyway. This technology isn't common knowledge. Can you imagine how we'll sound? We'll sound crazy. We need to go higher. We need to get to the president's inner circle – they'll know what we're talking about. I have to get to that rally."

"At Navy Pier?" Steven asked.

"Yes."

"How are you going to get there?"

"Is your car here?"

"Well – yes. It's a rental. My Camry was stolen, you know."

"Where's the rental?"

"Parked behind the garage."

"Then you're driving."

"Looking like this?"

Tom studied Steven. He was crusted in blood, like someone who had just crawled out of an automobile wreck.

"We'll get you washed up," said Tom. "We'll wrap that wound. I have extra clothes in my room."

"Good. Thank you."

"But we'll have to hurry," Tom said. He was anxious to get Steven cleaned up before The Cleaner arrived with his own methods.

★   ★   ★

The bullet had torn a hole in Steven's triceps, not lodging inside but creating a gory gash. Tom cleaned the wound with alcohol and wrapped him up with fresh gauze from a medicine cabinet. They scrubbed the blood off his face and traded his bloody clothes for a new shirt and pair of pants.

As they hurried to the front door to make a swift exit, Steven noticed Tom was having a hard time keeping up.

"Are you okay?" Steven asked.

"Yes, fine," Tom lied.

They started to open the front door, caught a glimpse of a vehicle stopped at the front gate at the end of the driveway, and quickly shut the door again.

"We have a visitor," said Tom.

He stepped across the foyer to a small security panel in the wall that displayed a camera feed from the gated entrance. The camera showed a branded van with a colorful, puffy-lettered logo: 'Thomson Cleaning Company'.

"It's The Cleaner," Tom said.

"There's a guy behind the wheel," said Steven, studying the security feed. "He looks really, really big. What do we do?"

Tom thought about it for a moment. "We let him in."

"Let him in?"

"We open the gate. That's what he's expecting. We leave the front door unlocked for him. He enters. We slip out the back. The gate stays open and we have a clear path to get out of here."

"What if he sees us?"

Tom lifted the gun he had taken from Cooper. It was the best answer he had.

Steven nodded. He took in a deep breath. "Okay."

Tom said, "Ready?"

"Sure," said Steven, more weary than enthusiastic.

Tom punched the green button that split open the iron gate. The cleaning van chugged forward, emitting a cough of exhaust.

Tom and Steven hurried to the rear of the mansion and exited through a set of porch doors that led to Bella Giamatti's Japanese garden. They stepped across a bed of stones, trampled colored moss, maneuvered around a small pond with goldfish and unlatched a door in the bamboo fence. Circling the perimeter of the estate, they were careful to avoid being visible from the front of the house.

The Cleaner appeared pumped up on steroids – thick necked, muscular and mean faced. He rolled large barrels from the back of the truck into the mansion's open entrance. Tom and Steven watched the activity from behind dense shrubbery. Once The Cleaner had completed moving the barrels, he closed up the truck and disappeared into the house to begin his work.

Tom and Steven scurried for Steven's car. They climbed in and Steven started up the engine with a quick crank of the key. The car took off, winding down the circular driveway and through the open gates.

Tom clutched the gun, getting used to the feel of the cold steel. He glanced at the time on Steven's dashboard and then stared ahead through the windshield at the changing scenery. "We should reach Navy Pier in less than an hour."

CHAPTER THIRTY-TWO

Navy Pier, a bustling summertime tourist and entertainment destination, took on an extra flurry of energy and excitement for the president's appearance. The celebrated pier jutted more than two-thirds of a mile from the Lake Michigan shoreline, offering restaurants, museums, a theater, cruise ships and an iconic Ferris wheel before culminating in the majestic, domed Grand Ballroom with its panoramic view of the lake and city skyline. Added layers of security took over the Chicago attraction, restricting access to a narrow, highly controlled pathway to the campaign fundraiser. The gathered visitors looked nothing like the usual T-shirt, shorts and sandals crowd. They were dressed up in their finest for the horde of TV cameras and photographers. In the hot sunshine, men wore jackets and ties, and women wore long, elegant gowns and heels. They funneled through a colorful archway of red, white and blue balloons, prepared to show identification and confirm reservations that started at ten thousand dollars a plate.

Navy Pier got its name from the pier's role in serving the military in World Wars I and II. Over the years, visiting dignitaries ranged from US presidents to Queen Elizabeth II. This latest milestone in Navy Pier's storied history promised to be an occasion to remember. President Hartel was riding a wave of popularity and expected to coast on a smooth ride to re-election for a second term. His donors arrived in a joyful mood on a picture-perfect day.

Tom Nolan watched the flow of pedestrian traffic from a safe distance, standing casually behind a lamppost. He noted the ample presence of Chicago police officers, private security and Secret Service. Admission required a picture ID, reservations on a guest list, and a trip through a metal detector. The meticulous screening process caused the line of incoming guests to swell.

Steven Morris stood next to Tom and asked, "How are you going to get in there?"

Tom had a ready answer. "I have connections." He took a cell phone out of his pocket – not his own. It was the phone belonging to his deceased robot replica, Alan/Alex. Tom accessed the number at the top of the Recent Calls list and dialed it with a poke of his thumb.

After four rings, Simon Giamatti's voice picked up – the same voice that had called earlier to announce the impending arrival of The Cleaner.

"Yes? What is it?" said the voice, sounding distracted and impatient.

"The Cleaner is at the mansion," Tom said in his natural voice while remembering to mentally become his attacker.

"Good. Excellent."

"I'm here at Navy Pier. I need to speak with you at once."

The voice on the other end became startled. "You're what? You're *here*?"

"Yes," said Tom. "I'm at the entrance. I'm at visitor screening."

"What the hell are you doing here?" The voice was aggravated. "Stay where you are. Don't move. I'll send Alina for you."

Tom almost said, "Who's Alina?" but quickly caught himself. He knew he should act as though he recognized the name. He simply responded, "Good. Thank you."

The call ended and Tom turned to Steven. "I'm going in. They still think I'm the other me."

Steven shook his head with a pained expression, conveying but not saying *I can't keep track of this*.

"They'll get me inside," Tom said. "Then I'm going to find the president's advisers – the ones who know what's going on. You stay here, don't let them see you."

Tom juggled the cell phones in his grasp, replacing Alan's with his own. "Give me your cell phone number, so we can stay in touch."

Steven recited his number and Tom entered it into his list of contacts. Then Steven said, "Tom, I'm sorry I got you involved in this. I never dreamed it would turn out this way."

"We're going to fix this," Tom said.

"I'm here for you. Anything you need...."

"Stay available, but not too close," said Tom. Then he took a deep breath and said, "Here goes nothing."

He gave his old friend a quick hug. Steven felt something in the embrace. "You have a...."

Tom nodded. He still had Cooper's gun under his shirt, tucked tight, out of view.

"Oh, Jesus," said Steven. "Be careful."

Tom turned and headed for the fundraiser entrance.

He stayed off to the side, trying not to draw attention to himself, avoiding being swept into the excited line of guests that advanced toward security clearance.

"There you are!"

Tom swiveled and saw Bella Giamatti coming at him, her shapely body draped in a beautiful, formfitting green dress. For a moment, it felt like she was the real thing, in voice and appearance, but Tom quickly corrected his instincts.

This must be Alina.

"Hello," Tom said casually. While she had a soft face, her eyes blazed hard at him.

She stepped very close and spoke in a low, intimate voice. "Yefim is angry. You never should have come here. Are you crazy? You're a wanted face. You should be back at the mansion."

"I have important things to talk about."

"Not here." Alina skipped a quick glance across their surroundings, lips pursed with frustration. "I'll take you in. We'll find a private room. Do not mingle. Just follow me."

"Yes," said Tom. "Of course."

She grabbed Tom's hand, smiled with phony affection, and led him to the security entrance.

Tom's heart began to pound. He lowered his face, pretending to be distracted by sights and sounds in the other direction.

"It's okay," Alina announced to the personnel at the security table, circumventing the long line. "He's with me. He doesn't need to go through security."

The trio at the check-in table responded to her with eager smiles and gracious permission.

"Of course, Mrs. Giamatti."

"Absolutely, Mrs. Giamatti."

"Go right in."

Tom bit his lip to prevent breaking out in a smile. The woman had major league clout and her relationship with the president was well known. Entry was a breeze.

Alina guided Tom past multiple security checkpoints and led him into a private entrance not far from the domed Grand Ballroom. She pushed through a door marked 'Events Office'.

Inside the office, a small group of people converged at a meeting table while a thin, older woman worked on a laptop. Alina gestured Tom into a corner.

"You really shouldn't be here," she said in a harsh whisper. "We'll have to keep you hidden. Now what's the trouble?"

"The trouble...." Tom hesitated, not having prepared this far. All his focus had been on just getting in. "Yes, the trouble. Back at the mansion. I think that...there's a security risk. I believe...there might be cameras still in operation."

"We disengaged them."

"But maybe not all."

Simon Giamatti entered the room. He was stuffed into a black tuxedo, face pinched in an unpleasant expression Tom had not seen on him before. Tom felt a quick shudder. *This must be Yefim.*

"What's the problem here?" Giamatti said, moving with swift ease, not bothering to fake the limp.

"He says there's security trouble at the mansion," said Alina as Bella Giamatti.

"Security trouble?" said Yefim as Simon Giamatti. Then his cell phone chirped in the pocket of his tuxedo. He pulled it out, stared at it for a second and muttered, "The Cleaner."

Tom's heart skipped a beat. He watched as the fake Giamatti accepted the call and listened to a long statement on the other end.

Tom knew it wasn't good. The fake Giamatti's eyes narrowed. Finally, he said, "I see." He looked up at Tom. "I'll take care of it," he said, and he hung up.

He addressed Tom. "The Cleaner has made an interesting discovery in the kitchen."

Tom knew exactly where this was going. He tried to twist the narrative. "Yes," he said. "I killed Tom Nolan in the kitchen. I stuck a fork in his eye. For fun...."

Neither one of the Giamattis looked convinced.

Then Bella Giamatti asked Tom a question in a low voice that the event staff on the other side of the room could not hear.

The question was in Russian.

Tom felt a chilled sweat on his scalp. He nodded, as if understanding. He spoke the only Russian word he knew.

"*Da.*"

The expressions he received from them indicated it was not an acceptable – or even coherent – response.

Bella Giamatti spoke more Russian at him. It was strange to hear fluent Russian coming out of her mouth in her soft, familiar American voice. As part of their efforts to work effectively undercover, the spies had perfected American accents and rarely spoke in their native language while on US soil.

Now both of them were speaking to Tom in deliberately thick Russian, expecting a response.

"*Da,*" said Tom again. "*Da.*"

He knew this was going very badly, and he was failing the test.

Finally, he spoke the only other language he knew – Spanish.

"*Adios,*" he said.

He punched Giamatti in the face, hurting his hand but startling his target. Bella Giamatti came at him and he punched her too, regretting that he was hitting such a soft, pretty face, feeling like a bully, but the punch probably hurt him more than her. She barely flinched.

Others in the room took notice of the assault, shocked. "Hey!" shouted someone from the nearby meeting table.

Tom took off, slipping away from the Giamattis. He tossed chairs behind him in a crashing tangle to block their path. He could hear noisy commotion in his wake but did not look back.

Tom stumbled into a long corridor and continued to scramble as fast as he could, fighting back the aches and awkward, stiff legs.

He had several doors to choose from and picked one at random. It led into a crowded lobby outside of the Grand Ballroom.

Tom moved across the lobby in a zigzag. He followed a group of lively, loud-talking supporters to the nearest ballroom entrance. He advanced with them inside, experiencing a burst of sights and sounds. The circular, cavernous event space was packed with people, a thousand or more, filling the gaps between dozens of white-linen tables that faced the elevated stage. Each table was decorated with crystal glasses, fanned-out napkins, china plates and shining silver. Big floor-to-ceiling windows admitted bright sunshine, forming a wide arc of light around the ballroom's perimeter. A cacophony of voices echoed off the domed ceiling. In a far corner, a jazz ensemble played chipper background music that could barely be heard over the layers of conversation.

Tom lost himself in the crowd, burying himself deep, becoming just another donor at the big-ticket event.

As Tom wormed his way through the crowd, he found a familiar face – a valuable face – engaged in a smiling conversation with a group of people off to the side.

It was Jarret Spero, the president's chief of staff.

Tom wanted to rush him and shout out a warning, but it looked unlikely he could get close to such a prominent political figure – and if he did, security would surely pounce.

Tom blended into a back wall, where a growing crowd gathered to browse a long table of 'Silent Auction' items to raise campaign money. Tom kept his head lowered and looked absorbed in the many offerings, giving himself a temporary activity to engage in so he could avoid looking suspicious. Some of the auction items were placed on display, like autographed sports memorabilia – baseball bats, football jerseys and basketballs signed by big-name stars. Other offerings were simply described in colorful summaries encased in clear plastic stands, such as a personal photo op with the president, starting at a mere fifty thousand dollars. Other significant draws, based on the volume of bids, consisted of a private dinner cooked by a celebrity chef; a one-week African safari; an intimate concert from an aging classic rock band; and original paintings by well-known artists.

Tom didn't care about these extravagant expenditures for the wealthy. His interest was much simpler: a pen and paper.

Tom found an item with only a few bids and tore off the bottom half of the sheet without disturbing any names. He snatched one of the fancy VOTE HARTEL pens and swiftly moved to the far end of the auction table. He found a clear surface and carefully wrote out a message in his uneven handwriting:

I need to talk to you about the Gemini Experiment.

As he folded the message for delivery, a loud, smooth voice sounded over the speakers, immediately hushing the crowd:

"Ladies and gentlemen, please take your seats. Our program will begin in five minutes."

Tom looked for the chief of staff and found him slowly moving toward a VIP table, front and center. Then he saw the Giamattis, not too far away, walking the ballroom with angry, searching eyes while trying to be polite and accommodating to the many acquaintances who approached to say hello.

"Shit," said Tom, seeing the Giamattis turn in his direction.

Tom quickly moved across the ballroom, dodging people on a path to find their seats. He slipped behind a large lighting truss, obscured from view as the Giamattis walked right past him. Tom quickly moved on, in a new direction. He stepped out of the ballroom and back into the lobby.

There, he saw several people in white catering uniforms marching back and forth between the ballroom and a service kitchen, carrying full trays of food. A team of security guards stood in measured intervals across the lobby with blank expressions and probing eyes. Tom put his head down and followed one of the catering employees into the kitchen.

Tom's presence in the kitchen was immediately met with suspicion. "Who are you, what are you doing here?" snapped a busy young man in a stained white shirt, with curly hair and dripping perspiration.

Tom made up a line about being from the president's security staff and 'checking things out'.

"Go about your business," Tom told the sweaty young man.

"I'm going to ask my manager about this," came the response with a doubtful glare.

Tom said, "Go ahead." He proceeded to walk through the kitchen area with a stern look of purpose. Once he was out of the young man's sight, he slipped into a storage room and closed the door.

Standing under a single light bulb, among shelves of bulk food supplies, Tom considered his next move. He could hear an amplified, muffled voice booming from the ballroom, delivering a set of evenly paced remarks. He guessed it to be the governor introducing the afternoon's special guest.

Tom's legs were shaking. He sat down on a box of canned pineapple slices. He was apprehensive about stepping back into the ballroom. He knew it was only a matter of time before someone discovered and apprehended him. Then, he had a premonition. He had a strong feeling he would not survive to see the next day.

The fanfare in the ballroom grew louder. Listening to the blur of words coming from the governor, mixed with large outbreaks of applause, Tom knew what he had to do. He thought about Emily and Sofi and fought back tears. He took out the note he had written for the president's chief of staff and added something to the bottom of it.

Under the message, *I need to talk to you about the Gemini Experiment*, Tom wrote Steven Morris's cell phone number.

Then Tom whispered a small prayer. He prayed to whatever waited in the afterlife.

The governor's voice rose to a boisterous bellow, whipping the crowd into a frenzy. He introduced President Gus Hartel. The crowd became a unified roar, followed by chants of "Four more years!"

Tom knew the president was taking the stage at that very moment. A loud, thundering ovation shook the east end of Navy Pier.

Tom stood up, ready to fulfill his mission.

He stepped out of the storage room. He moved out of the kitchen services area. He walked across the lobby and reentered the noisy ballroom as the president reached the podium.

President Hartel raised his hands, triumphant, gesturing with both thumbs up. The crowd stood and cheered in appreciation, packing the elegant, white dinner tables that filled the room. Tom observed the audience's happy, beaming faces. Every pair of eyes focused on the president, basking in his presence with unwavering loyalty.

Standing behind the podium, his face amplified on large projection screens, the president launched into his prepared remarks. He spoke in rich patriotic tones about America and freedom. His message drew frequent bursts of applause as he said all the right words, continuing on his well-paved course to re-election. Tom knew he was witnessing a massive scam. The phony president was holding back on showing any evidence of his true intentions – a secret agenda of evil that would change the world.

Tom calmly walked over to the chief of staff. Jarret Spero sat in his chair, eyes glued on the president. Tom dropped a folded piece of paper into his lap, startling his attention away from the speech.

"Excuse me, sir, this is for you," said Tom. The chief of staff stared down at the small white square in his lap.

Very quickly, security began to move in. Tom slipped away from the table. The president continued his speech, but a growing number of audience members became distracted from the stage to the odd, stiff man who moved around the maze of tables as security officials came after him from all around the room. These men wore no-nonsense expressions with arms half-raised, ready for some kind of action. Several spoke into headsets, trading information. Tom knew that most likely he had been identified, the crazy lawyer from Wilmette wanted for a long list of crimes that would put him away for the rest of his shortened life.

Tom saw Mr. and Mrs. Giamatti seated at a table at the front of the room, heads turned from the stage and eyes watching him, scowling. Their mouths moved, delivering directions to staffers, probably sending their own people after him, and it was anyone's guess who would get to him first.

Tom heard a man's voice nearby, possibly one of the private

security staff, offering a simple and civilized request: "Sir, please take your seat." Tom felt bad he would have to disobey, because the man's tone was surprisingly polite, not threatening, completely unaware that he was speaking to a very dangerous individual who was prepared to make international headlines.

The president was still delivering his speech into the lights, unaware of the commotion before him, when a man's shout erupted from the front of the crowd. It was Tom.

Tom approached the stage, pushing as close as he could get. He pulled out a gun.

"The president is a fake!" he yelled.

As screams ignited around him, Tom pulled the trigger and squeezed off as many shots as he could. His arm shook uncontrollably and he gripped it steadily in his other hand, successfully landing several bullets into his target to the horror of the crowd.

Tom could see the president's face contort as the bullets struck. He stared down at Tom with a fierce look, and for a moment he remained steady on his feet. Then he realized he could not act invulnerable on such a world stage and swooned from the shooting, performing a stagger of pain, responding like any mortal human would. He didn't have time to fall. Instead, he was caught.

The president disappeared in a large swarm of Secret Service, Chicago police, private security, event staff and members of his own entourage.

Tom stopped shooting but the sharp, staccato crackle of gunfire continued. He spun from the impact, pummeled by an immediate onslaught of bullets from multiple directions. Each hit delivered a new burst of pain, puncturing his body like needles of fire, penetrating ordinary flesh and organs, tearing up his mortal being, and it was fine. It was okay. He'd known this would be coming.

The crowd around Tom erupted into chaos, a thundering stampede with chairs toppling, tables shoved aside and glass breaking. Tom felt his entire body run slick with blood. Strangers began jumping on him, flattening him to the ground, breaking his fingers to extract the empty gun, and he didn't fight back. He wouldn't fight back. He couldn't fight back. He was done.

Mission accomplished. The president would be rushed to the nearest hospital where his artificial interior would be revealed, unraveling the Russians' plot.

Pinned on his back, unable to move, Tom stared up into the majestic domed ceiling, the direction of heaven, and shut his eyes. He listened to the sound of hollers and shrieks from near and far, a harrowing chorus from hell. Beneath all the noise, he spoke softly because he had no energy to talk louder. He gasped and sputtered a simple explanation that no one heard.

"He's not our president."

CHAPTER THIRTY-THREE

"You piece of shit, I hope you die."

Tom slipped in and out of consciousness in the back of the ambulance, hearing bits of commentary from the paramedics and his police escorts, none of it friendly. This was understandable, given the surface appearance of his actions. In a voice that croaked badly, choked up in his own blood, he tried to explain.

"That…wasn't the president. It's – it's a robot."

"What's he babbling about?" asked an angry, ruddy-cheeked policeman hovering inches above him, face dominated by a big mustache.

"Just nonsense," a disgusted paramedic said with a hissy voice as he steadied Tom's life-support tubing out of obligation, not compassion. "He's delirious."

After several blocks of wailing, the ambulance siren abruptly cut off. The vehicle began to slow down. It pulled over to the curb and rolled to a complete stop. It was the first time the ambulance had ceased moving since leaving Navy Pier.

The ambulance crew became still, as if waiting for something.

"What's—what's going on?" Tom asked, unable to see through the windows in his position.

"We pulled over to let an ambulance get through," said the paramedic.

"But *we're* the ambulance," Tom murmured, confused.

"This one is more important than you, asshole," the paramedic said in a hostile tone.

Tom heard the other siren as it grew louder, louder and then shot past, spraying flashing light through the windows.

The president.

"You have to listen to me," Tom said. "The president is a Russian spy. That's not the real president."

The police officer chortled, a brief escape of sad laughter. "I've heard some crazy conspiracy theories over the years, mister, but that's the craziest."

Tom wanted to say more but he was very weak from the loss of blood, and the damage to his organs was rapidly taking its toll. Every breath hurt inside. His torso felt ravaged. As a numbing wave of darkness crept over him, Tom heard the paramedic declare, quite confidently, that he probably wouldn't survive his wounds.

Tom accepted his fate. He was going wherever people go when they perish on earth. It was the common denominator for all of mankind. His mind swam.

We get old, we die.

We get sick, we die.

We get shot up by a half-dozen security people at the president's campaign rally and...we die.

Tom filled his thoughts with Emily and Sofi one last time. Then he lost all consciousness.

★   ★   ★

Feeling restless and confined, Emily put aside the magazine she was skimming and dropped it into a spilled pile of used reading material. Sofi had been complaining about boredom, quite rightly, and now requested a search for cartoons on the hotel room TV.

"Sure, honey, let's see what's on," Emily said, moving out of her chair. She had avoided watching television ever since stumbling across news coverage of her husband robbing a diner and stealing a police car. She still hadn't recovered from the shock, which lit her up with a terrible tension she couldn't shake from her bones. Perhaps cartoons were just what the doctor ordered.

Emily picked up the remote from the side of the television, aimed it and clicked ON.

The television popped to life with a red and blue BREAKING NEWS banner cutting across a live feed of aerial footage of Navy Pier shot from a helicopter. A male and female news anchor team spoke in unnaturally shaky voices, as if they couldn't believe their own words. They were recapping the latest developments in the shooting of the president.

"Oh my God!" said Emily.

Then it got worse. Much worse.

A photograph of the gunman filled the screen. He stared into the hotel room with big blue eyes as if trapped behind glass, the most gentle man she had ever known.

Emily began screaming and could not stop.

CHAPTER THIRTY-FOUR

Tom woke up.

He quickly sensed this wasn't heaven. It was a hospital room.

He was in a crisp, clean bed, surrounded by racks of medical equipment and monitors, facing a window with the drapes tightly pulled shut. Pillows propped up his head.

Tom was afraid to move. He knew he was not in the greatest condition, but he marveled over the complete lack of pain. He attributed it to heavy medication. His breathing felt comfortable. His mind felt a little foggy but rapidly sharpened like a lens being twisted for better focus.

"Hello."

The greeting came from Steven Morris. He stepped into Tom's view. He was smiling, cleaned up. His arm was in a sling.

"Steven," said Tom. His voice felt thick from sleep. "I'm so glad to see you. I didn't expect to make it out alive. I know you must think I'm crazy, but I had to do something…dramatic. They were going to kill everyone who knew. They could have gone all the way with it…."

Then Tom paused and asked, "The president – is he dead?"

"No. The president's not dead. But you are."

Tom realized that perhaps his mind was not as clear as he thought. "What?" For a moment, his environment became a surreal dream.

Steven held up a newspaper headline from the *Chicago Tribune*: *President expected to survive; shooter Tom Nolan dies.*

"I'm not dead," Tom said. Then he had to ask, "Am I?"

Steven put down the newspaper and moved closer. Tom stared at him. Steven was real, not an illusion. Tom could feel the texture of the bedsheets in his grasp. He was alive. He felt good.

"Your human lifeform has died," Steven said. "But before it died, we were able to digitize your brain and create a cartridge... like we planned to do all along."

"You did it?" said Tom, stunned. "You transferred me?"

"Yes."

"To where?"

"Very few people know about this. And it will stay that way."

"Know about what?" Tom asked.

Steven continued, "That note you gave the chief of staff. It mentioned the Gemini Experiment. Obviously that's highly classified. It got their immediate attention. They tracked me down through my phone. The president's inner circle – the ones who know about all this – they took me into custody. It was chaos, as you can imagine. But I told them everything, Tom. *Everything.*"

"Good," said Tom. "That's what I wanted."

"They went into lockdown mode. They took immediate control of the situation. The CIA moved in. They took over the mansion. They sealed it off, they locked down the lab. They took over a wing of the hospital, they set up a command center. They created a narrative that was delivered to the press."

"What narrative?"

Jarret Spero cautiously stepped into the room. He peered at Tom through his wire-rimmed glasses, serious at first, then breaking out in a big grin. He shut the door quickly behind him and approached the bed.

"You, sir, are a hero," he said.

Tom smiled a little. "I'm just glad to be alive."

"You saved the president of the United States," said Jarret. "He's going to be all right. In fact, he has a press conference in about twenty minutes to show the world he is safe and strong. This is monumental. With the addition of public sympathy over this terrible attack...the president is a lock for re-election."

"But wait," Tom said, head still sorting through the information. "The Russians...."

"All members of the Russian spy cell have been apprehended," said Jarret. "They've been removed from circulation quickly and quietly. Their digital minds have been ejected from their shells and isolated in a vault in an undisclosed location. It's all taken care of. There's no need for the public to become alarmed by any Russian threat. It's over."

"Then wait. Who is...?" Tom stopped and let his question hang.

Steven Morris and Jarret Spero glanced at one another.

"Who is..." repeated Tom. "The president?"

The two of them said nothing. They looked straight at Tom. Their smiles frightened him.

"And who..." Tom said, "am I?" He swiveled his head, looking for a mirror and found none.

Steven Morris and Jarret Spero continued to smile, holding back on saying anything, and in that moment Tom knew the answer.

"Oh my God," he said. "You didn't."

"Yes," said Steven. "We did. I personally handled the transfer."

"Tom," Jarret said, "and this is the last time I'll address you as Tom. Please understand that we had no choice. It was absolutely necessary in the name of national security."

"This can't be happening."

"The First Lady will be here in an hour. Don't worry – she's part of the inner circle."

Tom jolted up in the bed, looking at the two men in horror. "What have you done to me?"

"We saved your life," Steven said, trying to temper Tom's panic.

Jarret spoke in a calm, direct tone. "We have made you the most powerful man on earth."

Tom sank back into his pillows. He gave it deep thought. He touched his face.

"Oh no," he said. "No, no, no...."

CHAPTER THIRTY-FIVE

Maintaining a slow, even pace, Tom walked the long, cleared corridor at Northwestern Memorial Hospital, accompanied by his chief of staff, headed for a brief dialogue with the press at the conference center up ahead. He wore a dark suit and red tie that fit perfectly and smelled new. His hair was neatly combed in place.

Jarret talked rapidly in Tom's ear about what he should and shouldn't say, feeding him the key messages that the world needed to hear.

"You will commend your security staff for their fast response in bringing down the shooter. You will mention that you were wearing a bulletproof vest, which saved you from significant injury. You can tell them you are feeling good, headed for a full recovery. You may be out of the public eye briefly, but you fully intend on continuing your campaign and leading the country for a second term. There will be no mention of Russians or robotics or anything of that kind. Tom Nolan was a lone gunman, a crazy man, and you will express sympathy for his family. Avoid gun control questions or anything political for now until you have had a full briefing on the administration's position on key issues and public policy. Above all, *never* mention the Gemini Experiment. Do you understand?"

"Yes," said Tom.

Physically he felt reborn in his new shell, better than ever, no longer experiencing the drag of his crippling disease. His movements were swift, precise and pain free.

Emotionally he was a mess of fear and confusion. Would he ever see Emily and Sofi again? Could he truly leave them to lead the free world? What was more important?

Tom was cured, and now he had to heal a nation. It was a

huge responsibility but Tom knew he had a duty to his country. Besides, his very existence relied on cooperation. He didn't want his consciousness to wind up filed away in a vault.

As he neared the press conference staging, he could hear the growing buzz of the crowd, an overflow of media packed into the small room, anxious to receive the latest news and developments and see for themselves that the assassination attempt had failed.

Before Tom took the podium, Jarret Spero whispered parting words: "The future is in your hands."

Tom assumed his new role. Thrusting out his chest, he entered the room to an eruption of flashing cameras and shouting reporters. He broke out in a big smile and waved. The room filled with cheers and happy faces, some showing tears.

A representative of the hospital introduced him at the microphone, booming with patriotic pride and enthusiasm. At that moment, Tom Nolan disappeared forever. A new life was born in the shine of the camera lights.

"Ladies and gentlemen, the president of the United States."

CHAPTER THIRTY-SIX

Randy Phelan reported to an office in a Chicago high-rise with no identification on the door to indicate who he was meeting with or what he was meeting about. He only knew it was very important, totally confidential, government-related business and he was to report to the location alone. He wore his best suit – a cheap suit, rumpled with age – but at least it was a slight step toward appearing dignified.

He was convinced it had something to do with his debt and bankruptcy because there was no other reason he would be summoned like this. He was apprehensive but not fearful. He had nothing to hide. He had always been open and honest. And whatever these federal officials needed from him, he would comply.

The room was alarmingly bare, as if borrowed but not officially leased. There was a plain desk with two persons sitting behind it, a man and a woman in dark jackets. They gestured to a single chair across the desk from them.

Randy sat.

"Thank you for coming," said the woman.

"Are you the IRS?" Randy asked.

"No," said the man. "We're the CIA."

At that moment, Steven Morris entered the room. Randy let out a small gasp. "Steven, what are you doing here?"

Steven just smiled and pulled over a chair from the other side of the room. He sat opposite Randy, alongside Meg McGrath and Jason Wallers of the Central Intelligence Agency.

"Am I in trouble?" Randy asked.

"Not at all," Steven said. "You're here because you're family, and we need your help."

"My help?" said Randy quickly. "Yes. Anything. What is it?"

Steven took a deep breath. "Here goes...."

And he brought his brother-in-law into the biggest secret in the world.

He told him everything.

He had promised the president's inner circle that Randy could be trusted. They were desperate for the immediate resource. The cleanup of the damage and destruction caused by the Russians was moving fast and furious.

Simon Giamatti and Bella Giamatti were dead. Their murders could not be undone. Also, given their extremely high profile in the public eye and their secret ties to the Gemini Experiment, they could not suddenly become absent and leave a gaping hole that would prompt a lot of scrutiny and investigation.

Fortunately, the shells of Simon Giamatti and Bella Giamatti had been recovered – apprehended – and the cartridges of Yefim and Alina had been ejected.

This left two identities without an owner. Someone needed to assume these roles, preferably someone with close ties to Steven for a smooth transition into the Gemini project.

"You want me to *what*?" said Randy.

"We want you and Christie to become the Giamattis," Steven said.

"But what about the life we have now?"

"Randy and Christie Phelan would be phased out. Move away. Quietly slip out of society. Don't worry about that part – it's handled at government level. Like going into a witness protection program."

"But what about the kids?" Randy said. "There's no way I'm leaving my children. I'm sorry, but that is not negotiable."

"You wouldn't lose your children," said Jason Wallers. "The Giamattis would adopt them."

"I would adopt my own kids?"

"Technically, yes," said Meg McGrath.

"This is crazy."

"Yes," Steven said. "We know."

Randy slowly shook his head in bafflement, and then it increased in emphasis to become a response of no.

"I'm sorry," he said. "I'll keep all these secrets. I promise. You have my word. You can lock me up if I betray you. But this offer.... I just.... I just can't. I don't want to do this. I'm afraid I have to decline your proposal. Count me out."

Jason and Meg exchanged glances.

Steven sat back in his chair. "There's one more thing we haven't told you."

Randy said, "Steven, I'm sorry. Please respect my wishes."

"Absolutely," said Steven. "But hear me out. To truly become the Giamattis, you will need to inherit their assets and holdings. We would make it completely seamless. That means what belongs to them would belong to you. Including the fortune that Simon Giamatti amassed in his lifetime."

"And how much is that?"

"Seven and a half billion dollars."

Randy Phelan blinked and promptly responded. "Where do I sign?"

CHAPTER THIRTY-SEVEN

In a secured, concealed government facility nestled in solid rock in the mountains of West Virginia, Sam Mejos checked on his three prisoners. It was a daily routine, boring in the beginning, but he had found ways to spice it up for his amusement at the expense of his neutralized inmates. Humming to himself, the rotund man with thinning hair advanced through three layers of security before entering a long, narrow room with bare walls. The room was immaculately climate controlled, completely windowless, brightly lit and populated with rotating cameras hanging from the ceiling. The front section resembled a humdrum office with a desk, monitor and computer tower a little bit thicker than most. Sam sat down and began pecking at the keyboard to boot up.

Before long, an animated avatar of a male figure appeared on the screen, represented by simple, three-dimensional graphics. The cartoonish character paced within the borders of the monitor, head bobbing, mouth frowning and eyes alert.

"Good morning," Sam said.

"Go fuck yourself," said Yefim.

The captive Russian spy existed as a cartridge of digitized consciousness installed in a computer that linked him with a simulated human being created in pixels in a virtual environment. The computer-generated imagery allowed for user customization, which had enabled Sam to dress up Yefim as a small elf in a green jumpsuit with pointy shoes.

Sam's intention was his own entertainment and his cyber-prisoner's humiliation. It worked on both levels.

Yefim's avatar continued to spew profanity at him.

With a click of his mouse, Sam muted the audio.

"Watch your language," he said. "Don't forget, I can take away your voice."

The elf continued to move within the confines of his abstract, illustrated surroundings. He made several crude, offensive gestures.

"Okay, I'm putting you to sleep," Sam said. And he did just that, moving the cursor across a navigation bar and down a menu before clicking the avatar away. "You're lucky I don't drag you into the recycling bin."

He called up Alina next.

Alina was represented by an animated face embedded in the center of a big, colorful daisy flower. She didn't – couldn't – move. She just stared.

Sam had converted her to a daisy earlier in the week, just for fun.

Prior to that, she had been various other objects: a school bus, an octopus, a pomegranate, the number 4.

Awakened from sleep mode, she addressed her observer in a hard, direct voice that no longer attempted to conceal a Russian accent.

"Listen. I want to cut a deal. Get me back in the physical world. Put me in something real. I will see that you are rewarded. You will receive riches beyond your wildest dreams. I am very well connected. Name your price."

Sam chuckled at her. "You are a prisoner of the US government, for now and forever. You are serving a sentence of one million years. There is nothing to negotiate."

"This is not fair. This is torture."

"The United States does not torture," said Sam, and he moved the cursor across the screen. He clicked Exit.

Sam stepped away from the computer. It was time to check on his third prisoner, Sergei Vladin, the legendary spy known as 'The Stick'. The Stick stood at the end of the long, narrow room in a cage of thick steel bars. He stared at his fat captor with a simmering anger that never relaxed. It only intensified.

"Hello, Mr. Ugly," Sam said.

The Stick said nothing. He could not speak. He was a disfigured animal mutation, probably the closest thing to a living monster on the planet and definitely one-of-a-kind.

Pre-dating the creation of Tom Nolan's shell, the first experimental scan of a living mammal took place with a chimpanzee. The results were far from perfect. Its dimensions were wrong. Parts went missing. Its appearance was generally deformed with eyes at different levels, lopsided shoulders and arms of different length and size. The distorted facsimile was promptly abandoned and deemed useless until someone came up with the notion to test a human cartridge in it – specifically, the idle consciousness of a captured Russian spy.

Partly out of curiosity, partly out of cruelty, Sergei Vladin's mind was installed in the misshapen animal shell. It worked.

"Okay," said Sam to the prisoner. "Are you ready for today's joke?"

No response. This was to be expected – the thing in the cage had no voice.

"You're so ugly, you scare the crap out of the toilet," Sam said, following the one-liner with uproarious laughter. Sam provided a few more general taunts. Then he left the containment vault to begin crafting the next day's joke. Joke writing had become a daily ritual to kill some idle time in Sam's long, isolated, uneventful job in the middle of nowhere. As far as Sam was concerned, it was the easiest job in the world.

★　★　★

Sergei Vladin barely moved, perched on his two hairy, irregular legs, feeling no physical need to move or sit, content with remaining stationary while his brain did the racing. He festered with rage about his literally inhuman predicament and the smirking buffoon prison guard who constantly belittled him. He directed the crackle of all energies toward a single destiny that wholly consumed his thoughts.

I will find my moment and I will escape. It may happen in a week, a month, a year, a decade or decades, but I will be free. I will bring down my enemies with an unfathomable wrath.

There is but one certainty, America. My day is coming.

EPILOGUE

On the night of President Gus Hartel's re-election, Emily sat on the sofa with her second husband, Bob, and watched the voting results roll in on colorful maps from across the country. It wasn't even close. President Hartel won the popular and electoral vote in a landslide. Shortly before midnight he thanked his supporters in a rousing acceptance speech followed by a massive balloon drop and celebratory blast of rock and roll.

As they watched the president, Bob held Emily's hand. He comforted her as memories returned of a trauma from which she could never fully recover but hurt a little less every day. Emotionally, she continued to create distance from the deep shock of her first husband's attempted assassination of the president. Physically, she was a thousand miles away from where it all happened, long departed from Chicago to nestle in a calmer and more natural homestead outside of Casper, Wyoming.

While Emily would always love Tom Nolan very much, Bob Greshan had become equally special in her life and critical to her healing. They married seven months after Tom's death and moved with Sofi to a small ranch property that attracted few visitors and effectively discouraged the media. It was an ideal life – private and simple with bright days of sunshine and quiet nights of stars.

Following President Hartel's victory speech, Emily and Bob turned off the television and stepped out on the back porch while Sofi slept. A cool breeze swept across the prairie. Bob held Emily tight in the moonlight. She relaxed in his arms, and they felt good and right. He spoke softly to her in the darkness in that familiar, soothing voice.

Everything was in place, just like it should be.

"When do you think we can tell Sofi?" he asked.

"A few more years," said Emily. "She'll be old enough then."

"How do you think she'll handle it?"

"I think she'll be the happiest girl in the world."

Emily stared into Bob's eyes. She smiled because she could still see Tom. He was not lost. He was not gone. He was just hidden.

He was hidden beneath another man's face, a necessity for creating closure for a nation that still believed – and needed to believe – that Tom Nolan was dead.

Little did anyone know – except for a very small, closed circle – that Tom not only still lived, he lived twice.

A year ago, a digital representation of Tom Nolan's mind had been created for President Gus Hartel. Like all digital files, it was duplicable. Within weeks, an exact copy was made and installed in the refurbished Tom Nolan shell that had previously suffered electrocution damage. After several weeks of lab work, scientists repaired the scorched circuitry. They also altered the facial features sufficiently so they no longer resembled Tom Nolan and became a new identity entirely.

Bob Greshan.

Bob's mental starting point was lifted from Tom's first month as President Hartel. Once isolated in a new replica and life environment, the file quickly accumulated new data and analytics to shape its personality differently. While President Hartel and Bob Greshan had the same brain at the beginning, they evolved to become their own individuals. For Emily, the original Tom still existed as a familiar foundation, and he grew and developed in the ways people do during their lives. Sort of the same, sort of different.

In Wyoming, Bob took on a general manager position with a Casper accounting firm, distanced from the legal profession. Emily found a new teaching job at an elementary school. Sofi grew up remarkably well adjusted. While her new daddy was different, she found comfort in the many similarities: his voice, his physical build, his blue eyes and warm smile, his gentle personality and encouragement.

In the first year, Emily often found herself calling him 'Tom' and correcting herself while he chuckled. Gradually, she got used to 'Bob'. They enjoyed following the journey of Bob's secret twin in the White House, not always synchronized with his politics but well aware that his persona was being influenced by another environment, different people and separate life experiences.

Emily felt very fortunate. She was gifted with her own version of Tom in exchange for a lifetime of keeping quiet. That was a tradeoff she was happy to make. She came to terms with the morality of it all. Perhaps President Gus Hartel wasn't really the original Gus Hartel. But the general public didn't seem to recognize or question it. If he acted differently now and then, don't we all?

No one really knows anyone in this world, Emily thought to herself, as she continued to embrace Bob in silence. Together they watched the stars, experienced the moment in their own way, and held on.

FLAME TREE PRESS
FICTION WITHOUT FRONTIERS
Award-Winning Authors & Original Voices

Flame Tree Press is the trade fiction imprint of Flame Tree Publishing, focusing on excellent writing in horror and the supernatural, crime and mystery, science fiction and fantasy. Our aim is to explore beyond the boundaries of the everyday, with tales from both award-winning authors and original voices.

•

Other titles available include:
Junction by Daniel M. Bensen
Second Lives by P.D. Cacek
Thirteen Days by Sunset Beach by Ramsey Campbell
Think Yourself Lucky by Ramsey Campbell
The Hungry Moon by Ramsey Campbell
The Haunting of Henderson Close by Catherine Cavendish
The House by the Cemetery by John Everson
The Toy Thief by D.W. Gillespie
Black Wings by Megan Hart
Stoker's Wilde by Steven Hopstaken & Melissa Prusi
The Playing Card Killer by Russell James
The Siren and the Specter by Jonathan Janz
Wolf Land by Jonathan Janz
The Sorrows by Jonathan Janz
Savage Species by Jonathan Janz
The Nightmare Girl by Jonathan Janz
The Dark Game by Jonathan Janz
House of Skin by Jonathan Janz
The Widening Gyre by Michael R. Johnston
Will Haunt You by Brian Kirk
Kosmos by Adrian Laing
The Sky Woman by J.D. Moyer
Creature by Hunter Shea
Ghost Mine by Hunter Shea
The Bad Neighbor by David Tallerman
Ten Thousand Thunders by Brian Trent
Night Shift by Robin Triggs
The Mouth of the Dark by Tim Waggoner

•

Join our mailing list for free short stories, new release details, news about our authors and special promotions:

flametreepress.com